D1268138

SECOND ACT

MEG NAPIER

NAPIERPRESS

ISBN 9781735102436

Cover art designed and created by SALLY SCHAEDLER

❀ Created with Vellum

DEDICATION

With tremendous thanks and respect to N. James Whitehill III, of the American Ballet Theatre, who patiently answered my numerous silly questions and showed me around his amazing theater, and to Joanne Whitehill, who has spent years lovingly nurturing and honing the skills of young dancers through her magnificent Burklyn Ballet Theatre. The world is a more beautiful place thanks to the work you both do.

And to my beloved Nina, who surprised me with tickets to a performance of Giselle, and who stared at me in consternation when I pulled out a tiny notepad and started jotting down ideas. May we always find joy in dance.

Dear Reader,

This book was conceived and written in another time: a time when a seasonal flu could be serious but not often deadly, and a time when short disruptions to artistic performances were almost unheard of and always cost-prohibitive. Those of you reading it in the days, weeks, months, and God forbid, years, close to its publication, will know all too well that life has changed in more ways than I/we could possibly have imagined. I hope someday readers will be able to read this book and not think about how life has changed, or rather, think about how it has returned to a less frightening normal.

For now, I hope SECOND ACT can embrace you and take you to another time and place the way any memorable night at the theater should do. It was written with love and joy, and I hope that even as its suspense makes you shiver, it brings a smile to your lips and a lighter step to your day.

Tuesday

The spot of blood seeping through the pale pink fabric grew bigger.

"Stop!" Margot hissed, then glanced around, making sure no one had heard. Her chest heaving as she attempted to catch her breath, she glared at the crimson circle, just visible in the near darkness, willing it to cease its spread. There was certainly no time to do anything about it before her next entrance in less than a minute.

Don't think about it. No one will see it. This is it—your last entrance. Ever. A choking tightness pushed up through her chest, and she struggled to breathe. *DO NOT CRY!*

She tucked the ribbon she had been tightening into place and stood upright, grimacing ever so slightly as she made a quick circular movement with her foot. The ribbon was secure, and the blasted blister wouldn't matter at all after tonight.

Her final appearance as Giselle, a role she had danced at least forty or fifty times in her career, and here she was, bleeding like a novice. With luck, her performance throughout the evening had been so spectacular that no one would notice the stain on her heel. Okay, maybe not spectacular, but it had been damn good, and the commotion over her retirement with the countless curtain calls and flowers should prevent any eyes from straying to her stained tights.

She took one last deep breath. This really was it. She had to think young, be young—an innocent peasant girl, still besotted, even in death, with the handsome young noble who had literally broken her heart at the end of the first act. Dead, now, as throughout all of Act II, but still eternally young. *Please, please, let these last simple steps be the most beautiful ever.*

Andy, the stage manager, stepped from his position at the booth and came over to give her a smile and a thumbs-up, dimly visible through the dim blue stage light. He had stood at his station throughout her thousands of entrances and exits, and she was grateful for his compassion now.

Yuri completed his final solo as the bereaved Count Albrect. It was time. Margot's last entry. She inhaled and forced herself to ignore the tears that stubbornly refused to heed her will. This was her choice, and she *would not cry*. She moved from the wings in a graceful bourré and went as a ghost to bid her beloved count goodbye before he returned to the land of the living, and the curtain fell on her career.

Four Hours Earlier

The ding of the microwave and the ring of his cell phone were so close to simultaneous that Frank looked from one to

2

the other, momentarily confused. Then the phone rang again, and he snapped to attention.

"This is Sutton," he barked into the phone.

"Frank."

The prolonged enunciation of his name brought a scowl to Frank's face. He knew that tone. His boss was calling him back in, yet again. What was it about "off" that the son-of-a-bitch didn't understand? He had just finished his sixth twelve-hour day, and he was supposed to be "off."

"Yes, sir?" He made his tone as uninviting as possible.

"We have a . . . uh, a rather unusual situation, and I need your help."

"An unusual situation?"

"Yes. But I'm sure with the right attitude, you'll see it as a pleasant . . . diversion."

"A pleasant diversion? I'm supposed to be off, remember? 'Til Saturday?"

"Yes. I remember. But here's the thing. Conroy and Hernandez are both out with the flu. Mason was put on bedrest today for pre-term labor, and Blackman had to fly to Miami for his father's funeral. I need you to go to the ballet."

The microwave dinged again, insistently reminding him that his burrito was ready, so Frank figured he had heard wrong.

"The what, sir?"

"The ballet."

"Did you say the ballet?"

"Yes. We have two officers at every performance, and all our regulars are unexpectedly unavailable. I'm in a jam, and you're the next contestant on the new Price is Right."

"You want me to go to the ballet?" He tried to keep his tone polite, but the guy had to be kidding. His day had started at 4am when he had been called in after only a few hours of sleep. The flu was knocking out officers left and right, and no one healthy was being spared extra shifts. But the ballet?

"Yes, the ballet. The performance starts at eight, at the Columbus Theater. So you should plan on arriving at about 7:30. No uniform. You've got nice theater clothes, don't you?"

Frank had put the call on speaker while he got a beer out of the refrigerator, and now he glared at the phone lying on the counter.

"I'm sorry, sir. You've caught me a bit off guard here. What exactly do you mean by theater clothes? Are you asking me to put on a fucking tux or something?"

"No, no, of course not. Just nice slacks and a jacket to cover your holster. Regular undercover attire. Nothing too fancy. The whole idea is to blend in."

"Blend in."

"Yes."

"At the ballet."

"Yes."

Frank shook his head in disbelief. "I don't think I've been to a ballet since my sister was a mouse or something-or-other in *The Nutcracker* thirty years ago."

"Well then, it will be a nice change of pace."

"A change of pace."

"This conversation is getting old, Sutton. Go to the ticket booth, show them your ID, and tell them you're replacing Mason. The regular guys love the assignment, so I'm sure it'll be fun. Then you'll be off, and I'll see you on Saturday."

"Wait!" Frank's voice sounded desperate, even to his own ears. "What am I supposed to do there?"

"You watch the ballet. Isn't that what I said?"

"That's it?"

"Yeah. No biggie. As I said, we have two officers at every performance, but with all the shit that's gone down, you're all

I have tonight. You sit there like a good boy, watch the ballet, keep your eyes open for trouble, and enjoy the evening."

"Are you expecting trouble?"

"Of course, I'm not expecting trouble. It's a frigging ballet, for god's sake. The easiest assignment you'll ever get."

Chief Mackie was gone. Frank glared at the phone in his hand. The microwave dinged again.

* * *

Two minutes after the curtain had gone up, Frank was sure the night would be interminable. All the bright colors, the dancers flying around in every direction, and the god-awful boring music. Maybe if he closed his eyes, he could sneak in a few minutes of sleep. The young girl in the excruciatingly tight hair bun next to him was sitting on the edge of her seat, the woman on her other side smiling fondly at her enthusiasm. They wouldn't notice a thing, as long as he didn't snore.

Frank shook his head ever so slightly and sighed. He was supposed to be paying attention, because, who knew? Maybe a masked bandit would appear on stage and demand everyone's wallets. Good luck getting anything out of the dancers. What little they had on was so skin tight he doubted there'd be room anywhere for even a hidden coin, let alone a wallet.

He sighed inwardly again and glanced at the well-coiffed heads in the three rows in front of him. Didn't look like any armed bandits were hidden amongst those hoity-toity attendees. Nope. He was stuck for the duration, no doubt the most boring night of his life.

His eyes focused on the young girl dancing around and between the ridiculous huts on stage. He guessed those two pansies prancing about were supposed to be fighting over her, though what she could possibly see in either of them was beyond him.

God, she was gorgeous. He studied her more closely. Her movements were lightning quick, and she seemed to hang almost suspended in the air as she danced around. But when she held still, he could just make out the exquisite planes of her face, and he began to think that maybe she wasn't as young as he had first thought.

He watched her more intently. There was some silly game going on with a flower—some sort of 'he loves me, he loves me not' nonsense, he assumed, and as her brows drew together in a frown, he saw a maturity to her eyes that belied her girl-like portrayal.

He continued to watch her, almost spell-bound, as the dance went on. At times she sprang from the earth like a bouncing ball, and at other times she appeared more as a graceful butterfly. The postures she contorted herself into were unimaginably complex and stunningly beautiful.

A few minutes later he frowned in disgust as she suddenly appeared to be dying on stage, her long hair released from its pins, cascading over her convulsing figure.

What kind of fucked-up nonsense was he watching? The curtain came down to deafening applause, the lights came on, and people began standing and pushing to the aisles. He shook himself slightly and stood, moving out of the row and then off the side so that audience members could pass around him.

Intermission. Probably the best time to resume his lookout for pick-pockets or whatever other criminal-minded assailants might be lurking about. *Right.* He was stranded amongst hundreds of obviously wealthy idiots who had nothing better to do than watch the world's stupidest story played out by grown-ups in tights.

He plastered a pleasant expression on his face and moved slowly up the stairs behind the crowds. He'd wander around the lobby, watch the fools pay too much for the tiny glasses of alcohol they'd have to swallow down too fast, and then he'd cross his fingers that the second act would pass quickly and he could finally go home.

Ten minutes later he was back in his seat. The lights hadn't dimmed yet, so he turned to the printed playbill. That beautiful dancer must be Giselle, and . . . yup, from everything he was reading, she must indeed be older than the nymphet she was playing. Tonight seemed to be her farewell performance. What the hell? Did these prima donnas get to retire as soon as they were old enough to drink? His mother had retired last year after thirty years of teaching; this girl, or okay, woman, looked like she could pass as one of his mother's high school students without much effort. And damn. That meant the blasted thing would probably go extra-long, and he'd be stuck here 'til God only knew how late.

He read the synopsis. Giselle had definitely died, according to the notes, but she'd be back in Act II anyway. Pretty gullible, these ballet folks. He settled back and prepared for another hour of punishment. Willis came next, the program had said. What the hell were Willis? There were about a million names listed on the cast list, so maybe they were some kind of army. This whole thing gave him the willies. Maybe he had died himself and was now in some bejeweled version of hell. He breathed a quick sigh of relief as the lights dimmed. The second act was starting, which meant the end was in sight. Let it come soon, he hoped.

* * *

Margot lifted the bouquet that Jacob, as Hilarion, had left at her grave and sorrowfully handed it to Yuri, her heartbroken Count Albrect. This was it. She looked at him with genuine love and devastating sorrow, and a few rebellious tears slipped down her cheeks. And then, her arms lovingly

7

outstretched, she moved backwards into the shadows, her graceful en-pointe steps marking the end of her performing career.

She moved quickly back up-stage in the dark, swiping at her tears and begging her nose not to run. She watched Yuri's final sad steps as he moved back into the land of the living. He bent his head to theatrically inhale the non-existent scent of the stage flowers before turning back to replace them on her tomb.

Yuri crumpled to the ground.

Margot stared, confused. What was he doing on the floor?

"What happened?" Andy, the stage manager, hissed. "Margot, go back. Kneel next to him and cradle his head or something. Make it look like part of the show, and see if he's all right."

She moved instantly, still trying to sniff back her tears, gracefully coming to settle down next to Yuri. She lifted his head and felt a stab of fear. What was wrong with him? His eyes were wide open in unseeing frozen horror and his mouth was weirdly agape, his lips seemingly frozen in a desperate inhale. Margot forced her features into a gentle expression though he seemed completely unaware of her presence. She looked towards Andy's questioning gaze and shook her head ever so slightly as she lovingly cradled Yuri's head.

The music continued to its dramatic, slow finale, and just a few bars ahead of schedule, Andy brought the curtain down. The back-stage lights went on, and people rushed to the stage and surrounded Margot.

The heavy curtain muffled some of the uproariously loud applause, and Andy communicated on his headset while relaying instructions to the dancers and technicians.

"Dr. Han'll be here in a second. Jimmy said not to move Yuri until he gets here, so we're going to bring down the second curtain in front of him. Willis, move up quickly and make a single line to bow and then split and move to both sides so we can bring Liza and Jacob out before Margot goes out alone. Just put his head down gently, Margot."

The dancers obeyed, adjusting without hesitation to the new directions as if they had rehearsed them for hours, but none of them could resist turning their glances again and again to the motionless Yuri. After Liza, as the Queen of the Willis, and Jacob, as Hilarion, had taken their bows, Margot moved out into the center spotlight alone, the two principals separating to stand several feet off to both sides.

Afterwards, Margot would remember nothing from those shocked several minutes beyond a cold tingling of horror that seemed to stretch from her fingers to her toes. As she took her first deep curtsey, the voice-of-god announcement boomed out: "Ladies and Gentlemen, due to an unfortunate injury, Yuri Ossipov will not be appearing to receive your applause. He regrets most deeply that he cannot come out to join you in honoring this final performance of our beloved Margot Johnson."

Frank heard quiet exclamations of confusion and speculation, but the roar of the applause continued unabated. The heavy front curtain came down, and then the ballerina Giselle came out through an opening in the center of the curtain for curtsey after curtsey. Ushers brought her flowers, the conductor appeared, bowed to her and gave her a bouquet, and some young girls appeared in party dresses to present her even more flowers. The poor girl's face was almost obscured by all she was trying to hold in her arms.

She disappeared through the opening, but the applause did not stop. Then out she came again, arms empty, and

Frank rolled his eyes as the whole process seemed to begin anew. It was like a fancy-dress version of whack-a-mole.

He studied the ballerina's face. She was smiling graciously, but Frank was sure he saw distress in her eyes. Was something amiss in ballet fairy-land?

No one seemed ready to let go of their beloved retiring idol, but an usher suddenly appeared beside his end-row seat.

"Excuse me, but you're the police officer, right?"

Frank, already standing with the hundreds of clapping audience members, nodded, immediately tense.

"They need you backstage. Could you come with me, please?"

Frank followed the elderly gentleman out of the auditorium and into the side corridor he had ascended during intermission, but this time he was led down, and the usher opened a door barely visible through the paneling. They quickly climbed some steps, and Frank felt the aggravating twinge as his brace rubbed against his irritated flesh. He had been on his feet for too many hours this week, and now it looked like the week was about to get even longer.

* * *

The thirty-second reprieve from the spotlight allowed Margot to unload her flowers into the arms of the waiting assistant stage manager. One glance at the crowd clustered near the tombstone was all it took to know things were not okay. Dr. Han was on the floor next to Yuri, gasping for breath, and everyone else had moved back. Her eyes darted to the dancers holding each others' arms, some of them crying. A bone-chilling cold passed through her and she began to tremble. *What was wrong with Yuri?*

The clapping from the audience continued. She looked

towards Andy, and he nodded in silent agreement, holding up a single finger. One more time, and then he'd put on the house lights. The tribute was meant to be prolonged, with Paul, the Artistic Director, coming out to make a speech, but there was no time for that now. Calling on discipline she had been honing since the age of three, she forced her limbs to stop shaking. She had to smile. They were applauding the great Margot Johnson. One more time. And then she could go back to Yuri. *Please let him be okay. Oh God, please.*

Frank was momentarily taken aback by the chaotic scene on stage. What had been a darkened grave site moments ago was now brightly lit, and there seemed to be an extraordinary number of people milling around a cavernous area that had appeared quietly desolate only a few moments earlier. A few men dressed as he was, all with phones out, seemed to be acting as a barricade between the costumed dancers and two figures on the stage floor. The prince-dancer lay sprawled out, and another man, dressed in street clothes, was doubled over. A few feet away another man, probably in his 50s and dressed in an elegant tuxedo, was also speaking into his cell. Frank picked him out as the one in charge, and as he approached, he could make out the man's words.

"That's right. The doctor who started CPR now needs help as well. He's not able to talk, but he keeps gesturing for us all to stand back. No, I don't think so. Hang on." He turned from his phone and spoke to the crowd standing several feet from the two injured men. "Can anyone tell if Yuri is breathing?"

One of the buffer-men spoke. "It doesn't look like it, but I don't want to touch him to see if there's a pulse. I've got headquarters on the line, and they say a team with hazmat suits should be here in minutes."

Frank looked between the two and held out his ID. "I'm Frank Sutton, NYPD. Can you tell me what's happened here?"

"Where's Officer Mason?" The buffer-man spoke first.

"She couldn't make it. What's happened, and who are you?"

"Luis Enriquez. NYFD. We're here regularly, but this is totally bizarre. It looks like there might have been some kind of poisoning—it brought the first guy down instantly, and then the doctor got sick the minute he started giving CPR. That's why we're keeping everyone back."

The elegant figure spoke. "I'm Paul Cashman, Artistic Director. Yuri just collapsed. No one knows why." His words were even, but Frank could hear the fear in his voice as he continued speaking.

"And then when Dr. Han, our company doctor, started to help him, he came close to collapsing, too. He looks like he's having a hard time breathing."

"Yuri? Isn't that a Russian name?"

"Oh my God," one of the firemen hissed. "Do you think it's that numchuk stuff?"

Paul's eyes widened, but he answered Frank's question. "Yes. He's our guest artist. He's been with us all season."

Frank felt his adrenaline kick in.

"Whom have you called?" He directed his questions to Enriquez.

"Only headquarters, to report a possible poisoning. That's why they're sending a hazard team. But if it's that Russian stuff, we could all be in trouble."

"Yeah. Just trying to think—is it better to lock everyone down or clear the area ASAP?" He made up his mind, lifted his phone to take several quick pictures of the scene, trying rapidly to record everyone's positions, and then spoke to the director, Paul.

"I need you to get everyone out of this area as quickly as possible, but get them all together somewhere else in the building. Keep the doors closed, but no one is to leave, do you understand? No one. Do you have a large room where everyone can congregate?"

Paul nodded. "Yes. We'll go to the studio."

"Get everyone there—everyone that was here tonight. No one goes anywhere else— no changing clothes, getting phones, or anything. And we have to get this theater emptied. There's no telling what may be in the air. Can you get an announcement made?"

Paul nodded and went to speak to the man at the booth off stage with the headset.

As Frank lifted his phone to start making calls, he saw the ballerina come from the front of the stage, her arms again filled with flowers. She started towards the prince on the floor, but the director called to her and motioned her towards him. Her already large eyes seemed to grow enormous in her pale face, and Frank felt a stab of pity for her. This was supposed to have been her special night, and even he was pretty sure that she had done a spectacular job.

A voice boomed through the announcement system. "Ladies and Gentlemen, the entire Empire Ballet, and our beloved Margot Johnson, in particular, thank you for coming tonight. However, due to a problem with the electrical system, we ask all patrons to exit the building as quickly as possible. Thank you for your cooperation. Again, please exit the building as quickly as possible."

* * *

It was 3:30 in the morning before Frank and the FBI agents who had arrived within a half-hour of his initial call had finished getting contact information and statements from everyone who had been on stage or backstage at the time of the incident.

Frank was flabbergasted at the number of people needed to put on one performance. He had started a list with the director in the small notebook he always carried, writing down names and what each person did, but by the end he was trying to squeeze in so much info that he wasn't sure he'd be able to read his own notes. Carpenters, electricians, prop handlers, sound technicians, wardrobe, wigs and make-up, musicians, stage techs, and of course, all the ruddy dancers. And then there were the animal handlers and dancers from the first act who weren't even around by the end of the show. What a frigging nightmare.

Off to the side, though, the girl, no, *watch it, asshole,* the woman, was standing alone, wrapped up in a ratty, pale pink sweater that looked like something even his grandmother would have consigned to a charity donation.

Her name was Margot, he had been told, and it had taken him a few minutes to realize that the printed "Margot," which he had reasonably thought rhymed with "car lot" was whom they were talking about when they said what sounded like "car go." Crazy, effed-up dance people. They couldn't even have normal names.

She and that boy dancer who had died onstage with the Willis—the one who had died in the story before the other one collapsed—they had been the last two people to touch the flowers that were right now being tagged as the likely cause of the problem.

The forensic hazmat team had arrived and wrapped up and carted away all of the props that had been on stage. Margot and Jacob, the first male dancer, had been taken somewhere else in the building with a hazmat medical technician and an FBI agent, but Margot had returned and was now just standing there. She looked utterly exhausted and very alone. The director, Paul, had gone over to speak to her a few times, but he had left about ten minutes ago. Frank wondered what she was waiting for.

"Did someone tell you to stay here?" he finally asked, after looking around and confirming there were no others still waiting his attention.

She started, and her great round eyes narrowed in confusion as she looked at him.

"No, I don't think so. I'm not sure, really. I was hoping someone would come and tell me how Yuri is doing."

He stared at her, again puzzled by his inability to guess her age. She was still wearing thick stage makeup, and her eyes looked huge in her pale face.

He knew, of course. He had heard by text more than an hour ago that the dancer was dead. But she looked so alone and uncertain that he hesitated.

"I think it would be best to go home and get some rest. We'll know more in the morning, and I'd bet my last dollar that someone will want to ask you more questions by then."

"We're supposed to go to the wedding together."

"What wedding?"

"Paul's. He's getting married on Monday. Yuri's never been to an American wedding, so I told him we could go together."

"Was. . . is Yuri your boyfriend?" He was bemused by the sense of irritation he felt while voicing the question.

Her large eyes seemed to grow even bigger, and then she laughed.

"Of course not. His boyfriend is dancing in Paris right now. He's just such a sweet kid." She closed her eyes briefly. "Besides, I'm almost old enough to be his mother."

He seriously doubted that.

"Tell me about this wedding."

She seemed to focus on him for the first time. "I'm sorry.

Could you tell me who you are, again? I've spoken to so many people tonight."

Even in her exhaustion, she had a regal poise and beauty that made him stare, silent, for a moment.

"Detective Frank Sutton, NYPD."

"Can you tell me what they think happened? I mean, I know what I saw happen, but I don't understand what . . ." Her voice trailed off as her arms rose and spread out as though in an attempt to encompass the entire room.

"Right now, the working theory is that Mr. Ossipov inhaled some kind of poison when he smelled those flowers. Whatever it was also affected the doctor, though less severely, when he started CPR. The FBI should have mentioned the flowers when they spoke to you."

"Well yes, they did. They asked me questions about almost everything on stage. But they wouldn't say anything about Yuri. Are you . . . do they . . . did someone try to hurt Yuri intentionally?"

Again, those enormous brown eyes focused intently on him. He reached out and took her hand, the touch of her cold fingers against his the first awareness that he had done so.

"It's Ms. Johnson, isn't it?" Her fingers had tightened around his own, and he noticed how small her hand looked in his.

"Yes, but my name is Margot."

"Margot. I'm terribly sorry. Yuri died tonight. It looks like someone wanted someone dead. We don't know for sure if Yuri was the intended target. It could have been the other male dancer who brought in the flowers--Jacob Kattmeyer, right? Or it could even have been you. We don't know. But it definitely seems to have been intentional. Since Yuri is a Russian national, and the Russians have a history of using poison, that's our first line of inquiry."

A wave of shock and horror raced up from his midsection. What the hell was he doing, talking to her like this? She was a possible suspect.

He took a deep breath and tried to reassert an official tone to his words. "I've told you more than I should have, and I need to insist that you keep what I've told you to yourself."

Holy shit, he thought as he continued to stare at her. For all he knew, she could be a Russian plant herself. What the fuck had gotten into him?

Her eyes remained on him without wavering, but now he realized they were filled with tears, and one was moving down her pale cheek. Her lips began to tremble.

"Yuri's dead?"

He nodded gravely.

She seemed to cave in on herself, and he reached out instinctively and pulled her towards him.

* * *

Minutes ago Yuri had lifted her high in the air, and now he was dead? Margot couldn't breathe. A trembling seized her, and her entire body turned to ice. A whimper of horror escaped her throat. *How could what this man said be true?*

Seconds passed before Margot realized the stranger's arms had encircled her. He was tall, and his chest was broad, and as her face pressed into the scratchy fabric of his blazer, she inhaled a choking breath. He was so warm, and he smelled like a wintry campfire. She couldn't remember the last time she had been held like this—in arms meant only to comfort. For a moment she tried desperately to focus on breathing. He felt so strong and solid, and a sense of security enveloped her. She was safe. *But oh, God. Yuri was dead.*

Her tears flowed more quickly, and she pulled back in embarrassment. She didn't know this man, Yuri was dead, and she had to . . . she had no idea what she had to do. She swallowed convulsively and forced herself to focus.

She tilted her head back and looked up at him. The stage was only dimly lit now, most of the lights having been turned off at some point, but she thought his eyes were a golden-brown color, and they appeared filled with compassion. Amber, she thought. His eyes are like amber. A choking sensation rose up from her middle. She would never see Yuri's bright blue eyes again.

"I'm sorry," she said, trying to regain her composure. "I, uh . . ." She looked around, desperately knowing even as she did so that there wasn't anything nearby she could use to wipe her face. The towel she had used backstage from the second act had probably been picked up hours ago by the stage crew.

But then as if by magic, he was holding out a package of pocket tissues. She stared at him, astonished at his ability to read her mind.

"It's flu season, remember? I haven't caught it yet, but that doesn't stop my nose from running when I come in out of the cold."

She took two tissues from the packet, nodding her head in gratitude. After a moment she took a deep breath.

"Thank you. You've been remarkably kind. And I apologize—I know I just asked you this a few minutes ago, but what did you say your name was?"

"Frank," he said quietly. "Frank Sutton. I'm a detective. I was sent here tonight because the officers who normally would have attended were all unavailable. It was supposed to be a quiet, boring evening."

She watched him as he spoke. His face looked like he had weathered a lot in life, but his eyes were gentle as he continued.

"And I understand that this was supposed to be a special

night for you. It's a real shame things turned out the way they did because you danced beautifully. I've never been to a ballet before, but even I could see how great you were."

Margot sniffed and managed a small smile and slight nod of gratitude. She was used to ballet fans singing her praises and to the sometimes affectionate, sometimes snide, words of praise company members threw back and forth. But here was someone who seemed to know nothing about ballet, and it somehow warmed her to know he had liked it.

"Thank you," she said quietly. "I'm glad you'll have at least something nice to remember about tonight." She tilted her head in confusion as the words he had said sunk in.

"What do you mean, the officers who normally would have attended? Are there always police officers at our performances?"

Frank's eyes widened ever so slightly. He inhaled, seemed to hold his breath a moment, and then spoke in a less than successful off-handed manner.

"It's very late. How are you planning on getting home? Do you have a car here?"

Margot's lips lifted in a tired smile. "A car? No one voluntarily drives in this city. Normal people don't have fancy lights and sirens that let us come and go whenever we want. I take the subway like everyone else."

Frank glanced at his watch.

"It's far too late to be walking the streets by yourself. My car is in the garage. I'll give you a lift."

"You don't even know where I live."

"I assume if you dance here regularly, you don't live in Montana."

She looked at him in confusion. "Montana?"

"You're very tired. Get your things and I'll drive you home."

Margot drew the ragged sweater more tightly around

19

herself and turned to move off the stage. She hissed quietly as her first steps caused the point shoe to dig yet again into her blister. How could she have forgotten to take them off?

She shook her head slightly and resisted the urge to rub her eyes. Her eyelids felt unbearably heavy under the weight of her stage makeup and her fatigue. She had no clear recollection of the many hours that had passed since the ballet had ended. She had been herded into the rehearsal studio with what seemed like hundreds of people, and then so many questions had been thrown her way.

Figures in ridiculous-looking space suits had examined her, looking into her eyes, listening to her heart, and making her breathe out into some kind of weird tube. And then men in normal suits and two in FBI jackets had asked her again and again about the damn flowers, and about almost every other prop on stage. How was she supposed to know who had touched what? Her job was to dance, not to watch the stage crew.

But here she was, hours later, and she hadn't even taken her costume or shoes off. Bettina, the wardrobe mistress, would be pissed, and a pissed Bettina was never pleasant.

"Give me ten minutes, if you're sure it's no trouble." She looked back at the kind stranger and felt a twinge of guilt. He looked as tired as she was. "But I can catch a cab. You don't have to go out of your way."

His head tilted ever so slightly, and Margot thought she saw a flash of surprise on his face.

"It's no trouble," he said. "I'll feel better knowing you're home safe."

She nodded and turned to make her way to the dressing room. Everything that had happened since her last entrance had been so very, very wrong, but this stranger with the kind eyes stepping up to offer help somehow seemed to ease the panic that had been threatening to consume her.

* * *

Frank plugged his phone into the charger and hesitated. 4:57. Should he put it on 'do not disturb' – something he almost never did – or cross his fingers that he could get at least a couple hours of sleep before the damn thing did its best to ruin another day?

He was so tired it hurt to make such a minor decision. *Just do it*, he thought to himself. Let the world bother someone else for a few short hours.

A pair of haunted brown eyes flashed across his fading consciousness. Against all protocol and common sense, he had insisted she take his phone number.

"You might think of something," he had said, standing at the entrance of her Brooklyn apartment building. The neighborhood looked clean and well-lit, and the card-operated entry seemed relatively secure. He had been relieved she didn't live in one those hoity-toity uptown palaces but in a real building where normal mortals might live.

He left his phone on, even checking to make sure the volume was turned up. She wouldn't call; of course, she wouldn't. It had been absolute insanity to give her his private number. But she had looked so tiny and vulnerable, totally exhausted but resolutely carrying a huge black bag on her shoulder. He had taken it from her when they approached his car after descending to the garage from the theater and had been shocked by its weight – he'd guess close to at least thirty pounds.

"Jesus Christ!" The words shot from his lips without thought. "What do you have in here, bricks?"

Those huge eyes had widened and her eyebrows rose high into her forehead as a condescending smile made him catch his breath.

"It's my dance bag. Of course, it's heavy."

Silly him. What had he been thinking? She stood about five feet tall and probably didn't weigh even a hundred pounds. Carrying around a bag of bricks must be what all tiny little ballerinas did.

"Sure," he had muttered. Any semblance of eloquence had remained absent during the fifteen-minute drive. He normally loved the empty streets of New York at 3 or 4am, but Margot's silent and frozen figure of endurance distracted him. She had stared directly ahead, her back ramrod straight as if relaxing against the car seat would be an illegal offence.

When she got out of the car, he had walked with her to the front door.

"How about I put my number in your phone?" Even as he spoke the words, he mentally kicked himself. But the look she gave him was more confused than suspicious.

"It would make me feel more comfortable knowing you have it."

After a moment's hesitation, she whispered "thank you," and he wanted to pull her close again. He resisted but held her gaze in the bitingly cold night air.

"Get some sleep. I'll probably see you tomorrow back at the theater, but don't hesitate to call me for any reason."

She had nodded, pushed her card into the security slot, and then turned one last time before crossing the threshold. "Thank you again, Mr., uh, . . ."

"It's Frank." The vehemence of his words brought forth a puff of frosty vapor.

"Thank you again, Frank. You made tonight more bearable. Good night."

With that she was gone.

Now he lay on his bed, the sounds of the city muted by the hour and his distance from street level. He couldn't remember the last time he had thought of a woman with anything but professional detachment. Brenda had done such a number on him that he wondered occasionally if the nerves to his genitals had been severed by the IED that had messed up most of his left leg. He probably wouldn't have noticed.

Nope, the lying bitch had taught him that "love" was for gullible idiots. Brenda had been the cutest girl in their high school class, and all that marrying her had got him was a decade of deceit.

Tonight, though, he had been surprised by the strange sense of attraction and protectiveness the pretty little dancer seemed to have awoken in him. Going down that path would be stupid at best, and down-right humiliating all around. Frank moved his head back and forth against the pillow, trying to get comfortable and banish ridiculous thoughts. Women were poison to begin with, but a cop and a fairy-tale ballerina was bananas.

His mind wandered, though, as exhaustion set in. What kind of weird-ass name was Margot? And why did a tiny creature need to carry around a bag of bricks? And what in the world would be the motivation for killing a twinkle-toed Russian dancer? What kind of threat could he have been to anyone? And what if Mr. Twinkle-Toes had *not* been the intended target? What if the beautiful little ballerina was the target? Even worse, what if she was a murderess?

He struggled to push away the unease those last ideas caused and tried to quiet his thoughts so he could sleep for just a little while. He forced a few slow, deep breaths and pictured a pair of enormous brown eyes. Beautiful eyes. Maybe tomorrow he'd see her without all that make-up, and they'd turn out to be regular, everyday eyes. But then again, maybe not.

The trip back to Staten Island was its normal, late night/early morning mixture of exhaustion and tedium. An old white guy sprawled across two seats, his head back as he snored, several days' worth of stubble on his haggard face and his right hand still gripping the neck of a bottle covered in a wrinkled paper bag. A few young kids—they all looked like kids, though they were probably in their 20s—nodded sleepily in time to the sounds from their earbuds.

They were a mixture of races, and looking at them, it was hard to guess their origins. What did it matter, anyway? They were all stupid. It was a good bet none of them was just now leaving another endless day of work for a bunch of spoiled high and mighty artistes. A day of work that today had lasted even longer than normal. But at least the first step of the plan had succeeded.

Fuck-head Paul would see his precious ballet company in the news for all the wrong reasons. And with luck, after tomorrow the raging headlines in the city papers would be even juicier. He thought his happily-ever-after would be complete with his upcoming wedding to the lovely Miss Perfect. But no one merited a happily-ever-after, most certainly not the great and powerful Paul Cashman. When you pushed the little people aside on your rush to the top and forgot all about what should have been, you deserved whatever you got. Kind of a shame about pretty boy Yuri. It seemed he might actually have died. Oh well. Guess that stuff had worked better than expected.

2

Wednesday

M argot stepped hesitantly into the theater studio where company class was held daily. In theory she wasn't supposed to be here. She and Paul had agreed that after her "retirement" last night, she would take a week or so off and then return during his brief honeymoon absence to coach some of the newer dancers preparing for their first major company *Swan Lake*, scheduled to open in the spring. But everyone who had been at the theater last night had been told to show up this morning, and the company text alert this morning had said to assemble in the studio.

She hadn't been sure how to dress. Should she be prepared for class? She had even wondered where she should leave her stuff, but when she arrived, her name was still on the private dressing room she had been using for the last several seasons.

Yeah, right, she thought to herself. Like changing the

names on the dressing room doors would be anyone's priority just hours after Yuri had died on stage.

Another wave of despair swept over her. Poor Yuri. It wasn't possible that he was dead! He had been such fun to be with—like an eager young puppy, full of strength and vigor and ready for every new experience. He had never pretended to be anything other than a proud gay man, in love with ballet and the world around him, and his gracious warmth toward everyone he worked with had been infectious. He had made her feel young and attractive, always noticing a different leotard or telling her to eat more.

"I feel like I am not even working when I lift you," he had teased. "You need to eat more and make me feel like a man's man."

He had laughed uproariously each time he said those words, delighted with the silly English expression he had heard on some television show.

"*I* am a man's man," he had laughed. "But here people say those words and mean a *lady's* man. English is such a funny language!"

And now he was gone. He would never see his beloved Damien again.

Oh, no. Damien would learn of Yuri's death from the news, with no one to soften the blow.

She wondered whether word of his death was already out there. The strangely kind detective, Frank, had told her that Yuri was dead, but did everyone else know yet? She had been in such a daze that morning that she hadn't even thought to look at her phone after reading the text from Paul. Maybe she could get Yuri's phone and call Damien? Or would all of his things have been taken away?

The detective had told her he would probably see her today. Funny how that thought made her feel a little better. He had been such a reassuring presence last night, and she had fallen asleep remembering how good it had felt to be held against his chest.

She looked around the studio. Some of the dancers were in their regular practice attire, but some had street clothes on, as she did. They had still removed their shoes and were either barefoot or showing the white or pink fabric from the tights they wore under their jeans. Only the obvious non-dancers were brave or foolhardy enough to step on a studio floor in street shoes.

The various attendees had self-segregated into their own comfort zones: most of the dancers were in the far front corner of the room near the mirror, while the rest of the people standing around—and there were so many of them—were clustered close to the barres that were attached to the other three walls. All the suits and FBI jackets were in the middle of the room, and Margot saw Frank talking to a man and woman, both in NYPD uniforms.

His eyes met hers as if he had been waiting for her, and she thought he gave her a slight nod as he continued his conversation.

He had on dark slacks and what looked like a light brown shirt under his blazer. She wondered if it was the same one she had cried against last night.

Stop it, she scolded herself. What difference did it make what some detective was wearing? Yuri was dead, and some-one, maybe even someone right now in this room, had killed him.

Margot shook her head at the conflicting thoughts assaulting her. She should probably be frightened—terri-fied even, but the idea of someone intentionally hurting Yuri still struck her as absurd. Maybe they'd tell them it was all a mistake. Maybe Yuri had died from a heart attack or something equally obscene but natural. That was a horrible thought, but it was still better than thinking or knowing that someone had wanted him dead.

Liza came up behind her and grabbed her arm.

"He's dead, Margot! I just heard he really died! I can't believe it." Liza's voice cracked as she spoke, and a tear ran down her cheek.

Margot pulled her friend close. They had known each other for years, having met at a summer dance program they had both attended where Margot had been one of the senior students selected to serve as a mentor for the younger ones. From then on, they had continued to run into each other on almost a seasonal basis at auditions for intensive training programs or company try-outs. Margot had gotten into Empire several years before Liza, but she had been overjoyed when her younger friend had been offered a position. Their styles were different, and they had never been in serious competition for roles. Margot was far smaller and a more lyrical dancer, while Liza, at 5'7", was almost at the limit for how tall a female could be and still get good parts. It helped that her technique was lightning quick and almost always perfect.

Liza pulled back. The look she gave Margot was fearful.

"All those questions last night. All these cops and those guys in the white suits. Someone murdered him. Right here on our stage. Somebody actually wanted him dead. But I kept thinking all night, before I even knew Yuri had died, what if they had wanted to kill another one of us? Or all of us? Yuri never hurt anybody. No one could have wanted *him* dead!"

Margot shuddered, drawing Liza close again. The same thoughts had skimmed around the perimeter of her consciousness, but she had refused to seriously consider them. Now Liza's words struck her: whatever had killed Yuri might really have been meant for any of them. She tried to utter soothing words, but no sounds came out. A tightness gripped her throat as her arms clung to Liza, both seeking and offering comfort.

"Good morning, everyone."

Paul had been talking to the group in the middle of the room, but now he stepped away and looked around the packed studio as he spoke.

"Some of you know this already, but for those who don't, I am truly sorry to tell you that Yuri was pronounced dead at the hospital soon after his arrival. They did what they could to revive him, but nothing worked."

Gasps and quiet exclamations filled the room, but Paul cleared his throat, visibly devastated, and continued speaking.

"No official cause of death has been determined, but the police and the FBI are treating it as a possible homicide."

At his words, a chorus of murmurs and cries erupted. A tall, fit-looking man who appeared to be in his 40s or 50s and had caramel-toned skin and a well-tailored dark suit moved to stand next to Paul.

"My name is Robert Santini, and my colleagues and I," he pointed to the group of men and women still standing together in the center of the room, "we understand that this is all hard to take in. We represent a few different organizations," he gestured again to his colleagues, "but we have a lot we have to check out and many questions we need to ask. We spoke to some of you last night, but even if you talked to one of us already, we're going to have to talk to you again.

"So here's what we're going to do. It's 10:27. We want each of you to physically go to wherever you'd normally be at 10:27. I understand that besides dancers and musicians, we have craftsmen and women of numerous fields here as well as cleaning staff, cafeteria workers, and others. If you have work to do, please do it and carry on normally until we get to your area. If you're not usually here at 10:27, now 10:28, in the morning, go to wherever you would physically be when you are at work."

A rumble of conversation broke out again as people turned to each other, shifting positions but not moving toward the open doors. Paul looked around at the confusion and Margot saw him take a deep breath.

"Dancers. We'll start class in about ten minutes. Orchestra, we know this isn't your time to be here, and Jerry and I," his right hand moved in the direction of the goateed older man standing in the front of the thirty or so musicians clustered in the opposite corner from the dancers, "we want you to be able to get out as quickly as possible since many of you have other professional commitments during the day. The police and the FBI have agreed to begin their conversations with you in the pit, so the quicker they get started, the faster you'll be done.

"Everyone else, they've promised to speak with all of us as quickly as they can. I know being here now, like this, is an imposition, but we have no choice." He motioned to the assistant director who had come to stand next to him. "Angie will be coming around with a roster to check who's here and who's not. We'll have food available in the cafeteria by about 11:30, and that's an alternative place to congregate if you prefer.

"*Elite Syncopation* and *Firebird* dancers: green room as usual at seven. Thanks, everyone."

Liza squeezed her arm one last time and moved off, presumably to change for class. Margot chewed on her bottom lip as she watched Paul. The dancers for tonight's performance of the two shorter ballets would now have to be adjusted, given Yuri's death. Paul had wrangled with Yuri's agent for months to get him here, and after a great early season run, Yuri had been scheduled to dance in almost half their upcoming spring performances. Now Paul had not only a crime in his theater to contend with, but he would have to juggle cast changes and sensitive personality issues during his honeymoon.

Each of the principals had specific dancers they worked best with, and among his thousands of other tasks, it was Paul's job to see that the casts for each performance were optimally suited in terms of technique, appearance, and familiarity with the roles and with each other.

Margot and Yuri had danced together for most of the *Giselle* performances, and Liza had been paired with him for most of the upcoming *Swan Lakes*. Now Paul would have to put Jacob or one of the other male principals into Count Siegfried's role. Yuri had been a tall Russian bear, but many of Empire's male dancers were shorter and less visually impressive when paired with Liza.

People began moving to the wide double doors to make their way to other parts of the theater. Margot hesitated. Should she change and attend class? Sit in her—no longer rightfully *her*—dressing room? Go wait in the cafeteria?

As she stood thinking, the detective, Frank, broke away from the suits and came towards her.

"Are you feeling all right this morning? No breathing problems?"

Margot nodded but then shook her head, trying to answer both questions at once. "I'm fine. I was just trying to figure out where I should go. I'm not technically supposed to be here, so . . ."

His lips twitched. "Right. You retired last night. Are we keeping you from a move into assisted living?"

Margot narrowed her eyes. Was this guy making fun of her? He was! She glared at him.

"I was supposed to be off this week. Appointments, you know, with the geriatric doctors."

Somehow, they both smiled, and it struck Margot that

even smiling at someone in a normal conversation felt somewhat unfamiliar. Every day was a non-stop hamster wheel of class, rehearsal, physical therapy, and performances. When she got home, she scrubbed her face, showered, and fell asleep, just to start it all again the next day. She smiled on stage when her character was supposed to, and she smiled graciously at the end of every performance, but a smile as the result of normal discourse? Probably only when listening to some of Yuri's silly chatter.

Now her career was over, Yuri was dead, yet somehow this strange, world-weary-looking policeman was making her smile.

"Honestly, though, I'm not sure where I should go. I really wasn't supposed to be here. I guess I could take class . . ."

As she spoke, Frank took her arm. "If you might have time, I could use your help. We got a hastily put-together map and staffing list from Paul, but the senior FBI here need his full cooperation in sorting out Yuri's Russian connections. Angie . . . ." He stopped, peering at the top sheet of paper in his left hand. "Angie Gomez?"

Margot nodded. "Her name's Angelina, but she goes by Angie. She's the Assistant Director."

"Some of the other investigators need to talk with her and get any background medical information available on both Mr. Ossipov and Dr. Han."

"Oh God, right. Is Dr. Han okay?" Margot felt sick at having forgotten about the company physician.

"They're keeping him in isolation and running tests, but the last I heard, he was doing better."

Margot sighed in relief. Dr. Han had been at the company for longer than she had, and she knew he had a wife and at least one child.

"Thank God," she whispered. She looked at Frank and thought again that he looked like a man who had endured a lot in life. He was tall and seemed to carry very little body fat on his broad frame, and his eyes seemed to say that smiling was a rare experience for him as well. But they still reminded her of amber.

"I'm happy to help you, if I can," she said. "What can I do?"

"Is there somewhere we could go over these lists so I can get a better idea of who was doing what last night? And then maybe you could walk me around and give me an understanding of where everyone was."

"My dressing room seems to still be mine for the moment. There are a couple chairs and my make-up table in there. I took most of my personal stuff out little by little during the last few weeks."

"That sounds perfect. Lead the way."

* * *

Frank lectured himself silently as he followed Margot through the labyrinth hallways. Remember, he thought, she's still a possible suspect. Stop watching her ass in those tight jeans and concentrate.

But *fuck*, she had a beautiful little ass. Had he thought about it—and okay, maybe he *had* wondered about it just a bit—he would have guessed she was pretty much flat all over, kind of like the Gumby cartoon from his youth. But that bottom was deliciously curved, and he gave himself a hard, mental slap. Concentrate, asshole! This is a murder investigation, and the enticing female in front of him was the last one known to have touched the murder weapon.

They passed through a corridor with individual names on the doors, though the openings seemed relatively close together. When she opened the one marked 'Margot Johnson,' Frank could see why. The room was narrow and not very deep. There was a clothing rack that still held the white whatever—a dress? a nightgown? —he thought she had been wearing at the end of the performance last night. There was a table in front of a large mirror, a free-standing coat rack where he saw Margot's winter coat, and a few normal looking folding chairs, one of which held the black brick-bag. Several bouquets were propped up against the far wall, but most of the flowers looked sad and abandoned.

"This is it," Margot said self-consciously. "It's kind of barren right now, I'm afraid, and normally the flowers would have been taken care of, but today . . ." her voice trailed off.

"What normally happens to the flowers?"

"On a regular night, it's not a big deal. Sometimes I take a bouquet home, and I usually have vases in here. After a big night, like a final performance, an usher brings the bulk of them to a nursing home a few blocks away. But I guess we were all preoccupied last night."

She looked around as if confused. "I didn't think enough about last night ahead of time, in terms of logistics. I focused all my energies on making my last performance not suck, and I stupidly got rid of all my dressing room vases when I cleaned out my personal stuff."

He saw her teeth gnaw at her bottom lip and was struck again by how young she looked.

"Not suck? You're kidding, right?"

The look she gave him seemed honestly doubtful.

"Of course not. I didn't want to look like an idiot when everyone was coming to see the great Margot Johnson dance her last ballet."

"I can't imagine how you could ever look like an idiot. I don't understand anything about ballet, and even I could see you dance like a . . . like . . . Jeez, I don't know—like what a ballerina's supposed to dance like."

Margot gave a choked laugh.

"If you don't know anything about ballet, how could you possibly tell a bad ballerina from a good ballerina?"

"I'm a detective, that's how." He was laughing now, too, but he stopped and tried to make his voice sound authoritative. "I'm trained to see things and understand what I'm seeing." *Stop flirting, jackass!*

She raised her eyebrows while continuing to smile. He thought she had maybe a little make-up on, though nothing like last night. *But damn.* Her eyes were still enormous, and he could swear she looked about twenty-five.

Get a grip, he admonished himself, and tried to wipe the smile from his face.

"All right. Let's put aside my ballerina assessment capabilities for the moment. May I sit down?"

Margot nodded and moved to bring another chair to the table. She sat and angled herself towards him so that her profile showed in the mirror. He sat down, too, and was struck by the peculiar similarity to a police-questioning room. Here they both were, talking in front of a mirror. But unlike down at the station, he was confident there was no window on the other side for officers to watch their interaction. And he had certainly never sat so close to a suspect before or been aware of the light cinnamon scent that seemed to surround her. He had noticed it last night when he got into his car after leaving her apartment building. Nothing strong—just the merest suggestion of cinnamon.

He forced himself to focus. "How long did you know Yuri Ossipov?"

He pronounced it 'Óssipov,' with the accent on the first syllable, but Margot interrupted him instantly.

"It's Ossípov, with the i sounding like a long e. Yuri hates —hated—it when people said his name wrong. He loved America, but he hated it when people messed up his name."

"Sorry. It sounds like you knew Mr. Ossipov well." He said the name carefully and was relieved to see her nod.

"Yes, I did. I met him the first time when we performed in St. Petersburg three or four years ago, and then we danced together at an international gala in Paris two years ago. I encouraged Paul to try and bring him to Empire as a guest artist."

"And you said he had a boyfriend in Paris?"

"Yes. Damien Montrose. He's with the Paris National Ballet. They've been together for a couple years, at least. Yuri was going to fly back to Paris during our break, and then he hoped Damien would come over at some point during our spring season."

"So the Russians knew he was gay? They have a thing about that. I think the official word is that homosexuality doesn't even exist there." He filed the thought away to examine more closely later and spoke again without giving her time to answer.

"Did he have any other lovers here, that you know of?"

"Who? Yuri? Damien?"

"Yuri."

"Of course not. He loves . . . oh God." She stopped for a moment and looked down at her tightly clenched hands.

"He *loved* Damien. He was a total romantic and was always getting yelled at for having his phone around during class and rehearsals so he wouldn't miss any texts from him." Her eyes filled with tears and she looked around the small room. "I was going to try to find his phone myself and call Damien. Do you know what happened to Yuri's things?"

He could hear her trying to maintain a façade of calm in her voice, but her eyes darting around the room conveyed a growing sense of panic.

"Even my damn tissues are gone," she whispered, but once again Frank pulled a packet from his blazer pocket.

"Are you some kind of weird Boy Scout or something?" she asked, wiping her nose and eyes.

"Nope. Just a boy raised in a cold climate who learned not to go outside unprepared. My mother's a fanatic about stuff like that, and I guess it somehow rubbed off on me."

He gave her another second and watched how she seemed to force her facial muscles to relax. Was she performing for him now or displaying honest emotion? He pushed on.

"What about Damien? Could he have had other lovers? Could this have been a crime of passion?"

She looked at him, incredulous, the artificial calm gone. "Are you crazy, or just homophobic? They *loved* each other. What do you think, that there was some deranged jealous French guy hidden somewhere on stage last night, who somehow managed to put poison in a bouquet of plastic flowers?"

She almost snorted in derision and blew her nose. Frank admired the passionate defense of her deceased partner but tried to remember if he or anyone else had specifically identified the flowers as the source of the poison. Damn. He was so tired he couldn't remember what he had said to whom, but he had a feeling that he had carelessly spoken about the flowers to her last night. He looked at her and waited. Finally she answered, her voice cold.

"No. No other lovers. Yuri was a great guy, a devoted boyfriend, and a fabulous dancer."

"All right then. I'm sorry. I wasn't trying to impugn his character or insinuate anything. Were there any issues that you knew of with the Russian government?"

Now she gave him a seriously confused look.

"The Russian government? Like what? Spy stuff? Yuri was a dancer. He danced in Russia, he danced in Paris, he danced here, and I know he assumed he would dance in Russia again, eventually." She tilted her head slightly as she looked at him.

"Are you saying someone might have wanted to hurt him because he was Russian? Like those people in England?"

"I'm not saying anything. We have no idea who might have wanted to hurt or kill him, or even if he was the intended target. We're trying to find out as much as we can about everyone who was here last night, that's all. And right now, our primary focus has to be on the man who ended up dead."

Margot closed her eyes and inhaled, seeming to shrink into herself. Frank realized how harsh his words had probably sounded and tried to soften his approach.

"Did Yuri have problems with anyone here in this company? Any jealousies over roles? Or might he have owed anyone money?"

Her arms tightened across her midriff as if she were trying to hold herself physically together, and she silently shook her head.

"Okay, then. Let's look at the rest of the people who were on stage last night. Were you aware of any bad blood between other dancers? Or between dancers and stagehands or dancers and management? Can you think of any simmering resentments among anyone who was here last night that might have culminated in violence?"

Her head kept moving steadily back and forth.

"No. I can't. I really can't. This is a good company. There're always dancers who wish they could get better roles, or be cast more frequently, but by and large, I think everyone here is fairly happy. This is one of the top companies in the country—in the world, as a matter of fact—and everyone who's here worked super hard to get here."

"Okay, then, let's go back to that final scene last night. You were there, and Yuri. The character who brought the flowers on stage and then pretended to die from those Willi creatures," he paused to look down at his notes. "Jacob, right?

Did he and Yuri have any issues? Or did he have any enemies that you know of?"

Again, her head moved from side to side, her teeth coming out to chew on her lip once more.

"Not that I know of. Yuri and Jacob got along fine."

"Is Jacob gay?"

Her brows drew together and her response was cold.

"It's not true, you know. Not all male dancers are gay. A lot of them are, but Jacob isn't. His girlfriend is part of the chorus in *Phantom*. They have an apartment uptown. And I don't know of anyone who doesn't like him."

He looked at her steadily and told himself she was just another suspect. A suspect who had touched the bouquet of flowers before Yuri touched it.

"Then I need to ask you a few personal questions. Were you maybe in love with Yuri? Or with Jacob?"

Her eyes widened in disbelief.

"You *are* crazy! Haven't you heard anything I've been telling you? I loved Yuri. Everybody loved Yuri. But I wasn't *in* love with him; he loved Damien! And Jacob and Marissa have been together for years. What do you think this is, some kind of demented soap opera?"

"Do you have a boyfriend, Ms. Johnson? Or perhaps a girlfriend?"

Now her eyes truly were enormous, and the look she gave him could have melted ice.

"Why exactly are we here again, Detective whatever your last name is? I thought you asked for my help identifying staff members. For your information, I don't know anyone in this company who would want to hurt anyone else. And you know what? I don't even know anyone in this whole damn city who would want to poison another human being. Maybe you hang around with people like that, but I don't. I dance. Yuri danced. Jacob and Liza dance. We work hard, day in and day out because dance is our lives. We dance, and people who watch us get to escape the world for a little while and believe in princes and magic and true love and other such bullshit."

She had stood during her tirade, and now she walked towards the door.

"Unless I'm being questioned officially, I'd like to go to the cafeteria. I don't think there's any more I can help you with right now."

She held her scant five feet with the hauteur of an Amazon queen, and the glare she sent his way was scorching.

But Frank just looked back at her calmly. He stood, then, too, and followed her to the door.

"I didn't mean to offend, Ms. Johnson. Your dancing *was* magic last night. I can't even begin to understand why someone with your gift and commitment would consider retiring. You just said dance was your life, but my limited understanding is that you quit that life last night. The same night a fellow dancer was presumably murdered."

Margot stood still, her eyes narrowing slightly as she contemplated him. They stared at each other in silence, and he saw the fury fade as fear again took its place. It looked like fear. He had to remind himself that he was dealing with someone who was a master at presenting whatever she wanted to the world.

"I'm afraid you're going to be asked a lot of seemingly insane and rudely personal questions in the coming days. They're part and parcel of a murder investigation, unfortunately. Thank you for sharing your insight with me this morning. You have my number. Please use it if you think of anything, or if something else—anything else—happens that seems odd."

She nodded stiffly and moved out into the hallway. The

glare sent his way was devoid of anything save indifferent professionalism.

"Pull the door shut behind you, please. I'll be in the cafeteria." Her words were polite but clipped.

He tilted his head ever so slightly as he listened to her almost inaudible steps recede. She hadn't answered his question about a boyfriend or girlfriend.

* * *

Frank spent the next couple hours physically re-checking the backstage area. Many of the large prop pieces such as the village huts and trees were simply parked at the back and sides of the stage, shielded from sight by the numerous curtains and the vast reserves of space that were totally invisible from the audience.

Smaller props, including, presumably, the artificial bouquet that might or might not have killed Yuri, were normally kept in what resembled large wooden shipping crates, some with built-in shelves, but many of the actual props from the night before had been taken away for examination. The crates lined the passageways on both sides of the stage that led back to the wardrobe and dressings rooms— meaning passageways almost every damn person involved in the production would pass through.

He had spoken with several of the stagehands. The personnel list had been divided among himself and two other NYPD officers. State Department security officers sent over from the U.N. and FBI agents were attempting to deal with the Russian Consulate officials who had arrived, looking appropriately aggrieved and threatening.

The entire crime scene was a shit show. Far too many people had had access, if not obvious motive, and there were now far too many 'interested parties' trying to investigate.

Frank sighed and checked his notebook. No one he had spoken to had seen anything unusual. No one knew of any animosity towards Yuri or any of the other dancers who had been on stage at the end of the performance.

His stomach rumbled and he looked at his watch. 2:30. No wonder he was hungry. He needed to fortify himself before starting through the exhausting list of 'Willis' he needed to speak with. The director, Paul, had said the cafeteria would be open, and Margot had been going there when she left him in a huff. But where it might be was anyone's guess.

A middle-aged woman with salt and pepper hair pulled into a knot at her nape was standing with a clipboard by a clothes rack hung with capes and cloaks. Frank flipped through his pages of names. It might be the wardrobe mistress, Bettina Galick. She had been on Julio's list for an interview, but maybe she could point him in the right direction.

"Hi, ma'am. I'm Detective Sutton. I believe you spoke with one of my colleagues this morning. Is that correct?"

She glared at him as if he were an ill-behaving child speaking out of turn at school.

"Are you Bettina . . ." he checked again. "Bettina Galick?"

"Yes."

Amazingly forthcoming.

"Am I right? Did you already speak with one of the investigators?"

"Uh-huh."

"Okay, then. Great. So, I won't need to bother you any further. I was hoping, though, that you might help me find the cafeteria?" He tried to convey some boyish charm, but her continued glare made him summon patience before continuing.

"I see you're busy, and I know having all of us here is an

imposition, but this place is kind of a maze to anyone new to the theater."

He raised his eyebrows and stared at her, challenging her to respond.

"Follow me."

Well, he'd take that for a semi-win.

They left the stage area and walked down a long hallway, passing at least one corridor going off who knew where, turned down another, and then stopped in front of an elevator.

"Take this two floors down, then turn right."

She spun and walked off before he had time to thank her.

Lovely woman. Obviously not the company social director.

Fortunately, the cafeteria glass doors were visible when he turned right after exiting the elevator, and he could see a fair number of people sitting at the small tables that looked decades old.

His eyes scanned the room, and he caught sight of Margot. Her back was towards him, but he recognized her profile and her posture instantly. She was sitting with two men who obviously weren't dancers. They both looked far older than most of the male company members he had seen and had on faded plaid shirts, jeans, and well-worn shoes. The three were talking together like comfortable friends, and he was startled to feel a jolt of what almost felt like jealousy.

Get real, man. She's out of your league. But doubtless far out of those guys' league, as well.

Remembering her anger when she had stalked off earlier, he kept his head turned away as he walked towards the food. Pre-packaged salads that looked remarkably appealing, an industrial-sized tureen of what appeared to be minestrone, and a large assortment of protein and snack bars.

Frank had just picked up a salad and was looking around

for utensils when he noticed a change in the room's chatter. He turned his head and saw several people staring at their phones, and suddenly almost everyone was standing up, looking at each other with expressions of fear and confusion and moving towards the door.

His own phone buzzed, and he looked down. "An accident at the back of the stage. Left side. Get here asap."

He dropped his salad back on the counter and moved after the rest of the room's occupants who all seemed to have gotten a similar message to move.

Procedure and training kicked into place, and he called out loudly. "Stop, everyone. You all need to come back here. Whatever happened, we might need to know who was where, so to expedite things, I'll take a quick photo."

A grumble of responses came back at him: surprise, irritation, and confusion.

"Quickly," he said. "As soon as I have a picture of who was in here, you can go. Please stop anyone from getting on the elevator."

They moved back in. He saw the bewildered look on Margot's face and angry expressions on those of the two men she had been with. Why angry? What did they know? What had happened?

He motioned them all towards the food counter. The dancers were fairly easy to identify, but there were at least ten others. He recognized three stage hands he had spoken to that morning but didn't know the rest. They stood together warily, and he quickly took a photo and then waved them out.

"Excuse me, Ms. Johnson," he called out. She turned back and looked at him. He walked over and spoke more quietly. "Could you show me the stairs and the quickest route back to the stage?"

"Peter and Georgie said something happened to Rocco. Do you know what happened?"

"All I know was that there was an accident on stage. Can you get me there quickly, please?"

Her narrowed gaze held confusion and fear, but she turned and moved swiftly out the door. They turned left, pushed past the crowd trying to get into the elevator and half-ran down to the end of the corridor. She opened a door with the letters spelling "stairwell" barely discernable. The place was a fucking security disaster. How in hell had it passed safety inspection?

She moved swiftly and almost soundlessly up the two flights, and he struggled to keep up with her, holding the railing and trying to keep his gait even to avoid further aggravation to his leg.

Margot opened a door and he found himself facing one of the dressing rooms, but before he could even attempt to orient himself, she had turned right and was skimming down another hallway. Then there they were, once again amidst the huge dark labyrinth that was the backstage area. It had to be the enormous height that gave it such a cave-like quality. He had a sudden recollection of caverns his parents had taken him to on a long ago vacation, and how he had looked up as far as he could and seen only darkness. The backstage area gave him the same sensation.

But there was no cave-like silence now. People were shouting at each other and groups of women huddled together, crying. Frank pushed his way through to the area where a large group seemed congregated and then halted, jarred by the scene in front of him.

EMTs were lifting a figure onto a stretcher, a neck brace and backboard already in place. The injured person appeared to be a workman, but Frank was not close enough to see his features.

He saw his colleague, Julio Gonzalez, and moved over to grab his arm.

"What happened?"

"The guy fell while climbing one of the ladders to what they call the catwalk. He was apparently going to change a lightbulb, so he was probably only using one hand. These guys say they have backpack-type things they're supposed to use, but they never do. Except it seems the ladder broke while he was climbing."

Frank narrowed his eyes. "The ladder broke?"

"Yeah. Real interesting, huh? This place is giving me the fucking creeps, and I'm gonna get my little girl to give up ballet lessons. I think soccer would be safer."

Frank shook his head, annoyed at the scene around him and furious with himself. He had checked the whole stage earlier but had never thought to check the ladders. He peered over to the area behind where the EMTs and the crowd stood.

"Where's the ladder?"

"It's a built-in thing against one of those narrow walls. Not exactly a ladder-ladder, but I don't know what else it could be called."

"Any idea how badly he was hurt?"

"From what I heard, the EMTs think it's bad. I'm telling you, this place is messed up."

Frank sighed. "Okay. Tell me what you know. Who was around when he fell?"

"Those two made the first call." Julio pointed towards a pair of white men on the far side of middle-age who were casually dressed. One sat on the floor, and an EMT seemed to be checking him out. As Frank watched, the EMT attached a blood-pressure cuff.

"And they are?"

"Musicians. They were walking together from the pit on their way out, when Rocco yelled and then hit the floor."

"His name's Rocco?"

"That's what they're saying. Not the musicians; they didn't know his name. They heard him—they were further back on the side and didn't actually see it—and they ran over. They started yelling and one called 911, and it seems it only took a few seconds before we had a cast of thousands back on stage. I've got their names and their initial statements."

"The musician on the floor—what's his name?"

Julio looked down. "Andrew Gottlieb. He plays the oboe."

Frank moved toward the EMT and the musician. He pulled out his ID. "Is this man injured as well?" he asked the EMT.

"No, sir. He's just not feeling too well after what he saw. We're going to make sure he's all right before we pack up. The first patient's already on route to the hospital."

Frank looked down at the man. He seemed to be attempting to regulate his breathing, but his eyes kept darting around fearfully.

"Mr. Gottlieb?"

The man nodded, looked at Frank, and began speaking of his own accord.

"We thought we were finally going to get to leave. My wife had to stay home to take care of our granddaughter today because I usually do it. I don't come in 'till six, but I've been stuck here all day. And now this . . ." His voice trailed off and he shut his eyes.

"These guys will take care of you, and hopefully you'll be able to leave soon." Frank took the man's contact information, ascertained that he had told them all he could remember, and then stood up and moved back to Julio's side. "There's supposed to be another performance tonight. I think it has to be canceled. You agree?"

"Yeah. Something's definitely not right here." He gestured towards another older man standing a few feet away in workman's clothes. "Andy said three rungs of the ladder appear to have been tampered with."

Frank squinted for a second and then remembered. Andy was the stage manager.

"Christ. He didn't touch anything, did he?"

"Of course, he did. But when I told him to keep away and keep everyone else away, he snorted and said his fingerprints would have been there anyway, along with at least half the crew. But yeah, I think we gotta close this place down 'til we figure out what's what."

"Okay. I'll start with the director and see what needs to be done as soon as I call Mackie. I got a picture of the people who were in the cafeteria with me when Rocco fell. Get tape around the area close to where he landed and then try to get a concrete list of who was in this immediate vicinity when it happened and right before."

Frank rubbed the heel of his hand against his throbbing forehead as Julio moved off. Why the hell hadn't he ignored his phone when it first went off yesterday?

He looked around and saw Margot standing with a group of women. He'd pissed her off several times today already, so what was one more time?

"Ms. Johnson, could I speak with you, please?"

She separated herself and walked towards him, her expression wary. But there was fear there, too; he could see it in the way her arms were wrapped tightly around herself, as if she were freezing cold.

"Yes?"

"I'm sorry to keep bothering you, but could you bring me to wherever Paul Cashman might be?"

"He just left the stage with John Clay and Felicia Argon." At Frank's pained expression while he struggled to remember, she added, "They're our general manager and PR director."

"Fantastic. They sound like the exact group of people I need to see. Can you take me to them, please?"

"What happened? Did Rocco fall, or did someone do something to him? Is he going to be all right?" There was a catch in her voice, and he saw her teeth clench down on her quivering bottom lip when she stopped speaking.

"It's urgent that I find Mr. Cashman. As for Rocco, we're still trying to ascertain exactly what happened."

He saw her inhale and then deliberately relax her shoulders. A neutral, pleasant expression settled on her face.

"Of course, Detective."

"It's Frank, remember?"

"All I know is that I seem to have morphed from principal dancer into your back-stage tour guide in less than 24 hours."

"If it's any consolation, you're the most beautiful tour guide I've ever met."

The words were out of his mouth before his brain had time to engage, and he mentally kicked himself.

Focus, asshole. This is not the time or the place.

Those beautiful eyes widened once more, and Margot's teeth chewed on her bottom lip again for just a second. Then she turned and led the way back through the labyrinthine corridors.

* * *

Margot sat on the floor. Sitting was not something she was used to doing, but at the moment nothing was as she was used to. Yuri was dead and now something had happened to Rocco. Shivers of panic kept running up and down her torso, and she hugged her arms closer to her chest.

Almost every moment of life that she could remember

had been wrapped up in ballet. Yes, when she was very young her parents had encouraged her to try gymnastics, piano, soccer, and even softball. But the only thing Margot had wanted to do was dance.

It had been her mother's fault from the very beginning, of course. Yes, she had claimed that naming Margot was a gesture of respect to her great-aunt Margaret, but in truth, Margot's mom had been a ballet groupie and a passionate fan of Margot Fonteyn. Never a dancer herself, she filled her house nonetheless with ballet trinkets and memorabilia. And to her absolute delight, her daughter, Margot, had inherited her passion.

Family lore had it that Margot's mom had been invited by a friend with an older daughter to attend a *Nutcracker* performance one Christmas. The friend's daughter had been five while Margot was only eighteen months. And yet Margot's attention had been captivated while the five-year-old had whined and fidgeted. After that Margot's whole life had been ballet. When she leapt and twirled around the house, her mom bought her baby ballet video tapes and little tutus which Margot had worn everywhere until she was old enough for the youngest classes at her local studio.

Now, almost thirty-four years after seeing her first *Nutcracker*, Margot was, professionally at least, no longer a ballerina, and she had chosen to walk away of her own free will.

And yet again, it was to a degree her mother's fault. Of all the stories she had told Margot over the years, one that had struck her as horrifying had again involved her mom's beloved Margot Fonteyn. In the early eighties, desperate for money though essentially retired, the incomparable Ms. Fonteyn had taken a walk-on role as the nurse in a Nureyev production of *Romeo and Juliet*. As the nurse!

Margot had seen countless videos of Fonteyn and

Nureyev dancing, and she was sure her mother had somehow confused her memories. Margot Fonteyn had been one of the greatest ballerinas of the twentieth century. There was no way she had been relegated to the role of nurse.

And so Margot had searched for evidence to prove her mother wrong, all while loving every moment she spent training her own young body. Classes, at least five days a week, in tap, jazz, modern, but always, most wonderfully, in ballet. Margot was consistently the first one out of the dressing room to warm up at the barre, and the last one out of class after the final reverence. At home she stretched and plié-ed and swung her legs in grande battements while waiting for the microwave, brushing her teeth, doing homework, or talking on the phone.

Starting in ninth grade, she left school early every day to attend "academy" level classes, spent weekends rehearsing for performances, and departed for summer intensive programs the week school let out in June.

And then one day in the library, while supposedly on the computer doing research for a science project, she had found a mention in the NY Times and a video clip—from what appeared to be an illicit video—of Margot Fonteyn in the nurse walk-on performance.

Margot had been shocked and horrified at the images of the once-vibrant dancer reduced to a shadow of her former self. And right then, at the age of sixteen, she had vowed it would never happen to her. She would do everything in her power to become the best dancer she could, but she would never let herself grow old and diminished in the public eye.

So now she sat, thirty-six years old and "retired," wondering what the hell she was doing waiting for a detective while having no idea what she was going to do next with her actual life.

"Just rest and relax for a while," had been her constant

vague answer when her fellow dancers had asked what she planned to do after her final performance.

"You'll come home and stay with us for a while, won't you?" her mom had asked over and over the last several weeks, seldom stopping to notice Margot's lack of response.

But Margot had allowed herself to think only of her final season and had pushed even harder than usual in class, at rehearsals, and in each of her last performances.

Whenever thoughts of the future had crept up, she had pushed them aside. Just because she had built her own cliff and pushed herself to the very edge, didn't mean she had to look down. She would coach, or teach, or maybe even experiment with some of the choreography she sometimes imagined while listening to music. She had promised to help out during Paul's brief absence for his honeymoon, but beyond that, her future had hovered like the empty air off that giant cliff.

"You could always go to school, sweetheart," had been one of her mom's refrains. "Maybe let all those books you read and listen to bring you college credit."

While Margot knew that her parents were enormously proud of her, she also knew it had rankled her professor father just a bit that his daughter had not attended college.

Texts from her mother had been fast and furious last night, wanting to know what had happened and demanding assurance that Margot was all right. They had been at the performance and had been invited to the small celebration her closest friends had planned for her at "Alberto's" after the show—a celebration that had never taken place. Instead they had been shepherded out of the theater with the rest of the audience.

And now her mom was at it again. Margot's phone had vibrated numerous times with incoming texts, but so far, she hadn't been able to work up the energy to respond.

"What's going on, darling? You promised to keep me updated, but I just saw online that Yuri had died!!!! Please come home tonight, honey. We want to know you're safe!!!"

Somehow her mother never understood that one exclamation mark was more than enough. Margot typed a few reassuring words that she was fine, her parents shouldn't worry, and that she would be staying in the city.

Frank had mumbled something about canceling a performance while they were walking, but that was impossible. Margot had never heard of an Empire performance being canceled. She knew Broadway shows had been briefly halted after 9/11, and the Boston Ballet had had to cancel a couple programs a year ago due to crazy amounts of snow, but the Empire, which had had no performances scheduled during that long ago, sad September, had never closed. It couldn't happen. Could it?

Margot chewed on her bottom lip. She should get up and leave. She hadn't planned on being in the theater tonight, in any case, though she had made no other plans. But she found herself incapable of moving.

What was really going on? Could somebody truly be trying to hurt and even kill people working for the company? And if so, why? The trembling that had somehow become her constant companion began again as she thought about the events of the past 24 hours. Knowing it was ridiculous but unable to stop herself, she turned her head from side to side, checking to see if anyone was nearby. But no, she was alone in the hallway. She tried to force herself to relax, willing her muscles to stop quaking. There was no bogeyman waiting to jump out at her.

She had been telling the truth when she spoke to Frank earlier. She closed her eyes and leaned her head back against the wall. A strange sense of calm spread over her when she remembered being in her dressing room with him. He was such a warm, reassuring presence, and the memory of being held against his jacket last night filled her with an unfamiliar sense of . . . peace. How strange, since his only reason for being here was this total insanity, and he had certainly pissed her off with some of his stupid insinuations.

She went over in her head the questions he had plied her with. But no one had disliked Yuri; she was absolutely sure of that.

And now Rocco! She didn't know him well. He was just one of the many faces she was vaguely aware of in the darkened wings of the stage. Performing meant paying attention to the other dancers, catching her breath in her brief moments off stage, listening to the music, and counting beats. Always counting.

There was no music now. No music, no sounds of anything. She was in an upstairs level of the theater the dancers usually saw only upon initial hiring or perhaps firing —and she wasn't sure she herself had ever even been in most of the offices. Paul had mentioned a few times that she needed to meet with HR, but she had put it off, devoting all her energy to getting through her final performance. Maybe she should come in tomorrow; she certainly didn't know what else she was going to do with her day.

Was someone in one of these offices calling Rocco's family? And saying what? That there had been another incident? Was it possible that maybe his fall had been an accident after all?

Was there any connection between Yuri and Rocco? With her eyes still shut and her neck stretched back, her head against the wall, she struggled to remember anything that might point to a link. Nothing. Yuri had been about life, about joy. He loved to dance, he loved Damien, and he loved his little dog.

His dog! Damn! Was anyone taking care of Yuri's dog?

She pushed herself to her feet and tried to remember. Laska? Yes, that was it, she thought. A little white fluffy thing named Laska. Yuri had tried to bring her to the theater when he first came to Empire, claiming that there had been no problem with doing so in St. Petersburg or Paris. But Bettina had led the group of complainers. No one else brought their pets, and if rules weren't followed, the place would turn into a zoo. Or so they said.

And so Yuri had grumbled but then become fast friends with some dog walker he occasionally mentioned to Margot. She was a lesbian, he had told her with a huge smile, loving how he could say the word out loud. She was covered in fascinating tattoos, had bright pink hair, and he was under the impression she made almost as much money as Yuri himself. He had talked about her with wild enthusiasm and added the whole scenario to his long list of crazy things he adored about New York.

Margot couldn't remember the dog walker's name but felt a pang of sadness for little Laska. She had to find out if anyone was doing anything about the dog. Maybe Frank would know. She didn't really want to speak with him again, but he did seem the likeliest source of information.

John Clay's door opened just as she was debating knocking. John came out, looking thunderous, followed by Paul, Felicia, and Frank.

"I still think you're wrong," John was saying as Frank moved past him. "But the commissioner's given us no choice in the matter."

Margot was watching Frank's face and thought she saw his expression lighten as he caught sight of her. He stopped and then moved over to stand next to her as the other three moved down the hallway.

"Thanks for waiting." His face looked younger, suddenly, as he smiled at her, and she wondered how old he was.

"You knew I'd be lost if you weren't here to guide me out, right?"

His words were casual, but Margot knew instinctively that he was honestly glad that she was there.

"I needed to speak with you." She wouldn't mention that she had been sitting aimlessly, paralyzed by fear and indecision, before an actual need had come to mind. "I remembered that Yuri has a little dog. Her name is Laska. Do you know if anyone's been to his apartment?"

Frank's phone was already at his ear. Margot watched as he spoke with someone and then waited. Finally, "Yeah. I'll try to get over there with someone who can take her. Thanks."

He ended the call and looked at Margot.

"Can you take her?"

She stared blankly at him.

"What?"

"The dog. There were officers there today going over his whole apartment, and one of them took the dog out briefly and gave it some food, but they're wrapping up and were just going to leave it."

"They can't leave her alone!"

"That's why I'm asking if you can take her."

She continued to stare at him, her mind frantically trying to catch up.

"I . . . I don't know anything about dogs."

"Is there someone else here we should ask?"

Margot struggled to think. She had spent an evening at Yuri's apartment, as had some of the other principals and corps members, when he had a party for Russian Christmas a few weeks ago in early January. Had anyone played with the dog or showed it special attention? She couldn't remember anyone doing so.

"What about Damien?"

"The French boyfriend?"

She nodded.

"From what my boss told me this afternoon, he was questioned in Paris earlier today and told them he would fly to Russia to meet Yuri's body there. Maybe he'll eventually want the dog, but I don't think we can count on his help tonight, in any case."

He continued to look expectantly at her. When she said nothing, he asked, "Does your apartment allow dogs?"

"I think so. I think I remember a pets-under-20-pounds rule, or something like that, but I never paid any attention."

"So? Can you take her? Is she under 20 pounds?"

Margot stood frozen. A dog. She liked dogs, had always liked dogs. Heck, she had liked Laska and laughed with Yuri at her playful antics. But could she take care of one? But then again, Yuri had loved Laska. How could she not?

"I guess I'll have to." She whispered the words, but Frank had caught them and nodded.

"All right. Let's head over there and pick her up, and then I'll drive you both back to your place. Did you need to do anything else here?"

Margot's eyes widened. He was acting like her personal minder or caretaker and seemed to think he could direct her every movement. About to deliver a cutting retort, she saw him try to cover a yawn.

He had to be almost as tired as she was, and even though he was a cop, he had been nothing but polite and considerate. No doubt driving around dancers to pick up orphaned dogs was not part of his job description.

Instead of uttering the sharp retort that had come to mind, she reached out and touched his arm.

"You don't have to drive me again. I can manage."

He gave her a tired smile and unsuccessfully tried to hide another yawn.

"I'm sure you could, under normal circumstances, but even if you had a key—do you have a key?"

When Margot shook her head, he continued, "Even with a key, you couldn't get in because the apartment has to be sealed until the investigation is closed. If I take you, we can get in and out quickly, and then we can both maybe put today behind us."

She stared at him for a moment. His eyes held only honest kindness. She didn't think she had ever had even the briefest contact with any kind of policeman in her life, but he was not what she would have expected.

"This has been a poor introduction to ballet. I'm sorry about that. I hope someday you can come to a performance and just enjoy it."

"Well, I'd hazard a guess that today hasn't been what you expected your first day of retirement would look like, either. Let's get your stuff and go pick up the dog." He shook his head and smiled. "You yelled at me earlier for assigning stereotypes, yet here we are, going to get a teeny pampered dog from a male ballet dancer's home."

He rolled his eyes and shrugged his shoulders with great exaggeration. "Seems kind of frou-frou to me."

Margot narrowed her eyes back at him. "I didn't yell. I never yell."

"Oh, excuse me, your ladyship."

Margot laughed. She couldn't help it. Today had been an absolutely horrible day, but this guy was like a drop-in visitor from another planet, and almost everything he said or did surprised her.

"You're not like any of the detectives on tv."

"I'd say you're not like any of the dancers on tv, but I've never watched a dancer on tv. Now get going. You know I have no clue how to get out of this place."

Margot turned and led the way back to the elevator. She

quickly collected her bag and coat from the dressing room and helped Frank find his jacket from where he had left it outside the studio earlier in the day. She then found herself following him for a second night in a row to the unmarked black car parked in a yellow lined spot near the elevators in the underground parking garage.

"This really is totally bizarre," she murmured.

"What is?"

"I had never even been down to the parking garage before last night, and now you're driving me again. And I still say detectives on television don't give people rides."

"You don't strike me as someone who spends a lot of time watching tv."

"I don't!" Her voice was indignant.

"And yet you keep telling me how television police are supposed to behave."

"Well . . ." she dragged out the syllable, frustrated at not being able to come up with a response. "*Do* you usually drive people around the city?"

"Not at all."

"Then I was right. This is totally bizarre."

He had opened the passenger door for her, making a show of pretending to sag under the weight of her bag when he put it in the back seat.

Snow was falling as they exited the garage and he turned up the heat.

"What is most definitely bizarre is how we're all in danger of freezing to death thanks to the crazy weather brought on by global warming. Hold on a sec while I get the quickest route."

He entered the address into the GPS and moved the car smoothly into the evening traffic. It was only a bit after five, but what little sunlight there might have been that day was gone.

Margot shivered in spite of the heat blowing.

"No," she said softly, staring into dark, congested streets. Pedestrians had their shoulders hunched and their heads tucked down trying to avoid the wind and snow. "What's really crazy is that you're taking me to pick up Yuri's dog because he's dead." It kept happening: one minute she was fine, and the next minute it would hit her again like a smack in the face that her dear friend was truly gone.

His hand came out and touched her knee for just a second, and then he moved it back to adjust the screen on the complex dashboard. The volume of the almost constant police radio communications decreased slightly.

"Do you think the same person who killed Yuri tried to hurt Rocco today?"

"Do you?" His eyes didn't leave the road, but his head tilted slightly in her direction.

"I don't think any of this is even possible. And I can't believe tonight's performance was actually canceled. That just doesn't happen."

"We can't afford to take chances. Not until we have some idea what or who we're dealing with."

"How will you be able to figure it out?"

He gave her a quick glance.

"It's like a jigsaw puzzle. You keep picking up pieces and looking at them, trying to put things together, until finally you see the whole picture."

"And then everything just goes back to how it was? Except that Yuri's gone." Tears slipped down her cheeks.

"No. Nothing is ever the same after a murder."

Margot pulled off her glove and wiped the tears from her face with a fierce gesture.

"Did you find any of the puzzle pieces today?"

He made a sound like a soft snort. "You know I couldn't tell you if I did."

She turned her head and narrowed her eyes, studying him in the subdued light of the car's many electronics.

"I guess I'm still a suspect, right?"

His eyes met hers for the briefest second before returning to the road.

"Unfortunately, in a murder investigation, everyone is a suspect, at least in the beginning. But again, like with a jigsaw puzzle, as we fit pieces together, the pile of pieces remaining on the table gets smaller."

Margot stared at him a moment longer and then turned her head back to the snowy streets.

3

Wednesday Evening

L aska jumped around excitedly when they entered the apartment. The uniformed officer standing by the door said the FBI and Russian consular representatives had left about a half hour ago. He was to secure the premises and could leave as soon as Detective Sutton took possession of the dog.

Margot looked around. The apartment was quiet. Lights were on, but without Yuri's dynamic presence, it felt like the power was out. Yet Laska's excitement had a frenetic element to it. She kept yipping and running around from room to room.

"I'm going to check the kitchen for her stuff," she said to Frank. Entering, she noticed the spartan cleanliness, punctuated with whimsical color. A teapot with a brightly colored rooster design sat on the counter near the sink, a red toaster oven was tucked in the corner, and a large I 💜 NY mug rested in the sink, as if Yuri had just finished his tea. A box of expensive Belgian chocolates lay on the island. Yuri had loved sweets and had also loved teasing his female dancer friends that he could eat as many of them as he wanted.

Margot took in a choked breath. She had to concentrate on gathering up all of Laska's things. She found a canvas shopping bag on a hook in the pantry and put the dog's food and water dish into it along with the opened bag of kibble that was also in the pantry.

Margot narrowed her eyes, looking around. Dogs had papers like birth certificates or something-or-other, didn't they? Where would the dog's vet info and records be? She didn't see a likely spot in the kitchen, so she moved into the small living room area that fed from the entry into the kitchen. A large leather couch, a few contemporary chairs, and a glass coffee table, but nothing like a file cabinet. She moved towards the bedroom, feeling like she was trespassing into Yuri's private domain. Frank gave her a nod as she moved about, not interrupting his conversation with the other policeman. She knew she wasn't doing anything wrong, but she still felt guilty and uncomfortable.

Laska came running in behind her and used the little stepstool that was obviously hers to climb up onto the bed. She stood there, panting and staring at Margot expectantly. Margot stared back and sighed. Her own bed was probably about the same height. She wasn't sure she wanted a dog on her bed, but she didn't think she could be firm with her if she seemed to need it. She'd better take the damn stool, as well.

"Laska," she said imploringly, "where are the rest of your things, girl?" The dog cocked her head and gave another yip. Not much help from that quarter.

There was a small desk near the window with what looked like a laptop charger on it, but no sign of a laptop. No drawers, though, so not there. The closet door was open, and boxes were on the floor. Probably lots of people had been going through Yuri's things today. She assumed anything that could possibly be related to his death had been taken away, although she couldn't imagine how anything here could explain how or why he had collapsed on stage last night after smelling a bouquet of artificial flowers.

Margot forced herself to bend down and check the boxes. The folders had words written on the tabs in Russian, but there was one with a paw print sticker next to a Russian word that looked like it had five letters. She picked it up and let out the breath she didn't realize she had been holding. Vet receipts from a clinic not far from Yuri's apartment. In English. *Thank goodness.*

She took the file and put it in the bag, glancing again at the other folders. The way some were sticking up out of the box, it was evident that they had been examined. *Was* there something in them that could indicate why he had been killed?

Margot shuddered. She needed to get out of the apartment, needed to get away from the idea that maybe someone she or Yuri knew, or had known, was a killer.

She picked up the stepstool and took one more look around the room. Yuri had slept in this room, tired from performances, happy after parties, probably even nervous when he had first come to New York. Now it was just a shell, and the vibrant life it had sheltered was no more. She walked out, Laska jumping off the bed to follow her. Frank was standing by the door. He was still talking with the uniformed officer, but she was relieved to see he had the dog's leash in his hand.

"I think I've got everything . . .," she hesitated, feeling awkward at interrupting and making any kind of presumption.

"I'm fine with calling a taxi if you need to stay," she quickly added.

He turned his head and studied her for a moment, as if surprised by her words.

"No need. Let Officer Trebman see what you're taking, and we can get going."

Margot nodded and held open the canvas bag. Trebman took out the folder and looked at it, and then put it back and smiled.

"Good thing those are in English. The guys who were here earlier were frustrated when they had to wait for one of the Russian speakers to get here. And the dog's certainly been active enough, so I don't think there's any chance its food was tampered with." The man chuckled as if he had made a great joke.

Margot stared at him in horror. Was it possible there was other poison here in the apartment? She turned her eyes to Frank. She had known him only a few hours, but he seemed to be the only source of authority and reassurance left in the world.

Somehow, he understood her distress. "I think everything here is under control, and the dog will be glad to get away from all the commotion."

He bent down awkwardly and snapped the leash to Laska's collar. Margot remembered suddenly that she had noticed him limping earlier, and she wondered if there was something wrong with his leg. She'd ask later, if the moment seemed right.

"Let's go," he said, standing up. "Give me the bag and you take the leash. Thanks for your help, Trebman. Have a good night."

As they walked to the elevator, a door that had been partly ajar opened.

"Do you know what happened?" The speaker was a young girl—maybe twelve or thirteen. "Is Yuri really dead?"

Margot and Frank stopped, but Laska barked and pulled towards the girl excitedly.

"Hey, Laska," she said, coming out of her apartment and bending down to pet the dog.

"You're taking him away, so it must be true." She looked stricken, and Margot felt another wave of pain sweep over her.

"Did you know Yuri well?" Frank asked, his voice somehow both compassionate and professional.

"He knows how much I love ballet, so he got me tickets a few weeks ago." She stopped and looked at Margot.

"Wait! Are you Margot Johnson? Oh my God, you are, aren't you? I love watching you dance, and I told Yuri I wanted to meet you. But now they're saying he's dead!" Her voice rose and her face crumpled.

Margot felt tears come yet again to her own eyes.

"He is dead. I'm so sorry. We don't know exactly what happened yet," she said, glancing at Frank. "But if you want to give me your number or your email, I can try to get you some more tickets, sometime." Even as she spoke, she was jolted by the thought that she, herself, would no longer be performing.

"I can't promise," she added, "but I can try." Surely, she would still have some perks in the days and weeks to come.

Margot pulled her phone from her coat pocket and opened up the contacts.

"Here. Put whatever you want in here, and I'll get back to you, soon. And maybe you can come over sometime and see Laska, since she seems to really like you." A thought came to her. "Would you like to keep Laska for a bit, at least until one of Yuri's family comes for her?"

The girl smiled at Margot through her tears. "I can't. My

mother's allergic. I wish I could, cause she's such a sweet dog. But you're nice, just like he was. I'm sorry your friend is dead."

"Me, too," Margot said quietly. She reached out and hugged the girl, then checked what she had put on her phone. "I'll call you, Katie. I promise."

Katie nodded, and Margot and Frank moved back to the elevator. Laska seemed to want to stay with the girl, so Margot bent down and picked her up, holding her tightly to her chest.

"You'll see your friend, again, Laska, I promise."

* * *

The wind seemed to have grown even fiercer by the time they exited the apartment building to head back to Frank's car. Snow hit their faces like sharp pieces of confetti and Laska sneezed, pushing her little head against Margot's underarm as if seeking shelter.

"Lovely weather to bring a dog home for the first time." Frank reached out to take Laska and the stool while Margot got into the car. He handed the dog back to her, and Laska turned around twice on Margot's lap and then settled down, her little head between her paws on top of Margot's knees.

Frank laughed. "You may have a problem convincing her to use her own four legs to do her business tonight."

"Oh, damn." Margot closed her eyes and shook her head slightly. "I didn't even think about night time walks."

"You never had a dog?"

"Nope. We had cats, and my parents still do, but no dogs. My grandmother had a sweet dog I used to love playing with, and I spent a lot of time with him, but he died when I was about twelve."

"Probably best to postpone your move to the senior

center, then. You'll have to learn the fine art of coping with a pampered pet in a crowded city during a polar vortex."

Margot shivered. "Thanks." Then she turned her head and gave Frank an assessing glance. "You seem to know about dogs. Maybe you'd like to take her home?"

"Ha. Nice try, but don't even think it. My schedule is insane during a normal week—not that I can remember the last one of those. Besides, if I wanted a dog I wouldn't want a little pretend one the size of a cat. I've never understood the attraction."

Margot continued to study him. "I think Yuri simply enjoyed her company. Having her around, as tiny as she is, gave him a link to the real world—something totally apart from dance classes and performances. He was always talking about Jet's new hair color. . . Yes! That's her name. I couldn't remember before. I should probably try to contact her." She was silent for a minute, looking out at the falling snow and then turning back towards Frank.

"I asked you earlier and you never answered. What happened to Yuri's phone?"

"It was taken with everything else they picked up last night. It will probably get sent over to the Russian Consulate as soon as they release his body along with any other personal effects."

"Do you think there's any way I can get numbers off his contacts? I should call Jet and I'd like to maybe try and contact Yuri's family and Damien."

"Who's this Jet?"

"The dog walker he used. She was totally New York and completely unlike anyone from the ballet world. Yuri found her fascinating."

Frank didn't respond for a moment. Traffic was moving slowly as snow continued relentlessly to accumulate in the streets despite the non-stop movement of vehicles.

"I'll check and get back to you."

His words were clipped as if uttered reluctantly, and Margot was again contrite.

"I'm sorry. I keep seeming to presume upon your kindness. You've been incredibly generous with your time and help already."

"It's okay. All part of the job."

Margot considered his words while wondering how much of the chatter coming from the police radio Frank was meant to pay attention to. So much of it sounded like gobbledygook to her.

"It's not, though, is it? I know we were joking about tv police before, but what is your job really like usually?"

He gave her a quick glance and his lips lifted in a half-smile. "There's no 'usual' in police work. Every day's different. Sometimes a case will last a few days or weeks, but I never know for sure when I start my day what I'll end up doing. I know I'll probably be back at the theater tomorrow because we've got to figure out what's going on there, but beyond that, who knows? I'll be talking with my boss tonight after I drop you off and get a better idea where we need to focus next."

"Can I do anything to help?" The words came out of her mouth without thought.

Frank laughed. "When I asked you questions earlier, you stormed out, remember?"

"Stormed? I did no such thing."

"You most certainly did."

Margot narrowed her eyes. "You were asking totally absurd questions."

Frank snorted. "Well, excuse me, your princess-ship. They may have seemed absurd to you, but understanding relationships is what usually ends up allowing us to solve murders. Sure, there are random killings occasionally, but more often than not, the perpetrator knows the victim and has some kind of rationalized excuse, however twisted."

"So, you really think someone from the company wanted to kill Yuri?"

"Before this afternoon I would have said probably. But now Rocco's been hurt, and it seems just chance it happened to him and not one of the other stagehands. So that makes the whole picture more murky."

Margot saw that they were getting closer to her neighborhood. It was now at least an hour and a half since they'd left the theater, and Frank, who had looked so tired earlier in the day, had given all that time to her and Laska.

"I'm sorry I left earlier," she said. "But I didn't storm. It seemed that some of your questions were hurtful and biased. I guess you need to learn a lot, super-fast, about people you know nothing about."

"Yeah, we do. And we often have to dig into areas of peoples' lives they don't want anyone to know about. Everyone has secrets, and sometimes those secrets are enough to get someone killed or enough to drive someone *to* kill."

They pulled up in front of her building, Frank again stopping in the 'no parking' area with his hazards on.

"Is there some kind of secret marking on your car that keeps you from getting ticketed?"

"If I told you, it wouldn't be secret, now would it?"

She could hear the smile in his voice as he got out of the car. She opened her door and was hit by the blast of frozen air.

"Oh my God, it's cold."

"Why don't you put her down right now and walk her a bit before you go up. I'll stay here with your stuff."

Margot shivered but saw the obvious sense in his words. She looked down at her fashionably high-heeled boots that reached snuggly to the top of her calves but provided little real protection from the weather.

"Looks like I'm going to have to unearth my ugly Uggs," she sighed. She'd manage for now, especially if Laska acted like a smart dog and did her business quickly.

Fortunately, she did. Margot laughed at the little stream of yellow that made the steam rise out of the snow and then was relieved to realize there was some kind of container attached to the leash with bags in it when Laska made a more solid pile a few steps beyond the building's entrance. Where in the world did you buy bags to go in this kind of little plastic case? There probably had been more of them in Yuri's apartment, but she had never given doggie poop a thought. Why had she agreed to this? She knew nothing about dogs!

But Laska was looking up at her imploringly, her little body quivering in the cold.

"Oh, sweetheart," Margot said and bent down and picked up first her mess, and then the shivering dog. "I guess we'll learn together. It's just too bad we have to learn in the middle of a snowstorm."

Frank got out of the car again as she approached, obviously finishing a phone call, though she couldn't make out the words. He had parked in a space a few feet away from her door, in a spot Margot was pretty sure was reserved only for taxis.

"I'll carry your bag and the dog's bag up since you're once again carrying that silly animal. I know its legs work—I saw her moving on her own in Yuri's apartment."

"It's only because she's freezing. But I can get them. I don't want to keep you."

"Move! I know your bag of bricks weighs a lot more than that ball of fur, but with all her things, too, it'll be too much. I've got them."

Margot still felt guilty but decided he'd get back on his

71

way faster if she stopped arguing. She moved quickly to open the door and was relieved to feel the warmth of the foyer embrace her as she stepped in and held the door for Frank. Once again she noticed the slight limp.

"Have you hurt your leg?"

He gave her a look she couldn't read and shook his head. "The elevator?" was all he said.

"Yes. I'm on the fifth floor."

She hurried to push the button and Laska seemed to realize her feet were no longer in danger of freezing. She squirmed and Margot put her down. The dog immediately began sniffing around the floor of the foyer, but the elevator doors opened, and she pulled forward on the leash, obviously used to apartment living.

Frank stepped in behind them, and Margot pushed the button for her floor. They waited, and after a second, she broke the awkward silence.

"Can you go home now, or do you have to go to a police station? You don't have to go back to the theater, do you?"

"No, I'm done there for tonight. Ten hours on my first day off in a while is enough, even for me."

"Oh, no. Was today really your day off?"

"It was supposed to be. But that's part of the normal in police work."

The elevator doors opened and they stepped into a well-lit and clean hallway. Margot noticed Frank checking the area to either side of the elevator as she moved to her entrance a few steps down the corridor.

"It's a safe building. There's never been any trouble, and now I have a guard dog."

"Yeah, right. You'll be perfectly safe as long as the bad guys are all Barbie Doll size."

Margot smiled as she opened her door and flipped the light switch. "Here you go, Laska. Home sweet home." She turned back to Frank, not realizing how close behind her he was.

"Oh, sorry." She took a small step backward but then moved towards him again.

"Let me take all that stuff. Thank you so very much for all you did for us tonight." She looked around uncertainly. "Do you want something to drink or to use the bathroom or anything? This has all probably taken far longer than you planned."

Frank hesitated but then nodded a little sheepishly. "I actually could use a quick trip to the restroom, if you don't mind."

"Of course." She was startled to see him removing his shoes. "Oh, my goodness, you don't have to do that."

"They're wet and dirty. Of course, I do. It'll take only a minute." He had given a quick glance around her small but well-kept apartment and now moved unhesitatingly to the partially open door of the bathroom.

Margot took off her coat and her own boots, marveling at this strange man. He had been so considerate last night, seemed so harsh and impersonal this afternoon, and now had been the epitome of kindness all evening. Detective Frank Sutton was an extraordinary man, unlike anyone she had ever known before.

Laska seemed intent on checking out every inch of the apartment. Margot unpacked the two dog dishes, filled one with water and then looked pensively around her kitchen, wondering where the best place would be to put it.

Frank stepped out of the bathroom and gave her a small nod.

"Thank you." He turned and watched Laska for a moment and then gave Margot a half smile.

"Looks like your new roommate is happy. I hope for your

sake that she's well-trained and can make it through the night."

Margot smiled back. "I'm pretty sure I would have heard if she was the kind of dog who kept Yuri up. Thanks again. I really. . . um . . ." her voice trailed off. He had been a half-step ahead throughout the entire evening, anticipating her every need, and she had been inexplicably comfortable in his company despite the bizarre circumstances.

He was staring back at her as Margot stayed silent. He nodded again and moved to put his shoes on. "Do you think you'll be back at the theater tomorrow?"

"I don't know. I was supposed to have the rest of this week off and then help with the rehearsals next week after the wedding on Monday."

Frank straightened and his face grew thoughtful. "Tell me about the wedding. It's Paul, right? Whom is he marrying? And why now in the middle of the season and the middle of winter? And on a Monday?"

Margot remembered his words from only a short time ago. He had said they often solved cases by learning personal details, but she wanted to ask her own question first.

"What's wrong with your leg? Why do you have a brace?"

Frank colored ever so slightly and moved his left pant leg down even though nothing was now showing. But Margot had seen the bottom of a brace as he put on his shoes.

"It's nothing. An injury from my time in the military."

"It can't be nothing if you need a brace. And I noticed you limping earlier."

He looked at her and shook his head slightly.

"Margot, it's late. I know I'm beat, and given what the last twenty-four hours have entailed, you probably are, too. Tell me about the wedding, and I can give you all the gory details about my leg another time."

Margot tilted her head and assessed him. "I'll hold you to that, Detective Sutton." She straightened her shoulders.

"Paul is marrying Debi Judson. They've been seeing each other on and off for at least a year or so, which no one was supposed to know about, of course, though everyone did. I got the sense they were serious and would probably have ended up marrying anyway. But Debi's pregnant, and apparently, she and her family are closet conservatives, and it's important to them that they marry before she starts showing."

"Whoa. That was more than I expected. Does everyone know all that?"

Margot emitted a mirthless chuckle. "Yes and no. This is a ballet company, so rumors travel faster than the flu on the subway. Debi's been in the corps for three years, but just before Christmas she suddenly announced that she was giving up dance and returning to school to study personnel management. Then several of us got wedding invitations and understood why Debi had looked so green in the weeks after Thanksgiving."

"But why on a Monday? I've never heard of anyone getting married on a Monday."

"It's not so uncommon in the dance and theater world. We don't perform on Mondays, so if you don't want to take time off, or if you don't want to make your guests take time off, that's when you do it."

The right side of Frank's mouth scrunched up as he seemed to consider her words.

"You said several of you. Meaning some didn't get invitations. Would that kind of thing lead to problems? Is Paul liked? Might anyone else have been in love with him or thought he was in love with them? And what about Debi? Who are her friends?"

Margot bit her lip and regarded him. "Why don't you

come and sit down for a couple minutes? Don't worry about your shoes—" She caught the half-smile that returned again to his face. He really was quite attractive when he wasn't glaring, and he probably was a little younger than she had first guessed. And someone had taught him remarkable manners.

"I don't know about you," she continued, "but I'm hungry and thirsty. I can make a quick grilled cheese and something hot to drink—tea, coffee, or even soup. And then I can try to answer your questions. I heard what you said before, and I understand why you're asking."

Frank's eyes widened. "What kind of soup?"

Margot laughed. "Wow. You're easy. Let me check."

She looked in the kitchen cupboard.

"Minestrone, black bean, southwestern vegetable, curried lentil . . ."

"No Campbell's tomato?"

Margot looked at him with her eyebrows raised and said nothing.

"Curried lentil sounds good. I can stir the pot while you make the grilled cheese."

He had surprised her again. Just when she thought she had this guy figured out, he did or said something unexpected. She herself was starving, and she assumed he was too, but she had fully expected him to turn down her offer.

The kitchen was tiny, though spacious enough by New York standards, so they stood close together as Frank stirred the pot and Margot removed bread slices from the freezer and put the sandwiches together.

"You don't mind fake cheese, do you?"

"FAKE cheese?"

"Yeah. I'm a vegan, but the cheese is actually very good. You can't tell the difference, honest."

"Huh. I guess I should have clued in when there was no

chicken noodle on your list of soups. A vegan, though? How in the world can you work as hard as you do physically on a vegan diet?"

Margot rolled her eyes. "You're obviously part of the teeming masses of nutritional know-nothings. A vegan diet is the best diet for all levels of physical activity."

Frank snorted. "Yeah, right. I don't think any of my army buds would agree with you on that. None of my police colleagues, either, for that matter."

"As I said, teeming masses of ignorance."

She worked quickly and efficiently, leaving the sandwiches to brown while she got down plates, glasses, and bowls.

"So, to drink I have water, seltzer water, ice tea, hot tea, or instant coffee. I'm assuming you don't want wine or beer."

His shudder was exaggerated. "Instant coffee?"

"I don't drink it much myself, and when I do, I treat myself to something over-priced from the coffee shop. I only keep the instant here for when my parents are in the city. I do have red wine, and there're a few bottles of beer that I keep for my dad." She raised her eyebrows, waiting.

Frank smiled and shook his head. "Water's fine. The soup's ready, if you can pass the bowls."

She did so, and he carried them through to the small circular table in the open area beyond the kitchen. The apartment was compact, but Margot's parents had been insistent that she take some of their "extra" carpets, and the place had a quiet elegance that she loved. A multi-colored afghan crocheted by her mom covered the back of the comfortable love seat where Laska was already tucked in, and two small bookcases framed the television that stood on a beautiful chest of drawers.

Seeing Frank's gaze, Margot smiled. "My father made

that. My parents spoil me horribly, so the least I can do is keep instant coffee for them."

"I think anyone who can make furniture like that deserves at least an espresso machine."

Margot laughed. "I'll tell him you said that. Or maybe I won't because it will get him thinking he needs to get me one."

They sat down, and it occurred to Margot that their positions were similar to how they had sat that morning in her dressing room. It seemed like days had passed, but it had been less than ten hours. Somehow things had changed between them, though, and she now felt like she was sitting with a friend. Yet as she looked at him, she was struck again by how tired he seemed.

"Ask me everything you want to know, and I'll answer as quickly as I can so you can get home."

"You're kidding, right? This fake stuff smells delicious, and it's the first meal I've sat down to in I can't tell you how long. Now you're going to rush me through it?"

Margot shrugged. "It's up to you. I'm just saying, you look like you could use a good night's sleep."

"A home cooked meal, a cozy apartment, a dog nearby. . ." Frank waggled his eyebrows up and down in an over-the-top suggestive manner. "Watch it, lady, or I might be tempted to curl up right there next to Laska."

"Good luck with that. She doesn't look like she's ready to move anytime soon, poor thing, and you look a little big for sleeping on that love seat."

They gazed for a moment at the dog, and the sleeping animal somehow reminded them both of what had brought them there.

Frank took out his notebook, and as they talked, he jotted down notes about company members and their relationships.

This time Margot did her best to answer all his questions as completely as possible, stopping at times to correct herself or check that he had gotten down last names as well as first names.

Throughout their conversation he had monitored the messages coming in on his phone. One in particular caught his attention, and he held it out for her to see. Initial tests indicated an injury to Rocco's spinal cord that might leave him paralyzed, but it looked pretty certain he would live.

Margot huddled into herself, her arms wrapped tightly around her middle. The horror of all that had occurred in the last twenty-four hours was almost too much. She pushed her plate aside and looked up to see Frank staring at her, compassion on his face.

"And you don't know of any connection between Yuri and Rocco?"

She shook her head. "None." She thought for a moment. "It's probably not quite the same thing, but do you have a connection with the people who take care of police cars? Or with, I don't know, maybe with the guys who take care of the police horses? Or the station custodians? It's like that. We work more or less in the same place, but we don't really work together, if you know what I mean. I know Andy, a little bit," she saw the question in Frank's eyes. "The stage manager."

Frank nodded.

"He's been there forever, and he's the one we interact with the most. All the rest I know by sight, and I say 'good morning' if I see them in the elevator, but that's all. And Yuri's only been here this year, so he probably didn't even know Andy that well, let alone Rocco."

Frank nodded again, and they were silent for a moment or two. Margot looked over and saw that he had eaten everything on his plate.

"Can I get you anything else? I can make another sandwich if you'd like."

Frank started and looked guilty. "God, no. That was perfect. And you were right—it tasted great. Next time I'll have to let you go all propaganda on me and convince me how vegan is best."

As Margot stood up, she couldn't help but wonder at his words 'next time.' As if they were somehow becoming friends. The idea was preposterous, but nonetheless appealing.

"Let me help you clean up."

"Don't be ridiculous. If it weren't for Laska and me, you would have been home hours ago. Do you realize it's almost ten?"

Frank rose and collected the two plates and bowls as Margot picked up the glasses. "Yes, but now I've been fed and am far better informed than I was a few hours ago."

He carried the dishes to the sink and examined the still-orderly working space. "I'll yield this time, since it looks like it won't take more than five minutes, and God only knows how long it will take me to get home in this weather. But getting a good meal was just what the doctor ordered. I'm not sure what food, if any, I even have in my own kitchen at the moment."

Margot moved instinctively to the freezer. "Here. My mother bakes me muffins and breads almost every week, and they tend to back up." She opened the door, and as if to prove her point, a freezer bag fell out.

Frank grabbed for it and they both laughed.

"See what I mean? She doesn't believe me when I tell her I have enough. Take a couple—that bag you're holding has banana muffins, I think, but let me give you a couple more. That way you'll have something to eat in the morning."

"I can't take your food like that."

"Can you not see how much I have here?" She smiled. "You'll be doing me a favor. And don't worry, they're actually pretty good. But I can't get through them as fast as she can bake them, and she doesn't listen when I tell her again and again that I try to limit my carbs."

Frank looked at the frozen muffins in his hand and shrugged. "I'm not going to be an idiot and refuse free food. Thank you. And thank your mother for me."

"Oh, no. That would be far too dangerous. I tell my mother a man likes her muffins, and she'll be reserving a wedding hall. Just go on your way, Detective Sutton, and enjoy them."

She took a paper bag out of a side cupboard, added a few more plastic bags from the freezer, and handed it to him.

"Think of it as a token of my gratitude for all your help with Laska. And for trying to find out what happened to Yuri. And for telling me about Rocco."

The laughter of a moment ago faded as they looked at each other quietly. Frank nodded and moved to the door. As he bent to tie his shoes, which he had removed earlier in spite of her protests, Margot again saw the edge of a leg brace.

"You never told me about your leg."

Frank straightened and studied her for a moment. "I've got to get to the bottom of what's going on at this odd ballet company of yours, but how about we agree to get together after the case is closed? You can tell me about retirement, and I can give you the boring story of my leg."

Margot bit her lip. Was he asking her out on a date? She could barely remember the last time she had gone on an actual date. He was still looking at her, but she thought she could see a hint of surprise in his own expression as well. *Damn.* He was hot, he was smart, he was kind, but he was a cop, for god's sake. And they had only met because someone had killed Yuri and tried to kill Rocco.

"Let's see how the next few days go."

"Right. Thanks again for supper. Good luck with the dog."

"Thanks. Be careful driving home." The weather had been horrible enough when they pulled up more than an hour ago; the roads were probably a lot worse by now. She spoke again without giving herself time to reconsider. "Could you maybe send me a quick text when you get home? I don't mean to impose or anything, but I feel really guilty about keeping you out so late."

Frank looked at her again and then reached out and gently brushed a lock of hair off her face. Was he going to kiss her? Did she want him to? Margot felt an almost overwhelming urge to move towards him, but she resisted. Of course, he wasn't going to kiss her. She had to get her shit together. She pasted a professional smile on her face.

"I'm a retiree, now, after all, and have to be thinking about a second career. Maybe private eye? So, I'll need to know you're okay. I might need to hire you as a coach, or something. . ." she trailed off, giving a slight shrug of her shoulders. Oh, God. She was babbling.

She noticed fine lines around his eyes as he smiled at her again.

"Good night, Margot. I'll send you a text when I get home."

He pulled the door firmly shut behind him.

A canceled performance. Even better than expected. Lost revenue, lost confidence, lost prestige . . . exactly what the fucking Empire Ballet and its precious Paul Cashman deserved. Rocco—he hadn't been a bad guy. But that didn't matter. Cashman had made it to the top leaving lots of collateral damage behind, so whatever happened now was all his fault. What were a few more bodies on his tab? It was time they all got a taste of what it felt like to be sidelined and ignored. A few more days and the top brass might decide to clean house and get rid of all the garbage. It wouldn't be a moment too soon.

4

Thursday

The morning meeting at the precinct was heavy on detail: names, theories, and histories, but light on any real progress.

"The feds say they haven't found anything from the files they took from Ossipov's apartment."

Frank's head lifted at the incorrect pronunciation of Yuri's name, but he resisted the impulse to correct his boss. He didn't want curiosity aroused unnecessarily.

"And the autopsy confirmed what we thought. Apparently, he had asthma, and there seems to have been a totally bizarre mixture of poisons covering the plastic bouquet. It could have been a serious threat to anyone, but it was without doubt enough to bring down an asthmatic taking a deep theatrical sniff."

"What exactly was the bizarre mixture?" Julio asked.

"At least three different pesticides and antifreeze. We're dealing with some kind of real sicko."

"And the broken rungs of the ladder were definitely intentional?"

"Yup. Cut through and covered in matching duct tape. We need to speak with all the crew that would normally climb that thing and try to figure out who the last person to use it was. Is it something they climb daily? Several times a day? Once a week? Mason's been making phone calls this morning, and I should have her report soon. By the way, Sutton, she's kind of pissed at you."

"At me? Why?"

"She says she's been covering the ballet and opera regularly for two years and has never seen anything more exciting than a stuck curtain and a horse that got a little frisky onstage during some stupid opera. She gets put on bed rest, and you end up witnessing a murder."

"Yeah. Precisely what I always wanted. And think about what you just said. I was one of—what? a thousand—maybe two thousand—people who witnessed a murder, and none of us has a clue."

"Yeah, well, it's our job to get a clue, and get one fast. Gonzalez, I want you to check in with Rocco again at the hospital, find out if he can tell you anything else, and then, depending on what he says, you'll continue going over the list of everyone who normally handles props. It doesn't look like he was specifically targeted, but who knows?

"Sutton, I want you back at the theater as well. I think our guys did a pretty good job checking the place last night, but surprise, surprise, no vats labeled poison turned up. Duct tape, yes, in all colors of the rainbow. Apparently, it's used regularly for all kinds of things. And they've a huge tool collection, with several power saws that could easily have

85

been used to cut the ladder. Some of them were covered in prints, and one—get this—was miraculously print-free.

"So, we need to watch and listen and try to figure out who hates who and why. That ballerina that retired—what was her name? She was on her way out. A coincidence? Was she leaving voluntarily? Or was she forced out and is now getting payback through murder?"

"I've spoken with her a few times already, Sir. I'm pretty sure she was leaving voluntarily."

"Yeah? Seems kind of weird. She's what? Thirty-five? Check into her a little more. Smells kind of fishy to me. And then dig around and see if maybe Ossipov was carrying on with anyone at the company. I understand he had a partner in France, but maybe there was hanky-panky going on here as well, and somebody got jealous."

Frank took a deep breath and fought the urge to interrupt. Chief Mackie was only voicing some of the same questions he had had himself, and the chief would see the notes he had finished putting in immediately before the meeting started. He waited for his boss to give instructions to the others in the room and then pulled out his notebook.

"As I said before, Sir, I spoke with Miss Johnson for a while yesterday, and I updated my notes a few minutes ago. She gave me information on several of the company members. The artistic director, Paul Cashman, is getting married this Monday, and she filled me in on who's close to whom, and who might be holding grudges."

"And? You didn't call with a suspect, so I'm assuming you don't have one. Am I right? Which means you've got to dig deeper. Somebody there has already killed once, maybe tried for twice, and might be planning more. We gotta get this guy and stop him. Or her. Or them. So, go find out if this Miss Johnson is maybe hiding a violent side. And if she's not, find out who is."

"Yes, Sir."

* * *

Frank stood by his desk, trying to decide his next step. He thought he remembered Margot saying she wouldn't be at the theater today. The commissioner had said performances would be canceled for the rest of the week, unless the case were solved, but Frank was pretty sure rehearsals and classes were still scheduled. Mackie had ordered him to check into Margot, but Frank thought the notes he'd taken last night concerning various dancers gave him a good outline for those he needed to interview first.

An unfamiliar sensation of pleasure passed through him as he remembered the previous evening. In the nine meaningless years of his marriage, he couldn't remember a single evening that had been as quietly comfortable as last night.

He had been so young and stupid when he first met his ex, Brenda, the two of them intoxicated as much by sexual exploration as by the alcohol they had gleefully consumed as under-aged teens partying with their peers in upstate New York. Everything had been a lark, and the thrill of doing his patriotic duty after 9/11 had overcome any remaining sense. His little sister, just finishing elementary school, had made a horrible face when he confided his proposal plans to her soon after enlisting.

"Why would you want to marry her?"

"What do you mean why? She's nice, she's pretty, and she is smart. You'll be getting a big sister at last."

"You're an idiot. One: she's not really nice. She only pretends to be." Michelle had held up her hand, ticking off her points.

"Two: she's not all that pretty. She wears way too much makeup and her bra is padded."

Frank had stared at his twelve-year-old sister in horror. What kind of monster was she turning into?

"And three. . ." she smirked wickedly at him. "If she was smart, she wouldn't be going out with you."

He had laughed at her, and she had run off squealing, "You'll see. I'm right."

And she had been, but only on two counts. Brenda had turned out to be smarter than any of them had realized, stringing him along while he stayed in the military and she earned first a bachelor's and then a law degree, and then dumping him the moment he finally left the military, injured and disillusioned. And her bra had been padded. But he had known that long before the wedding and hadn't thought it important.

But one evening with a strange little vegan ballerina—even thinking the words make his eyes bulge—had given him a quiet contentment he couldn't remember experiencing before. Weird. Just over thirty-six hours ago he had known nothing about ballet and had never heard of Margot Johnson. Now the concept of ballet seemed somewhat more familiar—though still ridiculous—and Margot had somehow become important to him.

Chief Mackie was right, though. She was still a prime suspect. But he knew in his gut, beyond a shadow of doubt, that she had had nothing to do with any of the violence. Her grief over Yuri had been real, and her reaction at learning of Rocco's paralysis had been genuine distress and fear. So, he needed to take advantage of the information she had shared with him and check out the other company employees.

The snow had stopped, but the traffic lanes were narrow due to the piles on both sides of the streets the plows had left. During his excruciatingly slow drive to the theater, he had time to think about what Margot had told him. A few of the corps members—she had explained that corps was the name for the dancers who weren't soloists, like those damn Willi creatures and all those peasant people that had popped around stage at the beginning of the dance—had been jealous when they first heard rumors surrounding Paul and Debi. But Margot maintained that the jealousy had fizzled out when Paul continued to treat her the same as the rest of them.

But maybe there had been lingering resentments? Had someone else maybe had their eyes set on the artistic director? He knew that supervisor/underling relationships were discouraged in most professional organizations—his own most certainly included—but did these crazy artsy-fartsy people live by a different set of rules? Or maybe someone else had been in love with Debi and was seeking somehow to diminish Paul?

As he drove, he pondered whom the best person to seek answers from might be. Margot had given him copious details, but as much as his gut insisted she was innocent, his professional self demanded he regard her story as possibly suspect.

He tried to play the devil's advocate. Assume for a moment that Margot had a thing for Paul and was angry he was marrying Debi. He made a quick verbal note on his phone to check if anyone had spoken with this Debi yet. If she was no longer dancing, it was possible she hadn't even been at the theater the last two days.

He frowned as he drove. Margot had danced passionately on the stage on Tuesday night, and even he, a total dance ignoramus, had been moved by her display of what turned out to be—in the absurdly ridiculous storyline—a grief so intense that her character had died right at the end of the first act of unrequited love.

But nothing in his real-life encounters with the person pretending to be that same overwhelmed-by-passion-and-totally-deranged-Giselle bore any resemblance to the Margot Johnson he had become acquainted with over the past two days.

Yes, he told himself, but try to think with your brain and not your dick. Wasn't that proof-positive that she was a fabulous actor? She was young, beautiful, and unbelievably talented, and now her career was over. There had to be some resentment there somewhere. He hadn't seen any, though. He realized he had never received any explanation for her retirement—had he ever even gotten around to specifically asking? God, he was so tired. He shook his head and tried to concentrate. The speedometer had not moved any higher than ten mph since he had set out what felt like hours ago. Damn weather. Half the time he'd been driving, pedestrians had been picking their way right in the middle of the road due to all the piles of already ugly snow everywhere.

Why in the world *was* she retiring? The unit, and therefore this case, was still understaffed due to the same issues that had sent him to the damn ballet in the first place on Tuesday night, and everyone involved was behind in sharing the information they had collected. But he was pretty sure that he was the only one who had interviewed Margot, aside from the initial FBI interview immediately after Yuri's death. How could he not have checked out such an important question?

His eyes moved back and forth between the digital clock and the speedometer. At this rate he could have gotten there faster on foot, but at least he was warm and his feet were still dry. He reached over to grab his clipboard and flipped through the pages while waiting for the truck in front of him to move.

Paul was the Artistic Director, Angie Gomez the Assistant Director, John Clay the General Manager. . . He scanned down the staff list. Who was likely to know about relationships between dancers and management? What about between management and the tech staff? There was still a small chance the poison had been meant for one of the crew and not even for Yuri or another dancer after all. Given what had happened to Rocco, maybe this was all an internal techie vendetta.

Frank sighed and made it three quarters of a block before the traffic stopped again. He hated domestic violence and murder cases, but at least in those instances there was a limited pool of suspects. This case was just a damned shit-show.

He studied the list again. There was a Principal Ballet Mistress, three Ballet Masters, and eight company teachers. Then on the production side there was a list of names and titles a mile long. He saw Rocco's name: Assistant Lighting Director: Rocco Albertini. Poor guy. The chief had said that morning that his condition was unchanged. How was Frank supposed to divine the best source of information from this endless string of names?

"Oh, fucking hell!"

Frank watched as only a few yards ahead of him one of those stupid little mini cars took a left turn too fast, skidded, did a complete 360, and slid ass-first right into a bus stopped at a red light.

"Goddamn this fucking weather!"

He wasn't a uniformed traffic cop, but he had to stop, had to document what he'd witnessed, had to make sure no one was hurt. More fool he, for reassuring himself only five minutes earlier that at least he was warm and dry. And there wasn't even an inch of space anywhere where he could pull over. Fucking, fucking hell.

Eighty-five minutes later he hauled himself out of his car from his new favorite underground spot near the elevators beneath the theater and made his way up to the mezzanine level, hoping he could somehow yet again find his way to the backstage area.

He needn't have worried.

* * *

Margot woke on Thursday morning with a sense of disorientation. Her alarm hadn't gone off. The dim light in the room indicated it was no longer the middle of the night, but she was sure it was still fairly early. Sleep had been very slow coming. Laska had nestled in against her, and the sensation had been strange but also comforting. And yet she had lain there unable to sleep, thoughts of Yuri's frozen features as she had held him in her arms taunting her. Who had done that to him? And why? Why would anyone want to hurt Yuri?

Even after the amicable evening she had ended up spending with Frank, the questions he had plied her with yesterday continued to rankle. It didn't make any sense. She truly couldn't think of any horrible animosities hidden within the company that would cause someone to try to hurt, let alone kill, another member. But if he was right, there was a monster among them. Images of her fellow dancers, her teachers, the company executives, the stagehands—they all cycled through her head in an endless loop—but she dismissed each one again and again. And then the picture of Rocco's body being taken away on the stretcher came to her, and her tears had started yet again. She tried to pray for him, tried to think of his family, but all she could really do was cry and hold Laska more tightly. And when she had finally fallen asleep, Yuri had been there, holding Laska in *his* arms and looking at her with a stricken look on his face.

She had been sleeping on her side and felt something warm against her cheek. She lifted her head and gasped. The dog's face was two inches from her own, its little mouth open, tongue out, as it panted at her.

"Oh, God." Margot sat up, quickly displacing the dog who gave a little yip. "Laska, you scared me."

The dog continued to pant.

"Do you have to go out, sweetheart?"

More panting.

Yeah, that probably meant yes.

Margot groaned. What had she gotten herself into? She stood up and walked stiffly to the bathroom. She was always stiff in the morning, no matter how much she stretched or how often she had the company therapists knead her muscles. Maybe that would go away sometime soon, but for now, she was still stiff. She had to pee, and she had to find something warm to put on quickly so she could take the darn dog out. She tried to shake off the images of Yuri looking at her with pleading eyes. She had to focus and deal with the dog. *What in the world had she been thinking?*

An hour later she stood in her small kitchen, hands wrapped tightly around her mug of tea, still shivering slightly despite the warm sweatshirt she had on over her pants and turtleneck. It was effing freezing outside. The walkway leading up to her building's entrance had been cleared, but there was still ice everywhere and piles of snow wherever she looked.

Laska had picked her way around, looking up reproachfully at Margot.

"No. I am not going to carry you. You're the reason we're out here, you little fur-ball, so do what you need to do so that we can go back inside."

Laska looked up at her again, eyes pleading, but then finally did what she needed to do. She gave another quick glance towards Margot and then pulled back towards the entrance.

"Fine by me," Margot said, and they had hurried inside. Now she stood, wondering what she ought to do next. She had resisted her mother's pleas that she come down to spend time with them, saying she'd do so after Paul returned from his short honeymoon following the wedding. She had thought yesterday that she should use today to pull up her big-girl panties and finally go talk with HR, but she didn't want to. Could she just stay home? What she really wanted to do was figure out what the hell was happening at the company, but she couldn't think of a single idea. If secrets were the key, as Frank had indicated, whoever had them had managed to cover them up well. Maybe she would curl up on the loveseat with a good book or watch something on television. Margot looked at Laska, who had wandered back into the kitchen and was now staring at her, head cocked slightly to the left.

"I'm not that desperate, girl. If you see me start watching tv during the day, it really will be time for a retirement home."

Smiling a moment in memory of Frank's jokes about aging, she shook her head and decided to spend a few moments on chores she normally avoided. She flipped through the mail from the day before that she had picked up when coming in from Laska's walk.

Mostly junk mail, as usual. You'd think with all the ads popping up everywhere on the Internet, on social media, through spam calls, even arriving occasionally by text, that actual snail mail would die off. But somehow it was still going strong, filling up recycling receptacles around the country.

One envelope, however, was different. Margot stared at it, curious. Her name and address were printed in the center and there was a John Lennon "forever" stamp in the top right corner but no return address on the left. That was odd. Most ads didn't have actual stamps on them.

Margot opened the envelope and a chill ran though her as she stared at the sheet that fell out. A simple piece of paper, sized to fit in the envelope without folding, it had only a few words typed in bold, all caps: WILL YOU BE NEXT TO DANCE AND DIE?

She dropped the sheet in horror on the kitchen counter and backed away, a feeling of revulsion and fear moving up her chest. She stared at the paper, lying there, and tried to force herself to breathe. She had to do something, had to call someone, had to...

"Breathe. Think." She spoke out loud and tried to focus. It was a piece of paper. It wasn't a weapon and it couldn't hurt her. Someone had mailed it, someone who wanted to scare her. Well, they had succeeded. Was it the same person who had killed Yuri? What in God's name was going on?

She looked around the kitchen distractedly and saw her phone on the counter next to the rest of the mail. Should she call 911? Frank had given her his number. Should she call him directly? He had said he would be back at the theater again today.

She made up her mind. She didn't want to stay here, all alone, not knowing what was going on, and she wasn't going to waste time calling anyone and trying to explain. She'd take this thing in, give it to Frank or one of the other police, and try to find out what the hell was happening. Forcing herself to swallow down the feeling of nausea that swept through her, she went to get her boots and her coat.

Laska yipped, and Margot turned to look down at her. Yuri had died, and the poor dog had been left alone, forgotten, in his apartment. What if someone did indeed want to kill her? And succeeded? Laska would be alone again, this time in Margot's apartment. No, she decided, she'd take the dog with her, so that at least Laska wouldn't be alone if Margot was killed somewhere out there.

She looked around, knowing no pet carrier was suddenly going to appear before her, and scowled. Her dance bag still sat on the floor, unopened, since Tuesday night, even though she had taken it with her to the theater yesterday. But there was no room in it, and Margot wasn't planning on dancing, anyway.

She opened her coat closet and found an empty book store tote on the top shelf. She'd put Laska on her leash, but if need be, she could carry her in the tote like one of those Hollywood divas. And then neither one of them would be all alone.

* * *

When Frank stepped out of the elevator, a group of several people seemed to be milling around. A journalist he vaguely recognized from the city's all-news radio station gave him a hard stare as if trying to place him and then moved quickly forward, microphone outstretched.

"You're with the New York City Police, right? What do the police make of death threats being mailed to company dancers? Do you have a suspect yet in Yuri Ossipov's murder?"

Taken aback, Frank stared at the journalist. "Who got death threats?"

"You weren't aware? Apparently, they all did. What are the police doing to find who's behind all this?"

Frank tried to process the onslaught. Up until this point, the press had been kept at bay with vague assurances that the police were investigating Ossipov's death, and he wasn't aware that the word "murder" had ever been mentioned. What did this woman mean, death threats, and how was it the radio station knew about them before the police?

Frank motioned the mike away, and the journalist gave him a defiant glare before reluctantly lowering the mike.

"How did you know to come here?" Frank struggled to keep his tone civil.

"We got a tip at the radio station early this morning. *The Post* got it, too, and the local television news."

"What kind of tip and exactly what kind of threat are we talking about?"

A man with a film camera and a more fashionably dressed and made-up woman moved closer, attempting to listen, and Frank assumed they were the television reporters.

He looked around expectantly at all three while getting out his phone.

The woman answered. "We all got phone calls on our tip lines early this morning saying the Empire dancers had received death threats. And before you ask, yes, of course we checked. The phone number was unregistered—probably a burner phone."

"Jesus."

"So, the police don't know anything?"

Frank glared at them as he tapped his boss's number and moved a few steps away.

He had spoken to Mackie just a short while ago after filing the traffic accident report, but now he quickly filled him in on the press fiasco developing at the theater.

His boss's aggravated voice was loud in his ear. "Crap. You haven't seen any of these threats yourself, yet? Secure whatever you can—you've got gloves with you, right? Collect them all and I'll get the feds over there as well. Gonzalez should be arriving any time since all Rocco could tell him at the hospital was that he hadn't climbed the ladder since sometime last week. Stay in touch."

As Frank was ending the call, the elevator doors opened and Julio Gonzalez himself walked out. He looked around at the crowded scene and gave Frank a questioning look. Frank told him what he had learned and the two set off for the studio area, the reporters following. Frank turned back towards them.

"Okay, guys, you scooped us on this one. Good job. Why don't you wait here a few minutes while we check out exactly what we're dealing with, and I promise you, one of us will be back to give you a statement shortly. The backstage area is still officially restricted." It wasn't, technically, but he was hoping that none of them knew that.

The reporters hesitated, and Frank moved quickly, propelling Julio forward. He seemed to know the way and Frank was more than happy to follow. He was still perplexed by the "hidden" doors and corridors that separated the public and non-public sections of the mammoth theater. The case kept getting more convoluted, so it looked like he'd better start paying attention and learn his way around.

* * *

The lack of sound coming from the dozens of people hovering in and around the largest rehearsal studio was telling in and of itself. People looked terrified. They were clustered in small groups, some on the floor, huddled into themselves, some standing alone. A few were crying quietly. The only exception was one young woman who was sobbing hysterically, a group of other women gathered around her trying to comfort her. Off to one side, beyond the studio entrance, a group of young men, presumably dancers from their stance and attire, appeared to be arguing amongst themselves, but they were doing so in whispers, as though afraid of being overheard.

Frank almost growled in frustration. Another mob scene, with no one in charge and no obvious place to start. He didn't see Paul, Angie, or John, the only supervisory figures he could easily recognize. Well, he had no choice.

"Ladies and gentlemen." He spoke loudly, trying to sound simultaneously authoritative and non-threatening. It took a moment for the noise to die down, but then all eyes turned to him. "We understand that some of you may have received threats of some kind. It is vitally important that we know exactly who got what, when, and how.

"Officer Gonzalez and I will take your initial statements. We'll do a quick initial log and then either one of us, or other officers who will be arriving shortly, will probably need to speak to you again."

He conferred quietly for a moment with Julio, who nodded and left the room.

"There are a lot of you here, so to keep things straight and moving quickly, we're going to video record you saying your first and last name, your position here at the company, and your contact info. Then tell us briefly what you've experienced in the last several hours." He stopped to think for a second. "And to keep things as organized as possible, also please tell us where you were Tuesday night and if you've already spoken to one of us, and when."

Many in the crowd began speaking to each other again as Frank finished, and the din of voices seemed to help ease the tension in the room.

Out of the corner of his eye, he saw a diminutive figure approaching from one of the side corridors, and he felt a punch of relief in his gut. It was Margot. He reflexively berated himself at the pleasure just seeing her seemed to arouse in him, but that pleasure quickly dissipated as he saw the look of fear on her own face.

Their eyes met, and he thought he saw her relax ever so

slightly at seeing him. He inclined his head, and she seemed to understand his signal. She came up to him, bundled in a puffy parka with Laska's head sticking out of a bag carried over her shoulder.

Frank had an overwhelming urge to reach out and pull her towards him, but he forced his arms to stay down and gave her a tight smile.

"I thought you weren't coming in today."

"I got a letter—the same as everyone else, it seems—and I didn't know what else to do."

"Christ. You got one, too? Can you show it to me, please? I haven't seen anything yet."

He quickly donned a pair of thin gloves that were fortunately where they belonged in the inner pocket of his overcoat and reached for the folded envelope Margot had pulled from a small handbag she had tucked into the larger bag.

He opened the envelope and felt a sense of revulsion. Short, to the point, and brutal. Whoever they were dealing with was out to terrorize. They had to find this son-of-a-bitch and stop him.

He looked up to see Margot staring at him, a look of pleading in her eyes.

"Do you guys have any idea what's going on?"

"No. Not yet. I wish we did. Listen, can you help, please? Did you hear what I was telling everyone?"

"Yes. You had just started speaking as I came through the stairs, and I think I heard everything you said."

"Good. I don't know who's who in this bunch, but my guess is they all know who you are and will listen to you. Could you get them lined up and organized so that Julio and I can record them quickly? He just went down to get evidence bags from the car. We're going to have to collect these pieces of shit and test them, so tell them to have any letter or anything else they might have gotten ready to show us."

Margot nodded and looked around, scanning the groups of people. "Paul's not here because he went home to Debi. I got a text from Liza while I was on my way in. The dancers all had envelopes here this morning that had come in yesterday's mail but hadn't been sorted 'til today. When they started opening them and then began screaming, Paul found out and called Debi at home. Seems she got an envelope addressed to her at home, the same as I did."

"That's important," Frank interrupted. "Whoever's doing this knows exactly who is where. They knew to send yours and Debi's to your home addresses, but the others all came here." He stared at the envelope still in his hand. "The postmark is from this zip code. I have to check these things out as fast as possible so we can start trying to track them."

Margot held out her tote bag. "Can you hold her a second while I get my coat off?"

Frank smiled. He couldn't help it. He was surrounded by chaos and fear, and yet Laska's little head was calmly poking out of the top of the bag, the tiny dog seemingly content to watch the world from this new vantage point.

"You brought your bodyguard with you, I see."

"Of course. I wasn't going to risk going out on my own, unprotected."

They smiled at each other for the briefest of moments. She had no make-up on and looked barely old enough to drink, but she radiated a sense of calm professionalism. And she was so beautiful.

Frank forced himself to turn away. There was a psychotic killer loose, and he had to be stopped.

5

I t was after six when Margot looked around the hallways and realized everyone had been processed. She had been kidding last night when she joked about becoming a private eye, and yet she had, in fact, spent the entire day assisting the police—there had been seven, she thought, in all—and the four FBI investigators who had relentlessly hashed through everyone's life stories, past and present, and their memories and thoughts about other company employees.

Forty-nine dancers in all, including Margot and Debi, had received identical threats. All had been typed or printed in the same font, and all bore the same stamp and postmark. Four relatively new members of the corps—three women and one young man—had not received anything, and neither they nor anyone else knew whether to see that as a good sign or a bad one.

Two dancers who were home sick with the flu had received envelopes at the theater, and officers had been dispatched to speak with them in person.

It had been the strangest day. No one had danced or taken class, probably the first such day in the history of the company. No one in the crew had received threats, and except for a few conscientious carpenters who had continued to work on the pieces for the upcoming performances of *Swan Lake*, almost everyone had gone home.

Debi had arrived at the theater with Paul at about noon, her eyes red and puffy. She had spoken with Officer Gonzalez and was now sitting with Margot and Liza outside the studio where the police were wrapping up.

Laska had proved to be a godsend. She had compliantly moved from one anxious lap to another as dancers had waited to speak with the police. Debi now had her face buried in Laska's fur, telling her over and over what a good girl she was.

Only Bettina, the wardrobe mistress, had frowned upon seeing the dog. "I thought there was a no animal rule," she had said when she came by the studio mid-afternoon.

She hadn't received a threat, either. She and her staff were always simultaneously preparing for upcoming ballets and keeping everything perfect for the current show. Without an evening performance, though, there was little pressure, and most of her staff, too, had left.

"She's here to keep us company today, Bettina. It's been a hard day for everyone. Are you doing okay?"

Instead of answering, Bettina gave the dog another dirty look and moved off, mumbling something about a time and a place for everything.

"Well, I'm totally glad you brought her in today, Margot," Debi said. "I think it would make Yuri happy to know she was here."

Margot nodded. It was now still less than forty-eight hours since Yuri had died, and yet it seemed like years had passed. All the normal day-to-day activities of the dance company had been derailed. Paul had spent most of the day closeted with either the police or the countless business suits from the PR, finance, membership, and marketing departments who helped keep the place running. Money was always tight, and now with performance cancelations, eyes were starting to bulge.

Yet Paul had come by twice to check on Debi. Margot had been among several of the old-timers who had figured out something was going on between them months ago, but neither one had ever showed any public display of affection or unusual attention.

Today, however, Paul's concern for Debi was evident for the world to see. Margot couldn't help feel a twinge of jealousy. Her own panic had abated somewhat once she knew that others had received threats identical to her own, but Paul now didn't seem to care who knew that his pregnant fiancée receiving a threat was pushing him to the breaking point. He held her tightly to him, caressing her hair and whispering who knew what before reluctantly leaving again to help deal with the mess.

Liza sighed and stood up. "I need to go for a swim."

Margot and Debi stared at her incredulously.

"What?" Liza's tone was all New York, elongated and high-pitched. "Yesterday's class was a joke since even the teachers had to keep excusing themselves to wipe their tears and none of the rest of us cared—we were all so upset about Yuri. That means I've barely moved since Tuesday night. I've been sitting here all day answering the same questions over and over, and now I have to put on ten pounds of clothing just to make it home in this frigging cold.

"I want to go to my boyfriend's gym, take everything off, and jump in a pool and forget about this place."

"You go, girl," Debi said. "I simply want to go home and sleep. I'm getting married in four days, but all I want to do is pull a blanket over my head and hope that the last few days have all been a bad dream."

"Oh, Debi," Margot said, reaching out a hand to rub the younger woman's arm. "It will all get figured out. It has to. They have so many people working on it."

"Yeah, well, I don't know what kind of wedding it's going to be if everyone's looking over their shoulder for a killer."

"But the wedding's pretty small, anyway, right? I don't think anyone on your guest list is a killer."

"But we don't know that, do we? If it's not somebody from the company, how could they have known where to send all those horrible messages? And if it *is* somebody from the company, then it has to be someone we all know."

The three women looked at each other miserably. They had talked of little else throughout the day and had drawn the same identical conclusions every time.

Margot looked over to where Frank and the other police officers were talking. He still looked tired, but he was nevertheless exuding alert intensity and determination.

As though feeling her attention, he looked over and gave her a brief smile. Margot caught her breath. She felt like she was sharing a thought with a close friend—someone she had known and cared about forever. How could that be? They barely knew each other.

But he was coming over to them now, and Debi stood up and put Laska down, handing Margot the leash. "I'm going to find Paul. Goodnight, guys. If life goes anything according to plan, I'll see you all on Monday. Keep your fingers crossed, okay?" She took off.

"And as I said, I'm going to go find a pool. And then maybe Kevin and I will get rip-roaring drunk. Night, Margot." She leaned over and kissed her friend.

"I didn't mean to break up the party."

Margot got to her feet and looked ruefully at Frank. "Right. It's been a wonderful party. My parents go to those murder dinner parties sometimes, where they all play roles and then try to guess the killer. Only here we're not fooling around, are we?"

"No, we're not. I wish we were."

"Any progress?"

"Nothing front and center, but we have a lot more information to process. You were a huge help today. Thank you. I'm sorry it took a death threat to bring you in, but I'm glad you were here."

Their eyes met again, and Margot once more felt an odd sense of comfort and familiarity.

"I'm glad I was here, too."

He tilted his head and considered her a moment. "I'm heading out. Two guys have been up scanning personnel records that they'll be sending me later to go over, but I have nothing more I have to do here for the time being. Can I give you a ride?"

"I'm pretty sure I'm not on your way."

"That all depends. How do you know I'm not first heading to a place in your neighborhood that has really good Chinese food?"

"From where?"

"I was counting on you to tell me the best place."

He smiled at her and she couldn't help but smile back.

"There's no Chinese in your neighborhood?"

"None," he said, obviously lying but making no effort to pretend otherwise.

Margot laughed. She couldn't help it. Her entire world was collapsing, but this man—this cop of all people—was kind and gentle and made her imagine things she hadn't thought of in years.

"You're crazy, you know."

"Not at all. I've spent the entire day officially interviewing people, but you and Deputy Doggie here have been unofficially talking with everyone. Maybe if we compare notes, we can see a broader picture. And besides, I'm famished."

Margot smiled again. He had a childlike openness to him at times. She didn't understand how someone who had served in the military, been injured in some way she didn't yet understand, and now dealt with murder and mayhem on a regular basis could still be so normal—no, way nicer than normal—but Detective Frank Sutton pulled it off.

"If you're sure. I'm kind of hungry myself." It had been hours since she'd eaten. When had she eaten?

"Oh, and speaking of food, the muffins you sent home with me last night were delicious. I'm ashamed to admit I didn't wait until this morning. I ate one last night after I got home. I didn't want to offend the morning food truck guy outside the police station."

Margot just stared at him. He hadn't had a day off in forever, he was working insane hours, and yet he didn't want to offend a food truck guy.

"And you keep saying dancers are weird. I'd say that's the pot calling the kettle black."

He made a cutting gesture in mid-air in front of his chest. "Absolutely not. No pot. I'm a cop, remember? We're getting dinner."

They both laughed and set about bundling up for the frigid evening air.

* * *

Frank hadn't thought before inviting himself for dinner. This woman was making him do a lot of not thinking—something he hadn't done in longer than he could remember.

But he did a quick mental evaluation as they made their way back down to the parking garage. He had spent the drive here in the morning reminding himself that Margot was still a primary suspect. But after watching her help throughout the day, he was more convinced than ever that she was innocent. He had to understand the why piece of her retirement, though, both to reassure himself and to be able to convince his boss.

First, however, the dinner order. Margot named a Chinese restaurant not far from her apartment.

"They serve regular food, too, right?"

"You said you wanted Chinese."

"Yes, but they have real Chinese, right? With meat?"

She glared at him.

He raised his eyebrows and stared back.

"Of course, they serve meat. Here's the menu." She held out her phone.

"Good. You're not going to make a stink if I get Kung Pau chicken, are you?"

She gave him a condescending look. "I'm kind of a live and let live type of person. I happen to know beyond a shadow of a doubt that a diet that doesn't require eating dead stuff is the best you can eat, but what you choose to do is entirely your business. Just don't plan on leaving any of your leftovers in my refrigerator."

They were in the car now, Laska on Margot's lap, but he hadn't yet started the engine.

He looked from her to the phone she still held out towards him.

"What are you going to order?"

"Szechuan tofu."

"What other veggie dishes are good?"

"I've had the basil eggplant, the veggie Dan Dan noodles, and the Ma Po tofu."

"Are they spicy?"

"Yeah. Kinda."

"All right. Go ahead and order the Szechuan tofu and two other veggie dishes."

"I thought you were demanding Kung Pau chicken?"

"I never demanded anything. I'm merely trying to see what your parameters are."

Margot continued to glare at him and then she started laughing again. "You're going to eat vegan for a second night in a row?"

"Shhh. Not so loud. I don't want word getting out that I'm easy."

When she continued to look at him in amazement, he gestured with his chin while starting the car.

"Go on. Put the order in. Though given that the temperature's never gone above 25 degrees today, the roads will probably still be a nightmare, so it might take us a little while to get there."

* * *

They didn't speak much during the rest of the drive. As Frank had anticipated, the roads were still a mess. New York City was always miserable in the winter, but it wasn't usually downright frigid. Between all the salt, sand, and traffic, most of the asphalt was visible, but icy patches still popped up unexpectedly.

When they pulled up to the Chinese restaurant, he handed her his credit card.

"That's okay. I can get it."

"Nope. This was my idea. You spent the day helping me out, and I fully intend to pick your brain more tonight, so dinner's on me."

Margot started to argue, but Frank cut her off.

"Go get the food, please. I won't embarrass you by asking that you request a senior citizen's discount."

At that she shook her head and got out, leaving Laska on the seat.

When she returned to the car, bag in hand, Frank finished the conversation he had been having, disconnected his call, and lifted Laska up while she settled in.

"I cannot believe this cold." Margot took the dog and buried her nose in its fur.

"Me neither. Where did you grow up?"

"Northern New Jersey. So it's not like I'm out of my element. But this is still way too cold. How about you?"

"Upstate. So cold's not foreign to me, either. But that doesn't mean I like it."

They pulled up in front of Margot's building just as someone was pulling out of a spot.

"Whoa. Look at that. You'll get to leave your car in an actual spot like a mere mortal."

Frank parallel parked with annoying ease, and then gave her a self-satisfied smile.

"I was going to volunteer to walk Laska, but after a comment like that, I think I'll let you do it. I'll keep the heat going so the food doesn't get cold."

Margot groaned. "Shouldn't a dog her size be able to use a litter box?"

Frank looked at her, eyebrows raised expectantly.

"Come on, Laska. The sooner we get out there, the sooner we can get inside."

Wise dog that she was, Laska once again did her business quickly, and Margot and Frank made their way up to her apartment.

Seated again at her table as they had been the night before, Margot looked at Frank, her expression wary.

"Any chance you learned anything helpful today? I'd kind of like to know who threatened to kill me." She stopped for a moment. "God, even saying those words is horrible. Why in the world is someone threatening to kill me? Or the other dancers? This is all so damn surreal."

Frank looked at her thoughtfully.

"I've kidded you a couple times, but why did you retire?"

"What does that have to do with who's maybe planning to kill me?"

"I don't know if it has anything to do with it. But someone is trying to inflict pain and spread fear. Someone is acting out of some kind of rage. If we can figure out where the rage is coming from, we'll have our person."

Margot studied him. He was eating comfortably with chopsticks, as if it was something he did regularly. And it didn't seem awkward to have him here, which was strange, because except for her parents, she rarely had visitors. Her life was solitary. Always full, always busy, but solitary. Yet Frank seemed to fit in, somehow.

"Do you know anything about ballet?"

"Absolutely nothing. My sister used to take dance lessons, and I probably saw a few of her shows when I still lived at home, but they definitely left no lasting impression."

"Well, I grew up completely in love with ballet. I wanted to be a ballerina for as long as I can remember. My mother never danced, but she loved ballet, too, which is obviously how I first got the bug."

She told him briefly about Margot Fonteyn, perhaps the most famous ballerina of the 20th century.

"You said she became even more famous after she started dancing with this Russian guy, Nureyev?"

"Yes. He defected from the Soviet Union in 1961. He was twenty-three and already a phenomenal dancer. Then in 1962 he was in London and got partnered with Fonteyn, who was almost twenty years older than he was. Something magical happened when they were paired up. Two dancers who were on their own amazingly talented, became extraordinary when they danced together. There's never been anything like it, before or since."

Frank was quiet for a moment.

"So, bear with me for a moment and don't get offended. Could someone be drawing some kind of parallel between those two and you and Yuri? You were older than he was, right? I know not by much, but still. And again, I don't know what I'm talking about here, but were you two as good together as they were? I didn't notice anything special about his dancing on Tuesday, but you were incredible."

Margot felt herself blush. Ridiculous. She couldn't remember the last time she had blushed. People praised her dancing all the time, even after performances she knew had been less than perfect. But thinking back to Tuesday night, she realized she had been happy then, for a very short while, satisfied that she had given her final performance 100%. And then Yuri had died.

She closed her eyes and tried to quiet the panic she had been fighting to hold at bay all day. She had gone long minutes at a time without fear, and then suddenly it would bubble back up. Frank was asking questions because the more he knew, the easier it would be to figure things out. At least she hoped so.

"I was good—am good. Yuri was good. But we weren't anything like Nureyev and Fonteyn. Yuri looked great no matter who his partner was—he was scheduled to dance with Liza in *Swan Lake*, and they would have done a beautiful job. But a couple years from now, only crazy ballet fanatics will remember me. You'll be able to Google me and see a list of my major roles, but that will be it. I am," she paused. "I was, merely another top dancer at a topnotch dance company. But I didn't want to grow old on stage. I wanted people's memory of me to be when I was at my peak. I didn't want to have to go back to less demanding roles as I got older. It sounds horribly vain, and it probably is, but that's really how I've always felt and how I still feel. I never wanted to be the nurse."

At Frank's look of utter confusion, she explained about the *Romeo and Juliet* role.

"Okay. I'm going to pretend I somehow understand everything you said. That doesn't answer my question from before, though. You say you were just good, yada, yada, but could someone else be nonetheless trying to draw attention to the partnership between you and Yuri? Do you know if he had had any trouble with the Russian government the way the other guy did? Was there anything else unique about the Fonteyn/Nureyev thing that could relate to you and Yuri?"

Margot shook her head, baffled. "No, not that I can think of. All of that was so long ago, anyway. They've both been dead for years."

"Were they romantically involved?"

"No, not really. People talked, and there was some speculation, but the general consensus was that they were just very simpatico. She was married to some old politician from Panama who had been shot and paralyzed, I think, and he was gay."

Frank smirked.

"Just stop. Yes, he was gay, but he was, without doubt, the most spectacular dancer ever. His strength and his speed and his artistry have never been matched. Yet despite that, he danced during a time when being gay was something you were supposed to hide, and it was during a time when it could be a death sentence. Which it was, for him."

Frank raised his eyebrows, questioning.

"He died of AIDS. It was horribly sad."

"Huh." He was silent for a moment. "Okay, back to the Russian thing. Were you aware of any problems Yuri might have had with the Russian government? They still don't like gays, as far as I know. I think it may even still be considered a crime."

"No, not that I'm aware of. I suppose there could have been something I didn't know about, but he never said anything or seemed worried about anything. He talked to his family regularly, and I know he always assumed he'd go back there."

Frank stared into space for a moment and then sighed. "This whole Russian dancer thing being the motive was kind of a long shot, anyway, because it certainly wouldn't explain the ladder being sabotaged or the death threats."

They both continued to pick at their food.

"This stuff is good, by the way. You were right. And I suppose I don't miss the chicken all that much."

Margot rolled her eyes. A thought hit her, causing her to put down her chopsticks and look at Frank.

"You know, I just realized. I will forever be linked to Yuri now, anyway. Not big time, like Fonteyn and Nureyev, but if anyone ever *does* Google me, it will always be there that he died during my final performance." She bit her lip and squeezed her eyes shut, but a tear slipped down anyway.

"That's not how I wanted it all to end."

Frank reached out and uncurled her fingers where they were clenched tightly together. He held them gently, his thumb stroking the back of her hand.

"You're not all that old, you know. I don't think the Google dump on you is necessarily complete. Maybe you'll find a cure for cancer or be the first ballerina to go to Mars."

She gave him a grateful smile but had to reach for a napkin to wipe her eyes and nose.

"Or maybe I'll simply sit here and grow old watching reruns on television."

"My. Aren't we the melodramatic princess? I guess you do have some of that Giselle ridiculousness in you, after all."

Margot pursed her lips but didn't answer.

"Come on, Ms. Johnson. You've gone some distance in convincing me you ended your career willingly and intentionally, but you haven't told me what you actually plan to do next. You must have hobbies or interests outside of ballet that you've always wanted to pursue. Give me something I can give my boss so we can move you off the prime suspect list."

Margot stood up abruptly and began to collect the cartons from the table. But Frank stood up, too, and grabbed her arm.

"Hey, don't get mad, and don't walk away in a huff. I'm serious. You're a suspect. I don't think you did it, but I need some solid evidence I can use to back up my hunch. Are you independently wealthy? Do you have a ticket to travel around the world? Are you writing a sexy tell-all about the secrets of the ballet world?"

Margot laughed, still sniffling, and leaned against the table.

"Not at all, no, and no."

Silence.

"I'm waiting."

Margot sighed and sat down again, folding her hands in front of her and looking across at Frank.

"I feel like some kind of one-dimensional paper doll when you ask me these questions. I've never had hobbies. My whole life has been dance. I know there are good tv shows on that people stream in all kinds of ways that have nothing to do with a regular television. I know there are good movies. I know some people love to cook, or travel, or I don't know. . . .quilt."

Frank's look was doubtful.

"But all I've ever truly cared about was dance. But you've got to understand: retiring now isn't an idea I just had last week. I've been planning this for years. I told Paul about a year and a half ago that this would be my last season. He argued for a little while, but when he understood how serious I was, he was really wonderful and even tried to make sure I got to dance exactly what I wanted to this past year."

"But still. You're what? Thirty-five?"

"Thirty-six."

"Oh, *that* old."

She gave him a withering look.

"Last time I checked, thirty-six is still a little ways away from being able to collect Social Security. How're you going to support yourself?"

Unbelievably, Margot felt herself blushing again. She shook herself slightly and tried to get a grip.

"As I told you last night, my parents spoil me rotten. My grandparents have also always spoiled me because I'm their only granddaughter. So, they've given me a lot over the years."

"Geez. You're an only child and an only granddaughter? So, one of those fairytale East Coast trust fund kids?"

Margot looked down at her hands. "Not a trust fund, but yeah. Spoiled to the gills. Kind of unusual, I know. But I've also saved a lot. And like I said, this wasn't some idea I dreamed up yesterday. And I've also done some work with a shoe company."

"A shoe company? Like Nike?"

"No. A dance shoe company. You know, pointe shoes."

Frank sighed. "Oh, God. Now we're going to get back into stuff I don't understand, aren't we?"

It was Margot's turn to raise her eyebrows.

"Are toe shoes that scary a concept? It's not like I'm going to ask you to wear a pair."

Frank made a strangled groan and waved his hand. "Just tell me what you're talking about."

"I've been working with a company developing a new line of pointe shoes."

"Hold on a sec. Are toe shoes and pointe shoes the same thing?"

"You really don't know anything about dance, do you? Of course, they're the same thing."

"Yeah, well, I'm assuming you wouldn't be able to explain the finer differences between a shotgun, a pistol, and a rifle."

She looked at him blankly. "Why would I want to know any of that? I hate guns."

"Oh, don't even get me started. But my point exactly. Why the hell would I know anything about dance shoes?"

She held her hands up as if trying to fend off a wild animal.

"Okay, calm down. You're the one who asked the questions, and I'm trying to explain."

She stood up and went over to her bag, pulled out several pink pointe shoes, and then brought two over to the table.

"See how these two are different?"

Frank looked at them and shook his head.

"No, really look. They're completely different."

Frank continued to stare and shook his head again. Then he pointed. "This one's a darker pink and the ribbons are dangling down, and this one's a lighter pink."

Margot laughed. And then she couldn't stop laughing, holding the shoes to her waist and almost bending over double.

"Thank you. That's probably the silliest explanation of the differences I've ever heard, but it was worth it. It's going to be part of my job in the next several months and maybe even years to explain to dancers why this shoe," she held up the darker pink one, "is better than this one." She held up the other. "And now I'll know exactly what to say."

She continued to laugh, tears once again coming to her eyes, and Frank held out a napkin.

"Happy to be able to help."

"Seriously, though. It's all about how the toe box is shaped, the material it's made with, and the length and depth of the vamp. This one, from the company I've been working with, is using a whole new cushioning technology that was developed for drone deliveries from restaurants and companies like Amazon, but is now being repurposed for its superior spring-ability."

He looked at her as if she were speaking a foreign language.

Margot shook her head.

"Never mind. But this is something I had sort of laid the groundwork for doing. I've been working with this company's development team and testing their shoes."

"Okay, then." Frank tilted his head side to side ever so slightly. "So, I'll just say product sponsorship and maybe throw in a dance tell-all for good measure. Let's move on."

"That's it."

"That's it? How can that be it? Haven't you been explaining to me how you've devoted your entire life to ballet?"

"Yes. But I did what I wanted to do. I suppose it's like running a marathon. I've never done it, but my dad did. You train and train and train, and then you run it. And you either finish or you don't, but then it's over."

"Yes, but most people don't stop at one marathon. Especially one that they've been training for for thirty-six years."

"Don't they? Do you know that for sure?"

"I don't have statistics at my fingertips, no, but I've never heard of anyone doing only one. They get that competitive thing going and want to go on and do the next one in better time. Try talking to one. It's incredibly boring. You have to nod and pretend you're enthusiastic and supportive when you're really standing there thinking, 'Get a life, dude!'"

Margot sat quietly for a moment. How could she make him understand what she couldn't explain rationally, even to herself?

"Well, I guess one marathon was enough for me."

Frank continued to look skeptical.

"I love dance. I love it with every fiber of my being. Balanchine said you have to see the music and hear the dance, and that's something I wish everyone could experience, and an idea I always hoped people could understand through my dancing because it comes down simply to a fundamental expression of joy."

He cocked his head, confusion showing again.

"Oh, God, I'm babbling. I'm sorry." She looked down at her hands, clenched together tightly on the table. "He was a famous choreographer. Don't worry. You don't have to know who he was. It won't be on the test."

He nodded, smiling, and motioned for her to continue.

She tilted her head and gave him a doubtful look, but his eyes reassured her.

"I want to understand. Don't stop."

She waited a moment, searching for the right words.

"It's magical being on stage and being part of an ensemble where everyone's working together to do something extraordinary. And it's incredibly satisfying to work at something that's really hard—like a new role with complicated choreography—to work, and work, and work, and curse, and sweat, and finally accept that you'll never be able to do it right, and then suddenly, it feels like it's a part of you. And some ballets, like *Giselle*, demand both pushing yourself to

119

the limit technically but also somehow sharing love, and pain, and loss with your audience."

He was watching her intently, caught up in her passion.

"But it's like a bouquet of beautiful roses. You get them, and they're not quite open. You keep them in water, and then one day, right before your eyes, they open up completely, and they're exquisite. Or like a nectarine. You buy it when it's still a little too hard, and you wait until it's just perfect, and you bite into it, and it's the most delicious thing you've ever had. But if you wait only a day or two too long, all of a sudden, the nectarine is mushy or moldy. And before you know it, the petals are dropping off the roses, and they look so very sad. I didn't want to look sad, and I didn't want to get mushy or moldy."

She stopped, realizing she had been going on for far too long and feeling utterly exhausted.

Frank's eyes were still on her, his face thoughtful. He stood up then and moved to her side of the table, pulling her up to join him.

They stood together, no more than a few inches separating them, and Margot felt a quiet calm move over her. She was utterly exhausted, and her neck and shoulders ached from tension. But looking at him, looking up into his eyes, which seemed somehow to show an understanding of all she had said, gave her a sense of peace.

Frank leaned down and touched his forehead gently to hers.

"Okay, Ms. Johnson, you've convinced me. But I can say for certain that you will never be moldy or mushy, you're absolutely nothing like a paper doll, and you've got far more ahead of you than dropping toe shoes from drones."

Margot sniffed, teetering between laughter and tears. "They don't get dropped from drones."

"Hey, I'm a detective. I caught every word, and I absolutely remember you mentioned drones dropping toe shoes."

"I did not." She strove for indignation, but her voice cracked.

He moved back the tiniest bit and lifted her chin.

"Speaking of being a detective, I asked you yesterday if you had a boyfriend. I'm pretty sure you never gave me an answer."

She gazed into his eyes, so close to hers, and so filled with warmth and gentleness. She shook her head.

"I very much want to kiss you," he said quietly.

Margot felt tears well up and threaten to spill over. Through the blur she saw care and tenderness, and the thought swept through her that if she stayed right here, like this, gazing into his eyes, she would never be alone again.

His lips were so close, and she couldn't help herself. She wanted desperately to kiss him, too. She moved forward and up across the chasm of differences between them and felt the warmth and softness of his lips as they touched hers.

It was a gentle exploring. His lips moved ever so lightly against hers, tasting, feeling, caressing, top and bottom, one side and then the other. Margot felt like she was dissolving and sinking into him, pulled into the wonder of his taste and touch. She parted her lips, wanting more, and his tongue danced softly with her own.

All too soon, it was done. He lifted his mouth from hers and rested his forehead once more against hers. She heard his deep sigh and felt its echo in the depths of her being.

"I need to go. I need to get to the bottom of this case so I can come to your door with a bouquet of roses, and we can watch them bloom together."

Margot smiled, tears threatening yet again.

"Okay. I'll hold you to that."

He stepped away, reluctance written on his face. "You've

convinced me that I need to keep looking for my killer, but we managed to forget the part where you were supposed to tell me anything helpful you learned today."

Margot shook her head and shrugged. The reality of why they were together crashed down on her once more.

"There was nothing, honestly. Everyone is scared. Everyone. If I spoke to whoever's doing this today, then that person is the greatest actor that ever lived."

Frank sighed. "Yeah, that was the impression I got, too. So, the next step is to go over everyone's background, trying to find some kind of motive. Do you know what you'll be doing tomorrow?"

Margot shook her head, still raw and shaken by all they had dredged up.

"Tomorrow's Friday, right? I don't know. I really, really need to go to class and move. I can't remember the last time I went forty-eight hours without dancing, and my body feels like it's turning to stone."

He tapped her ever so gently on the nose. "Not even close to stone from my perspective. And still so very far from mushy, my would-be retiree. I may know nothing about dance, but I think you're nowhere near finished. No matter what you may think right now. But I hear you about moving. If I don't get to the gym myself, I won't be able to walk by the weekend."

Again, she wondered about his leg but kept her tongue.

He gave her a thoughtful look. "Are you planning to go back to the theater for class?"

"No. A woman I danced with years ago works at a studio uptown, and I go there whenever I end up with days off or during the off-season when I'm not dancing elsewhere. The teachers are good and no one bothers me."

"You need to be careful. I don't like the idea of you off somewhere alone."

"I won't be alone. I'll be at a studio filled with dancers who have nothing to do with the company. I can't just sit here and be afraid. Besides, it was pretty clear from the fact that so many of us got letters that none of us is a specific target. Right?" She couldn't help the desperate plea she could hear in her voice.

"We don't know that. We don't have any idea what is motivating this guy or what he may still have planned."

"How do you know it's a guy? Couldn't it be a woman? Or maybe a few people working together?"

"As I said, we still don't know much of anything. That's why it's so dangerous."

As though unable to stop himself, Frank reached out and pulled her against him, holding her head tightly to his chest.

"Be careful. Don't go out too early, stay in crowds, and get home well before dark. And text me in the morning when you're getting ready to leave."

Margot pressed herself to him for a brief moment, her cheek tight against the warmth of his chest. She nodded.

"I will. And thank you."

Frank put his hands on her shoulders and moved her back just enough to meet her eyes.

"Nothing to thank me for. Text me in the morning." He bent and brushed one more kiss ever so lightly on her mouth and then turned away.

Neck and shoulders tight from constant shivering, eyes heavy from so many days, weeks, years, with little sleep. "God damn fucking cold." Maybe when this business was finished and the great King Cashman had been dethroned, it might be a good time to finally say good-bye to this part of the world. People said Arizona wasn't bad. Maybe that'd be worth checking out.

It hadn't been too hard over the years to put away a little nest egg. Orders padded a little here, comp tickets marked up and sold on scalping sites, and of course, the tidy little side funds brought in from Ebay sales of discarded costumes, props, and shoes. Technically forbidden of course, but no one ever checked.

But there was still more to do here in New York. It had been mildly interesting, watching them all quiver and quake with their oh-so-scary death threats today. Maybe not quite as satisfying as anticipated, but diverting. But now it was time to get serious. With luck, today's work would pay off well. Time to show the never-to-be Mrs. Cashman a little fun. She, too, could learn what pain felt like. And afterwards . . . the pain inside might finally ease. Maddie had never gotten a happily-ever-after, thanks to that son-of-a-bitch, so Paul certainly wasn't going to get one of his own.

6

Friday

F rank had gone over files again and again until he fell
asleep and woke to find his left hand and wrist numb
from holding up his head, squished into the corner of his
couch.

A different part of his anatomy also felt compressed, but
that was because he had fallen asleep still clothed, and his
morning boner was straining against his jeans. He gave a
half-second thought to trying to ignore it, but then reached
down and rubbed his aching crotch, a momentary vision of
Margot's soft lips filling his head. *Focus, asshole!*

Damn, but he was tired. And so fucking frustrated. Hours
of study, and nothing. His team had divided the staff up into
groups: he had the dancers, Julio, the tech workers and musicians, and Fatima Harris had the management, custodial, and
clerical staff. But they all had copies of everything. Yet so far,

he hadn't seen a single red flag. And no burst of insight had popped forth while he slept, unfortunately.

The dancers came from all over the world, but the majority of them were US citizens, and they had nary a speeding ticket among them. Of course, from what he had seen in the last few days, he doubted that many of them even knew how to drive. Their whole lives seem to revolve around dance; their resumés showed enrollment at dance programs sometimes going on simultaneously with high school and sometimes somehow instead of high school, with many of the dancers moving frequently around the country during their teenage years. And a good number of them seemed to have begun to dance professionally in one capacity or other without attending college.

Frank gave a disgusted glance at the pages of notes that had remained open while he and his laptop slept. Lines and lines of facts stared up at him with defiance, with not one iota of motive stepping forward. Over the years he'd found jealousy, time and again, to be at the root of countless crimes. Yet he hadn't heard or observed any real signs of competitive problems at the Empire. No one had hinted of significant friction over roles, nor had he caught rumors of personal scandals, aside from the director intending to marry a pregnant, and now former, dancer.

He pushed himself to his feet and groaned. There was no point in delaying the inevitable. It was morning, though still early, and time to go in and face the music.

He looked around his barely furnished apartment. It was a far cry from the comfortable haven Margot had made for herself. A haven that had felt strangely welcoming, as if the seat at her small table and the space next to her on the loveseat had been waiting for him.

His own abode was a place to sleep, eat, catch up on computer "paper work," and occasionally watch games on television. The rest of the time he kept the news on, but he had been so intent on digging deeper into the files when he returned home last night that he hadn't bothered to turn it on.

Margot. Just thinking her name sent an unfamiliar wave of happiness through him and set his hard-on twitching again. She was such a bundle of contradictions. Young and innocent looking, but emanating a mature wisdom. Tiny and delicate, but strong in both body and spirit. And so astonishingly beautiful up close. He had noticed her beauty while bored out of his mind during the performance, but face-to-face, eye-to-eye, and most wonderfully, lip-to-lip, she was breathtaking.

Was he a complete idiot? Hadn't he learned anything from the lessons his oh-so-beloved wife had taught him? Trust was a commodity like anything else in life, and if promises made in a church in front of family and friends meant so little, why should the words of a stranger he had met—could it only be days ago, hold any weight? Brenda had treated their commitment and their promises like bubble gum you chew for a few delighted seconds and then spit out as soon as the sparkly taste is gone. What kind of fool was he to imagine this fairy-tale princess would be any different?

He groaned again. His back, neck, and shoulders ached, his leg was as stiff as the cane he tried never to use, but his long dormant sexual organs were telling him that almost a decade without attention was far too long. He wanted Margot with a physical yearning he hadn't felt in years. He wanted to spend time with her, listening to her voice and marveling at her passion. And he desperately wanted to feel that small, alluring body wrapped around his. Maybe she was the same as other women, and maybe even if they got together, she'd betray him just as Brenda had. But maybe not. Maybe he was nothing but a horny fool. But if there was even a chance in hell of exploring the possibility of a future for the two of them, he had to find out who was behind the violence at the ballet company.

First, though, he had to come clean to his boss.

He stretched, trying to ease his tight muscles, and peered out the blinds. He was momentarily startled by the cold seeping in from the window frame. Still freezing out there, apparently.

He took a quick shower, attempting to simultaneously discipline his raging fantasies and alleviate his discomfort, and then frowned at his overflowing pile of dirty laundry. Laundry was for days off, a concept his department seemed no longer to understand. After today, he'd have one change of underwear and socks left. Either he'd get it done tonight or he'd have to start turning things inside-out. He was too old for this shit.

The roads were slightly better than the day before, but the cold still hit him like a slap when he walked from the garage to the station. How the food truck guy survived was beyond him.

"Morning, Manny."

"Usual, Mr. Frank?"

"Yes, please. You're not frozen in there?"

"As long as the stove works, I'm okay. Not too many people out on the streets, though."

Frank handed over a ten. "Keep the change, Manny."

* * *

"You've got to be fucking kidding me."

Frank winced at the derision in his boss's voice.

"No, sir."

"Do you realize how stretched thin we are right now? Gonzalez called this morning. But he couldn't even talk. He had to put his wife on the phone to tell me that now he, too, has the fucking flu."

Damn. With Julio out of the picture, this whole thing was going to be even harder.

Mackie was pacing the small office which was shrinking even smaller in the face of his angry energy.

"I can't take you off this case. I have no one else available. And yet you decided it's appropriate to go all Romeo with one of our prime suspects? Jesus Christ, Sutton, did your dick swallow your brain?"

Frank cringed at the image. "No, sir."

"No, sir what?"

"My dick did not swallow my brain, sir. I know it looks like she's a prime suspect, but she's not. Or she shouldn't be. I've checked her out thoroughly, and she's not the one we're looking for."

"I bet you've checked her out thoroughly, asshole. Jesus."

The chief sat down and blew out his breath in an angry huff.

"What the fuck is going on? You're supposed to be the department eunuch. There's been a wager going on here for months over whether you're a closeted gay or you had your junk blown off in the military. I personally don't give a crap what you all do in your spare time, but everyone says you do nothing except work out. And now, all of a sudden, you're carrying on with a suspect. What makes you so goddamn sure she's not the one?"

"She's frightened."

He saw the sarcastic skepticism on his boss's face.

"No, she really is. And she's heartbroken over Yuri. I know what I've done isn't professional, sir, but I do know a little about reading people. And she's not faking her sorrow."

Mackie stared at him, incredulous.

"So now you're a goddamn fucking expert on when women are faking it? Holy shit, Sutton."

"Chief, listen. I haven't slept with her. I know I'm in a grey area here, one I probably shouldn't be in, and that's why I'm talking to you about this. But she's not the one. She's actually given me a lot of information, and she's just as determined as we are to find out who's done all this."

"Wonderful. A fucking dancing Nancy Drew. Is that her appeal?"

Frank stayed silent.

Mackie heaved an exhausted sigh.

"Damn it all, Sutton. The commissioner's breathing down my neck because he's apparently buddy-buddy with some of those rich people running the ballet company. Gets invited to their galas and all that horse shit. He wants this solved yesterday cause the company needs to open up again. Like we're not busting our asses as it is with no one available to work. Goddamn fucking flu."

Frank studied the floor, absently wondering during which decade it might last have been washed.

"All right. Stay away from Nancy Drew, would you? If it looks like we need more from her, I'll deal with her myself if no one else is available."

Frank steepled his fingers and steeled himself.

"By stay away you mean . . . "

Mackie raised his eyebrows. "Now you're having trouble with English?"

"Walter, one person is dead and another is in the hospital paralyzed. Margot's lost one close friend and has received a death threat. I told her to keep in touch with me today, and I fully intend to do everything I can to keep her safe, without sacrificing the integrity of my position or this investigation."

"Ooooh. Listen to you, all righteous indignation. You can

protest all you want, Frank, but you've already compromised your objectivity."

"No, sir. I've studied the facts at hand and am using the skills the department pays me to use, to sort out what's what. Margot is not the killer, and her life may well be in danger."

Mackie studied him and finally shook his head. "Don't fuck this up."

Frank nodded. "Understood, sir."

"Okay. Assuming we never had this ludicrous little conversation, where are we?"

Frank studied his hands again, hoping something impressive would spring from his lips.

No luck.

"We've gone over all the personnel records at least twice, and nothing stands out. My thought was to do some online searching today and see if anything looks fishy."

His boss shook his head. "Mason's been checking with exterminators and their distributors to see if there have been any odd requests for chemicals, but anyone with a credit card can get anything they want now online, so that's probably a dead end. Personnel's probably going to come after me for having her work from home, but she hates being on bedrest, and right now I'm out of options."

"How's the ballet doctor?"

Mackie shuffled through the piles of paper on his desk. "There was definite damage to his lungs and bronchial tissue, and blistering on his lips and throat, but they think he'll be okay in the long run. He's still on oxygen and intravenous meds and fluids since he's not able to swallow much."

"And there's no indication he was anything but an incidental casualty?"

"None. Everything you, Gonzalez, and Harris have taken in and carefully recorded, as well as what the doctor himself and the stagehand has said, have given us absolutely nada."

"There has to be something we're not seeing." Even to his own ears, Frank's whispered words were pointless.

"So, go back and look some more. If the Russian dancer had been the primary target, the ladder rungs wouldn't have been tampered with, assuming the second incident wasn't meant solely to distract us. If nothing else, we've got to get this damn thing solved so the feds stop breathing down my neck about an international incident. Who's the ultimate target here?"

Mackie was practically shouting now. He had risen and was pacing the small room, Frank backing up as much as possible to give him space. "Was it the Russian? Then why all those death threats? Is it the company as a whole? If so, why? If it's an outsider with a grudge—maybe someone who wanted to dance with them and couldn't get in—then he or she would have to have an inside accomplice. So, who would that be and why? If it's someone on the inside already, what's the motive? And has the perp finished what he set out to do, or is there more to come?"

Mackie stopped and looked at him. "Any answers?"

Frank shook his head.

"Then get out there and get me some. And whatever you do, don't catch the fucking flu. Wash your hands and take some vitamin C. Oh, and here's a thought: stop kissing murder suspects."

Mackie shook his head as he waved Frank out, and Frank heard him muttering about how useless it had been to give officers time off to get the flu shot when they were all going to get sick anyway.

Frank reached into his pocket for his phone the minute he was far enough down the corridor from his boss's office. He had felt the vibration of incoming texts but hadn't wanted to further inflame Mackie's temper.

· · ·

Heading out now. The studio's on 73rd and Lexington and I should be done about noon. Hope you had a good night. Don't freeze!

For an instant he imagined her in front of him, wrapped in a fur-hooded jacket, her nose red from the cold. He let out his breath. She was so unlike anyone he had ever encountered—a barely five-foot beacon of light and energy. Why in the world did the very thought of her carry so much intensity? The last time thoughts of a pretty female had so preoccupied him, he had probably been in high school.

The chief had been right—he didn't do women. Didn't talk about them, didn't date them, didn't look for them. He'd tried it, failed spectacularly, and learned his lesson. But Margot was different.

Frank hauled himself back to reality, hoping no one had noticed his momentary vacancy. The station was noisy and grimy and the florescent lights were harsh, as far removed from ballet princess-land as anyone could imagine.

There was a brief text from Julio apologizing for being sick and dumping it all on him and one from his mom saying she hadn't heard from him in a while and hoped he was staying warm.

Frank smiled. Two women were worried about him surviving the cold. That was something new.

He looked at the time and thought for a moment. He could work here for about two hours, first identifying a dance studio at 73rd and Lexington and then looking into the backgrounds yet again of his mile-long list of possible suspects. Then he could head uptown, meet Margot outside her dance studio, make sure she was okay, and then go work out himself at the rehab gym he went to on 56th St. Definitely not on his way, but worth it to see her for a few minutes. And who knew? Maybe he'd strike gold in the next hour and find out that dancer So-and-So owed stagehand So-and-So money, and solve the damn case. And maybe pigs would fly overhead in celebration.

Frank rolled his eyes and went to find an empty desk where he could work.

* * *

Margot sat up in bed with a cry, and it took her a moment to realize where she was. She had been dreaming that Yuri was caught in some kind of quicksand, and no matter where Margot had turned, she couldn't find anything to help him. Her dream mind had ludicrously produced first a chopstick and then a slinky, and she had cried in horror as Yuri gasped and sank down until he was gone.

Tears ran down her face as she reached for the dog, who was once again standing on the bed staring at her and panting slightly.

"Oh Laska, what are we going to do? I'm so sorry I couldn't help him, little girl. So very sorry."

She buried her face in the dog, who kept trying to lick at her tears. After a few moments, she forced herself to focus.

"Okay, sweetheart. I'll get up. I'm going to have to start setting an alarm again so I don't keep you waiting in the morning, won't I?" She reached for her phone and peered at the time. "This is earlier than I had to get up before I retired."

Margot shivered, pushing Laska gently aside as she untangled her sweat-drenched limbs from under the blankets. She felt exhausted from her nightmare and so damned angry that the waking reality was almost as bad as the dream.

The dog followed her as she moved to the bathroom. "It might as well have been quicksand, for all I did to help him." Laska appeared to listen but didn't reply. Margot sighed—

still tired, frustrated, and weighed down by grief, but also disconcerted by a barely ten-pound audience to her morning routine.

"Laska, darling, I'm sorry, but you have to step out while I pee." She bent down, moved the dog back into the bedroom, and closed the door. Laska whined and Margot shook her head, wondering for the 100th time what she had gotten herself into. *A dog? Couldn't Yuri have chosen a cat?*

Twenty minutes later she was putting together a quick breakfast and still shivering from their walk outside. She chewed her lip while she thought about what she was going to do that morning.

Margot's entire life had consisted of moving from point A to point B without diversion: classes, rehearsals, performances, auditions, more classes, more rehearsals, and so on. Her occasional breaks between engagements were often crammed full of the neglected routine activities her mother considered vital: dental and medical check-ups, visits to grandparents, and the ever-so-rare day at home with nothing special to do.

Now she stared at Laska, worrying again about this new responsibility. She, Margot, wasn't really in any kind of danger, was she? If she left Laska home while she went uptown to take a dance class, she'd be back to take care of her that afternoon, wouldn't she? She pictured the stark letters that had stared at her in yesterday's mail: "Will you be the next to dance and die?"

A feeling of nausea rose up in her, and she put down the piece of toast she had been holding. That stupid paper had meant nothing; almost all the dancers had gotten one, and Frank had assured her that it was just an attempt to spread fear.

"So, mission accomplished," she said out loud. She *was* afraid. Part of her brain insisted she shouldn't be; the studio where she planned on taking class today was one no one else from the company visited, as far as she knew. So that meant she'd be safe, didn't it? And she'd be back in a few hours, and Laska wouldn't be left alone again, locked in an apartment and forgotten about. As she had been three days ago. When Yuri had been killed and Margot had watched him die.

Margot crouched down on the floor, softly crooning her sorrow and uncertainty. The dog bounded over and once again began licking at her tears.

"I'll come back, sweetie. I promise. I can't take you with me today, but I'll be back in a few hours."

Thoughts tumbled through her head. Did she really need to go take a class? *Yes!* Of course, she did. Her body needed it, and she had to prove to the world that she wasn't afraid. *To the world?* What world? Who the hell cared if the now retired Margot Johnson took a dance class or not?

"Oh God."

Margot forced herself to stand and leaned against the kitchen counter, trying to regulate her breathing.

All that mattered was that she, herself, not let fear paralyze her. She would go take a class, forget about the nightmare of her world for a few hours, and then maybe she'd have a fresh mind, and she'd remember something that would explain all this horror.

That was what Frank had said. Someone had to know something that wasn't coming to mind, something about someone, or multiple someones, that would explain what had started this nightmare.

Frank. Her own bad dream had pushed thoughts of Frank from her mind, but now the memory of last night swept over her. He had kissed her, and it had been perfect. No kiss had ever been perfect before, but that one had. It had felt like coming home, like being in the one place in the world where everything was as it should be. He hadn't pushed her to go further, hadn't attempted to touch her breasts or her ass, but she had felt like she could have stayed in his arms forever, with only their lips and tongues intertwining for all eternity.

The dog brushed against her legs and Margot realized her fear was gone. Just the thought of that kind, ordinary man and that kiss had banished her terror, and she could breathe again.

"He's a pretty neat guy isn't he, Laska? Wouldn't it be crazy if I ended up without a career but with a detective for a boyfriend?"

The very concept was other-worldly. Everyone she ever associated with outside of school had been part of the ballet world. And she had paid so little attention to school that she could barely remember any of her classmates. Her one close high school friend, Miriam, had convinced her to go to the junior prom, so Margot had gotten one of the two boys left in her dance class to go with her. They had had fun, but she and Patrick had never been more than friends. And then Margot had left school and her hometown dance studio behind to study in New York, finishing her high school credits online with as little applied effort as possible.

She had lost her virginity at sixteen with a cute guy she had been partnered with in a summer intensive program, but neither one of them had minded saying good-bye at the end of the summer. Last she had heard, he was dancing on the west coast and had had a string of girlfriends.

Margot had affected annoyance at Frank's stereotypical assessment of male dancers, but the truth was, many of them were gay. The straight ones, though, lived like Hollywood princes, with dancers and fans always ready to fall into their beds. Margot had watched these chick magnets from afar, never feeling the pull herself. The dance world was too small, and anything beyond flirting took way too much effort.

Margot's last romantic interlude had ended more than

two years earlier, but it had been so underwhelming that it barely merited remembering. The Empire Dance Company, like so many artistic institutions, was perennially short of funds, and so the principal dancers were presented almost on auction to major businesses looking to sponsor a "star" and garner a hefty tax write-off.

Margot had been sponsored for the past four years by an online tech security company. In "gratitude," she attended their annual holiday parties and company spring picnics. At the first holiday party, three years ago, a mid-level executive named Owen had spent time asking about the company and fetching her champagne, and she had accepted his invitation to dinner a few times—Monday nights only, of course. But his interest in dance had been limited to polite conversation, and all Margot cared about the tech world was whether her phone worked when she needed it. When she had gently brushed aside his tentative forays into physical intimacy, he had acted surprised and a bit taken aback but then seemed to shrug it off.

The last time he had called it had been to oh-so-reluctantly cancel a dinner date because of a work emergency, and that had been that. She had seen him last spring at the picnic with a smiling pregnant woman at his side, and a feeling of relief had washed over her.

But a police detective? They would have even less in common, wouldn't they?

Margot thought about the hours she and Frank had spent together while she showered and dressed. She had been irritated at his prying when he had come to her dressing room on Wednesday, but looking back, she now understood his questions.

And since then, he had shown her nothing but kindness and respect. She had joked about his job description, but the truth was, he had spent hours of his valuable time with her, and she had felt somehow different during every one of those hours. There had been none of the awkwardness she had felt with . . . what was his name? Owen.

She shuddered. Owen had been good-looking, but when he had put his hand on the small of her back, she had had to force herself not to move away. His tongue trying to force itself into her mouth had been nothing short of revolting.

But Frank, with his tall, sturdy, but fit, physique, his barely-noticeable limp, and his beautiful eyes, somehow made her insides wake up and come to attention. He had said last night he wanted to bring her flowers and ask her out on a real date once this nightmare was over.

Did he really mean it? Would they have anything to talk about? He knew how to kiss, and she had a yearning deep down to know what else he knew how to do. But what did she know about him besides the fact that he had grown up in upstate New York, had a sister who once took ballet lessons, and a mother who had taught him to carry tissues?

Margot laughed, and Laska tilted her head to study her. That last bit really was funny. If she had to make a list of what constituted the perfect guy, tissues would most definitely never spring to mind. But they had proved handy more than once, so maybe her perfect-guy-attribute-list, that had never existed in the first place, needed to be re-written.

His eyes were always so intense, and looking into them felt inexplicably familiar and right. Even when he had stared at her appraisingly, as if mentally weighing her possible guilt, she had seen honesty in them. And his arms around her had felt like a refuge—albeit one she would secretly like to take to bed. God, but it had been a long time.

"Enough," she said aloud. She went to get her jacket from the closet and Laska ran over, ready to venture forth.

"We're going to run outside for one more quick potty trip, in case I get held up later, but that's all, little one."

Once back inside, Laska continued to look up at her, apparently confused by Margot's failure to take off her coat and come further into the apartment.

"I'm sorry, sweetheart, not this time."

Laska stared at her, head tilted and panting slightly, and Margot felt a pang of anxiety. How working mothers managed it was beyond her. She bent down and rubbed the little dog's head.

"I'll be back soon. I promise. You be a good girl, and we'll go out into the cold again as soon as I get back."

Laska lay down right at Margot's feet, her head tucked between her paws, and gave Margot a mournful look of reproach.

"I can see you're going to try to be the boss in this family, aren't you? We're going to have to have a talk when I get home."

She straightened, sent Frank the text she had promised to send, and zipped her jacket. How weird. She hadn't communicated with a guy about personal plans in who knew how long. What an oddly comforting feeling in the midst of all this horror.

She tried to make her tense muscles relax. She was going to her dance class, and she was not going to look over her shoulder the whole time watching for a boogey man. And she would be back soon to keep her promise to Laska. Margot squeezed her eyes shut for a second and then forced herself to walk out the door.

* * *

Margot chatted with the woman at the desk before heading back into the cold. Her friend Oksana wasn't going to be in until later, but the woman promised she'd let her know Margot had been there.

It had been a good class. Nothing strenuous, at least for Margot, but a good work-out with regular people who loved dance but hadn't received death threats or had their close friends die in their arms during a performance.

The routine of a ballet class had been an unchanging part of her life for almost thirty years: pliés at the barre, tendus, relevés, grand battements, followed by center work that included adagios, jumps, and then allegros across the room. The level of difficulty varied, but the pattern, the reassuring sameness, the sense of completion at the end of class, with a reverence directed at the teacher—be it a part-timer at a small-town studio or a world-renowned artist—were all as much a part of her day as brushing her teeth. As Margot walked out of the changing room, she rolled her shoulders and sighed contentedly. Three days had been too long to go between classes. She was going to have to figure out a way to satisfy her muscles in a post-ballet life.

Her bag over her shoulder, she pulled her hood up and stepped out on to 73rd Street. A blast of frigid air hit her face and she flinched. Would this obnoxious cold never end?

She bent her head against the wind and walked right into a solid chest that appeared out of nowhere.

Margot gasped and pulled back.

"Hey. It's me."

What the heck?

"Frank? What are you doing here?"

"I wanted to make sure you were okay. I was in the neighborhood . . ."

She narrowed her eyes. "You were in the neighborhood?"

"Okay. Maybe not this exact neighborhood, but close enough. Can I give you a ride?"

"Where are you going?"

"Eventually I'm going to my gym on 56th, but I can drop you home first."

She looked at him, considering. His nose was already turning red from the cold, and he was shifting from foot to foot, obviously trying to stay warm.

"How about I ride with you to your gym, and then I'll decide where I'm going from there."

His eyes narrowed. "Are you always so argumentative? Can we get in the car, at least? It's too damn cold to stand here negotiating."

Finding herself yet again in the passenger seat of his unmarked police vehicle, Margot pursed her lips.

"You're making me feel guilty. I feel like I'm using a highly skilled New York City detective as a chauffeur."

"Ah. At last you're finally recognizing my superior detective skills."

She laughed. "Did I ever doubt them?"

"I seem to remember some opposition to my initial line of questioning."

Unthinking, she reached out her left hand and touched his thigh. He took in a sharp breath, and Margot realized what she had done. She lifted her hand, embarrassed.

He caught it and pulled it back, giving her a small smile.

"But now you acknowledge my talents and have joined forces with me to fight for Truth, Justice, and the American Way."

'Slow down there, mister. I never called you Superman! I merely said you were a skilled detective."

"I'm not proud. I'll take what I can get." They smiled at each other, both a little tentative, oblivious to the traffic around them.

It didn't last. A horn sounded from the adjacent lane, and New York's normal cacophony jolted them back to reality.

"Why don't I take you home?"

Margot looked at her watch. It was a few minutes shy of

one, and she didn't want to be alone in her apartment for the rest of the day.

"Show me your gym. Please," she added guiltily. "I'm going to have to find ways to stay fit now that I won't be dancing every day."

"I'm happy to show it to you, but I doubt it's the place for you. It's not anywhere near your apartment, for one, and it's a rehab gym, not a regular one."

"Distance obviously isn't of paramount importance, seeing as it is closer to my apartment than where I just took class. But tell me about it. What kind of rehab?"

He shot her a quick sarcastic smile before turning his attention back to the street.

"Not substance abuse, obviously, although I suppose a gym could help with that, too."

She returned his look.

"Ha ha. You said you'd tell me about your leg, so tell. I assume that's what the rehab is for?"

Frank sighed.

"Yes. I had a fair amount of my leg blown away in an explosion outside Kabul a while back. I was lucky that they didn't have to amputate, though it was touch and go for a while. But I left a good deal of bone, muscle, and tendon tissue to mingle with the dust of that lovely paradise."

His voice had grown hard, and Margot studied him.

"That must have really sucked."

Frank snorted. "Well, yes, it did. That's an apt way of putting it. But I'm here. I'm alive, I'm mobile, and I've got a good job. That's more than a lot of grunts ended up with."

"How bad is your leg?"

"Let's just say I wouldn't do too well leaping around a stage in tights. But I get by."

"I'd like to see your gym. Really."

Margot glared back at his continued skepticism.

143

"Dancers spend a lot of time in rehab, buster. We try to make it look like a walk in the park, but I don't know anyone who hasn't fractured something or other along the way."

"Have you?"

Margot laughed. "Of course. I've had stress fractures in the metatarsal area of both feet, and when I was fourteen I broke my wrist when an asshole dropped me from a lift."

Frank's look was horrified. "Someone dropped you?"

"Yup. He was a guest performer from a local college. Dance studios never have enough male dancers, so come performance time, they put out calls for volunteers anywhere they can find them. And by volunteers, I mean guest performers they'll pay, unlike the females in their own companies. This guy arrived, said he was a dance major, and presto, he was our prince.

"Of course, it would have helped if he had been a little stronger. His footwork was good, and he could jump, but every time he lifted me, I felt his arms trembling. I said something to the director, she talked with him, and then she came back and said everything was going to be fine. That afternoon he dropped me."

"Holy shit. And you broke your wrist?"

"Yup. It hurt like anything, at first, but what really pissed me off was having to miss our performances. They ended up changing the whole show anyway, since they were short both a prince and a princess, but it was still incredibly annoying. At fourteen you believe every performance is the most important of your life.

"And then on top of all that, it took a long time for me to trust my partners again, and even though I knew in my head I wasn't fat—" she ignored Frank's incredulous snort—"I still felt like maybe it had been my fault." Margot bit her lip and turned her head to look out the car window.

"I was never afraid with Yuri. He was big and strong and . . ." her voice trailed off.

Frank put his hand down on top of hers and squeezed.

"I'm sorry, Margot. I really am."

She nodded, not saying anything for a few minutes.

Finally, she spoke again. "But all that was simply to explain to you, Mr. Macho Soldier-Man, that regular people need rehab too. Though not for explosions, I guess. Oh, God, that sounded totally obnoxious, didn't it?" Margot hung her head. "This is where you say, 'shut up, idiot.'"

But Frank laughed. "So, we're even. I'll show you my gym, and you can wait if you want, and then I'll drive you home. There's a coffee shop next door—in fact, it's right in front of you."

Margot looked out the window and realized they had arrived.

"Getting around this city is a lot easier in this car than using public transportation. I'm starting to feel extremely spoiled."

Frank pulled into a parking garage and showed the attendant some sort of I.D.

"Wait! You don't have to pay to park?"

"I'm still working, even when I'm here. I only use the car when I'm active. If I have a real day off and need to go somewhere, I use the subway like everyone else."

She glared at him suspiciously. "Does that mean you're working—keeping me under surveillance and just pretending to be nice?"

He raised his eyebrows. "Do I need to keep you under surveillance?"

"Back to square one again. Oh well." She gave a huge theatrical sigh. "Just show me your gym."

They went in, and Margot was surprised by the diversity of ages and handicaps. She hadn't been lying when she had talked about dancers and rehab, but now she realized how separated she had been from others' suffering. Her therapy had been handled by dance specialists and massage therapists in private centers with Pilates machines, dance barres, and highly specialized equipment.

This was a massive center with tables, pullies, weights, climbing walls, balance balls and machines she had never seen before. There were men and women of all ages and even a few children. She looked around in fascination, but Frank touched her arm.

"I've got to get back to the precinct fairly quickly, so how about I get you from the coffee shop in a little over an hour?"

"I can get home on my own. Really."

"Of course you can. But you can use the next hour trying to think if there's anything we've overlooked, and I can go back to work knowing you're safely in your apartment."

Again, that unexpected feeling of warmth suffused her. He seemed to really care. How extraordinary.

She nodded. "Okay, I'll see you in an hour." She rose up on her toes and kissed his cheek. "Thank you."

She turned quickly and moved out of the gym and upstairs to the street-level entrance hallway. She would let him do what he needed to, get a latté, and sit in a café like a normal person who had nowhere else to be on a Friday after-noon. She thought back to what her day had been like only one week ago and felt like she had somehow ended up in an alternate reality.

"Excuse me."

She turned and saw a woman about her own age holding the back of a wheelchair not far from the set of elevator doors. A young girl was in the chair, her eyes and mouth both open wide in what looked like surprise or anticipation.

"This sounds, crazy, I know, but my daughter asked me to ask you if you're a ballerina."

Margot smiled and tilted her head inquisitively.

"What makes you think I'm a dancer? she asked kindly, smiling directly at the girl.

"You walk like one and your hair is in a ballerina bun." The girl's voice was shy but still certain.

Margot instinctively reached up and touched her hair. She had, indeed, left it up after class, and her bun had stayed more or less intact, even after her hood had been pulled on and off in the cold.

"Well, you are absolutely right. I just finished a dance class a little while ago. Do you like ballet?"

"I love it so much!" The girl spoke with reverence, her eyes shining. "Were you dancing here, downstairs?"

"No. I was at a studio uptown. I loved ballet, too, when I was little. I begged my mother all the time to let me take dance lessons."

The girl nodded in understanding. "If I could walk, I'd want to take lessons, too."

Margot felt a pang of sympathy.

"Have you gone to any dance performances?"

"Oh yes. Mom takes me to the *Nutcracker* every year. I wish I could dance like the Sugar Plum Fairy. She's so beautiful. Can you dance like the Sugar Plum Fairy?"

A strange feeling of guilt and embarrassment swept over her. "Yes, I can. It's possible I even was the Sugar Plum Fairy one of the times you came."

"Oh my God!" The look of wonder on the girl's face was almost too much to bear.

"Mom, did you hear that? She might have *been* the Sugar Plum Fairy."

"Yup. I heard. That's exciting. But we have to go downstairs, honey. Sara's probably waiting for you."

The girl sighed. "Okay."

She looked at Margot curiously.

"How come you're here?"

"I came with a friend of mine. He's still downstairs, but I'm on my way out."

"Will you ever come back?" Her voice sounded wistful, and Margot hesitated.

"I might. Do you come here often?"

"Every Wednesday and Friday."

"Maybe I'll see you here again sometime. I'm not sure how often my friend comes." Even as she spoke, Margot felt a twinge of remorse. She'd probably never come back.

"I wish I could see you dance."

Oh God. Now the guilt was worse.

"Well, I don't dance anymore, at least not in front of an audience, anyway," she added quickly at the girl's confused look.

"But maybe I could come here one day on a Wednesday or Friday and show you some dancing you could do with your arms." *What the heck had she just said?*

"You can't dance with your arms." The girl's voice was dismissive.

"Of course, you can. Good dance is all about understanding the music and making it come alive with your body. You can do that with your arms and your hands and your head. You like music, don't you?"

The girl looked at Margot sympathetically. She shook her head as if sorry for Margot's misunderstanding.

"I like music, but you can't *dance* with your arms. The Sugar Plum Fairy goes up on her toes, and spins, and jumps, and gets twirled around high in the air . . ." her voice trailed away sadly.

"Yes, she does. But there are all kinds of dancing in the world. The Sugar Plum Fairy is only one kind, but there are hundreds. Thousands, even."

The girl still looked doubtful.

"What's your name?" Again, Margot was surprised at her own words.

"Nida. What's yours?"

Nida's mom looked embarrassed and moved as if to try to distract her daughter.

"I'm Margot, and I'm really glad to meet you, Nida. And I'm going to try to come back next Wednesday about this time. I can't promise, but I'll try."

What in the world was she saying? Frank was going to kill her.

But Nida's eyes were shining, and the look on her face was rapturous. "Really?"

"I'll try." Margot stood up from the crouch she had assumed without even realizing it. She looked at the girl's mother and held out her hand. "I'm Margot Johnson. It was wonderful to meet you both."

"Allison Grevely. And thank you. Nida will be talking about meeting you now for weeks."

"But I'll try to come back. I really will."

Margot smiled at the woman and felt a lurch in her midsection. How was it that someone who had lived her whole life so methodically was now acting on one crazy impulse after another?

"Margot. We've got to go."

She turned in surprise. She hadn't even gotten out the door, let alone to the coffee shop.

"What is it?"

Frank was zipping his jacket.

"I'll tell you as we go." He looked at the woman and child with some confusion. "Excuse me for interrupting, but we need to leave."

"Not at all." Allison shook her head. "Thank you again, Margot."

"Bye, Margot!" Nida's voice was a happy promise.

"Bye, Nida. I'll see you soon."

Margot zipped her own coat and turned to Frank. He nodded at Nida and Allison and pulled her towards the door.

"What's going on?"

"I'll tell you in the car."

As they were pulling out of the garage, he gave her a quick, intense look. "Were those friends of yours?" When Margot shook her head, he continued abruptly, "Are you feeling all right?"

"Me? Yes. Why?"

"You're sure?"

"Of course. What are you talking about?"

"Four dancers and six other staff members from the company have been hospitalized for severe vomiting. There may be more."

"Oh, my god. What's wrong with them?"

"We don't know yet. It could be some kind of crazy fluke," his voice indicated how dubious that idea was, "or it could be the tip of another fucking iceberg."

Margot stared at him, the horror of his words slowly sinking in.

"Wait. Are you saying someone may have made them sick? On purpose?"

The look he shot her expressed his own frustration.

"I don't know what the fuck is going on. People all over this damn city are ending up in the hospital from the flu, but these cases are different."

Margot sat silent, stunned. Finally, she shook her head slightly.

"So where are we going now?"

"I'm driving you home and then meeting another hazmat team back at the theater, since right now that's the only commonality."

"Let me come with you."

"No. If there's something in the theater that's making people sick, that's the last place you want to be."

"No, Frank. Let me come. Let me try to help figure this out. If they're throwing up, it sounds like it's from something they ate. We're not going there to eat anything, right?"

He shot her an incredulous scowl.

"Obviously we're not going to eat anything. Or touch anything." He drove in silence for a few minutes, his mind evidently weighing choices.

"All right. Maybe you can help. I've got a list of names that, the way this week is going, is probably going to grow. You can help us sort out who's who and what they might have been doing at the theater or what else they might have in common."

His sigh sounded so exhausted that Margot again reached out instinctively, this time touching the side of his clenched jaw.

"We'll figure it out. We've got to."

"Sure." The word was more hissed than spoken. "We spend our days and nights putting out one bush fire after another. And as soon as one case is closed—and keep in mind that more cases than we admit are never fully closed—but as soon as one is, there are twenty more waiting to take its place."

Margot looked down, absently registering the mucky mess that had puddled at her feet in the passenger seat of his car. His world was bleak and unlike anything she had ever imagined. But she felt pulled to him with an intensity that she could not remember ever feeling about anyone. His pain and exhaustion reached into her aloof, professional heart and made her want to comfort him, to make the lines of tension around his mouth and eyes disappear, if only for a while.

She looked out at the gray city streets and felt like a

visitor to an unknown planet. There was the horror of all that was going on, and then there was the change in her own sensibilities and behavior. She was used to keeping a distance —being friendly, but not intimate. Now it seemed she was opening her heart to anyone crossing her path: a dog, an unknown girl in a wheelchair, and first and foremost, this driven detective. Maybe it was she who had fallen on Tuesday night, and this was all some kind of concussed illusion.

But no. She was alive, she was strong, and she was incensed by the nerve of whoever was perpetrating such evil. A dear man and spectacular dancer had been ruthlessly killed, a father and hard worker had been left perhaps permanently disabled, and now, who knew how many more were sick. Whoever the fuck was behind this had to be stopped, and she was going to do all she could to help that happen.

The theater was strangely quiet. No workers moved around backstage, and even the smell was somehow different. The air on stage was always a unique but familiar mixture of glue, sawdust, toe rosin, and stale body odor. Always body odor. But today there was an impersonal scent of disinfectant hovering above it all, and Margot instinctively moved back a step. She and Frank had been handed face masks when they entered the building, and she had put hers on reluctantly. But as the strange smells reached her, she was glad for the barrier.

The stage no longer felt like home. Margot looked around, bemused. How could everything have changed so drastically in such a short time? She had probably spent more hours in this building than anywhere else in her life, but now the shadowed space off stage looked menacing.

Workers in outfits that resembled hospital scrubs were moving around with handheld devises that incongruously made Margot think of the *Star Trek* episodes she had watched as a child with her parents.

"Are you all right?"

Margot started. Frank had grasped her elbow through her puffy coat sleeve. She stared at him. The company members who had danced with her, around her, in step with her, in this very spot, had been as familiar to her as her own facial features. But today, the eyes of this man she had known for only . . . what? three days? His eyes were a beacon of strength and reassurance. His face, with its look of never-ending strain and fatigue, was the force that centered her.

She straightened her spine and stood tall.

"Yes, of course. What can I do to help?"

In the backstage semidarkness, she saw his cheeks redden slightly.

"Could you take me to the cafeteria again? I know you showed me the way the other day, but this place is still a maze to me."

Margot laughed. "Margot Johnson, Columbus Theater tour guide for the Empire Ballet Company, back in service."

Frank reached down and took her hand. Margot felt a pulse of warmth as their fingers intertwined.

"Lead on then, Lady Giselle."

Margot rolled her eyes. "Giselle's not a lady. She's a peasant girl. You did get at least that much from the ballet the other night, didn't you?"

"All I saw was beauty and energy. In my book, Giselle was a princess at least, if not a queen."

Margot shook her head, smiling. "I'm sure my mom still

153

has one of my ballet stories for children books. I'll have her look for it so you can be better informed."

She had begun walking while she spoke, aware as she hadn't been a day or two before of Frank's almost unde-tectable uneven gait. She paused at his snort.

"I think this week will have more than fulfilled my ballet world quota for a lifetime."

Margot bit her lip and continued down the corridor. She fought to quash the dismay his offhand words had wrought. She was being a fool. A few days—maybe today even, if they could catch the monster doing all this—and he'd be done with this case and moving on. They'd most likely never see each other again. He had mentioned a proper date in the future, but those had probably just been words, dropped casually in conversation with no real intent behind them. He was a police detective, and she was . . . a pointe shoe consul-tant. An involuntary shudder ran through her.

They were in the stairwell now, and Frank had evidently seen her shiver.

"Are you cold?"

"No, of course not. Just lost in thought."

They entered the cafeteria, where several more of the sci-fi types in white were poking around. Margot saw Maria, the grandmotherly woman who ran the food center. A dark-haired man was speaking with her, his mouth and nose covered with a white mask, and Margot could tell by the frustrated look on Maria's face, her brow contorted above her own mask, that she was having difficulties. The man held a tablet with an attached keyboard, and from the little Margot could see of his eyes and forehead, he, too, seemed aggravated.

She turned and looked up at Frank.

"Should I try to help? I bet it's a language thing. She always has trouble with people who speak with an accent.

Yuri used to tease her by trying to learn words in Spanish, since she insisted he couldn't speak real English."

"They were friends, then? Maria and Yuri?"

"Yuri made friends with almost everyone. But Maria adored him. Sometimes she even brought him special dishes from home. They wouldn't be out with the rest of the food, but suddenly she'd come over with a little plate wrapped up specially for him."

Frank had taken out his notebook and written a few words, but he motioned with his chin.

"If you think you can help, go ahead."

Margot walked over and reached out, touching the older woman gently on the shoulder.

"Oh, Margocita! How are you, my darling?" Maria reached out and embraced her. Margot hugged her back, smiling into the woman's scratchy apron. Maria was always loving, but the embrace was unusual, likely brought on by the several days of turmoil.

"I'm fine, Maria. Are you okay?"

"Yes, yes. But this man is asking me many questions, and he does not seem to understand me."

Margot turned and looked at the man, who eyed her suspiciously.

"I'm Detective Frank Sutton, NYPD. You're one of the forensic investigators?"

Margot hadn't realized Frank was so close behind her. The masked man's brows relaxed as he looked at Frank.

"Yes, sir. We've been called in to try to find out if the food was tampered with. I've been trying to get a list of all that was prepared and served here this week."

"And?"

"And Mrs. Bofil has been telling me about different soups, but she seems not to understand that I need to know exactly what was prepared and served this week—particularly what was brought in pre-packaged and what was prepared on site. We need to know who orders the food, how it is delivered, and how it is stored. And specifically, we need to know what was served on each day this week and who ate what."

Margot opened her eyes wide in exaggerated commiseration and looked from Maria to the obviously impatient man.

"Maybe we could sit down and go over your questions one by one? Mr. . . . ?"

"Nguyen."

Frank spoke up. "A lot of what you need to know overlaps with what I need to know, so the four of us can sit down. And sorry to pull rank, but I have to check certain things right off the bat."

Frank had moved to a table while he spoke, a gentle hand on Maria's shoulder. Margot and Mr. Nguyen sat down, Margot on Maria's right, Frank on her left, with the forensic inspector sitting opposite.

Frank held out a list on his phone screen.

"Ms. Bofil, do you remember when these people last ate here?"

Margot saw the names on the list and a flash of horror ran through her yet again. These weren't just names; they were people she knew and cared about and worked with— had worked with—on a daily basis, including—oh, God. Debi and Liza were on the list.

She turned horrified eyes to Frank. "Debi's in the hospital? Is she going to be okay? Why didn't you tell me?"

Frank's eyes drew together slightly, and Margot caught her breath. He was the detective working the case, and she was a suspect, and here she was, talking to him like he owed her information. But Liza and Debi were in the hospital.

"I'm sorry, Detective Sutton." She tried to make her voice sound steady and impersonal. "I'm concerned about my friends. Do you know how bad they are? Are they going to be okay?"

Maria was staring at the list on Frank's phone, a look of concern and confusion on her face.

"Yes, yes. They all eat here. They were all here yesterday. Normally the girls eat only salad or fruit, but yesterday I made a big pot of potato soup. It was so cold and everyone was so upset. Almost everyone who came in had soup."

"Is there any left?" The inspector's words were sharp.

"Yes, of course. I didn't put any out today because Ms. Munroe told me not to bother with fresh food. She said everyone had been told to stay home. But she and the people upstairs are here," she gave a tilt of her chin to indicate the company's management. "And I wanted to make sure there was coffee and food in case they needed anything."

Mr. Nguyen stood abruptly. "I need the soup, and any other in-house prepared food that was out yesterday."

"One moment." Frank reached out and touched Maria's forearm. "Ms. Bofil, were you here all day yesterday? The whole time the cafeteria was open?"

"Yes, of course. Where else would I be?"

"Do you have an office of some sort? What about when you need to use the restroom? Do you leave the room unattended?"

Maria furrowed her brows in confusion, looking at the three faces staring at her.

"I do not understand. Of course, I have an office. It's back off the kitchen. And of course, I must use the restroom sometimes. But I take care of my kitchen. I never leave my work."

Her tone was anxious, and she continued to glance from one of them to another, obviously fearful they were accusing her of something.

Frank's tone was gentle.

157

"Please, Ms. Bofil. I saw myself on Tuesday how many people were eating together here in your cafeteria. No one is saying you don't do a good job. But I need to know if you were here the whole time the food was out yesterday, particularly when the soup was out."

"Yes, yes, of course I was here. Every time the people came in to talk to me and ask me questions, I told them I didn't know about anything. People are telling me that Yuri is dead, and the doctor is sick, and Rocco is hurt . . ." her voice had become choked as tears rolled from her eyes.

"And a policeman came and asked me questions on . . ." she stopped and thought a moment. "On Wednesday. And then they came again yesterday morning, and everyone was upset again, and a lady showed me this terrible note and asked if I knew anything about it."

Tears were streaming down her face now.

"And I told her I know nothing. All I want to do is to feed my dancers and make them feel better."

"Where did this lady talk to you?" Frank asked.

"In my office. She said she had to show me something, and she took out that paper with those terrible words." Maria shuddered.

"Who was in the cafeteria when she was talking to you?"

Maria looked around as if searching for yesterday's diners.

"I'm not sure. People were coming in and sitting and talking much longer than normal. I suppose because no one was dancing. . ." her voice trailed off.

"Was the soup out when you went to talk with her?"

Maria gave him a quizzical frown.

"Of course. I got everything out early yesterday because, like I said, no one was dancing. And it is so cold."

She shivered and hugged herself tightly.

Frank inhaled slowly, evidently trying to keep his impatience from showing.

"Ms. Bofil, I know this is difficult, but if you could try to remember, it would help us a lot. Think about it a minute. Who was in here when the lady took you back to the office? And how long were you in there? And who was here when you came out again?"

Maria's whole forehead seemed to crinkle up as she struggled to remember.

"There were several girls sitting over there," she pointed to the far side of the room where there were round tables with four chairs at each of them. "They had moved tables and were sitting close together. Some of them were crying. Debi was there. I remember because I haven't seen her for a few weeks, and I wanted to know how she was feeling." Maria clapped her hand to her mouth and looked horror stricken.

Margot sensed what was wrong and interrupted.

"It's okay, Maria. We all know about the baby."

Maria let out her breath. "Oh, Diós mío. I was afraid I had told her secret. She told me before Christmas but made me promise not to tell anyone."

"Okay. Debi was over there with some of the women dancers, right?" Frank's tone remained gentle. "Do you remember which ones?"

Maria closed her eyes and then named a few first names, and Frank jotted them all down.

"And who else was in the room? Do you remember?"

"Some of the men were over there, and they were talking about Rocco. I know because I asked them how he was, and Andy just shook his head."

"And then there were a few other people. . ." she looked about the room.

"Miss Bettina was over there," she pointed to a small table by the bulletin board. "And Miss Angie and Miss Felicia were over there." She pointed to another small table close to the door.

"So, it was Andy and who else over there?" Frank pointed to where Maria had indicated.

"Andy and . . . Peter and . . .I'm not sure. I had asked Andy about Rocco when Debi came in, and her poor face was all red from crying. . ."

Maria's own tears started to fall again, dripping onto the light blue face mask and leaving wet splotches.

Margot couldn't stop herself. She reached over and covered the older woman's hand gently with her own. "It's okay, Maria. You're helping so much."

"But I still don't understand. Was there something wrong with the soup? I ate some before I put it out and it was fine."

"Excuse me, Detective Sutton. If Ms. Bofil could show me where the soup and the other food is, I could at least get started and leave you to your questioning." Mr. Nguyen's voice was polite but firm.

"Yes, of course. Ms. Bofil, please show us where the left-over food is."

Maria stood up and brushed non-existent crumbs from her apron.

"It's in the refrigerator. I was going to get it out if anyone wanted it, but all anyone seems to want today is coffee."

Maria moved to one of the industrial-sized refrigerators that were part of the kitchen behind the food counter, with Nguyen following closely behind her.

Margot remained in her chair, uncertain what to do. She watched the forensic expert reach into his bag for what was probably a sample kit and heard Frank, who had risen and moved a few feet off, talking into his telephone. He was speaking quietly, but Margot heard "fingerprints."

Once more the horror of the situation assailed her, and

she realized she was rocking back and forth, her arms around her midriff. Frank hadn't answered her when she asked about Debi and Liza. Mother of God, was it actually possible that someone had deliberately put poison in the food? What kind of evil was lurking in this place where people worked day in and day out to bring dance to the world? And why?

She stayed seated, thinking about the questions Frank and Mr. Nguyen had asked. She stared around the room, trying to picture the people Maria had named. They were all colleagues she had known for years. Could one of them really be trying to hurt or kill the rest of them? The very idea seemed inconceivable.

But there was security or carded entries at every entrance of the building. Could it be one of the security staff? But again, why? If it was a crazy lunatic from outside the company, determined to kill or maim, why pick on a ballet theater when there was a city filled with innocent people all around them?

A small whimper escaped her lips as she continued to rock. It had to be someone among them, someone hiding an unfathomable amount of hate and insanity.

Margot stood abruptly. She had to get out of here. She had begged Frank to bring her with him, but now she just wanted to escape this place. She wanted to go back to her quiet apartment and hug the little dog who had only her, now.

Frank was in the doorway speaking with two uniformed policemen. He looked at her quizzically, evidently noticing she had zipped her jacket.

"I'll see you later," she said as she went to move past the three men.

"Margot, wait. Where are you going?"

"I'm going home. I've been gone longer than I planned,

and I need to take Laska out." Her words sounded strained, even to her own ears, and his brows drew together.

"If you wait a while, I can give you a lift."

"No, no. There's no need. I'm fine."

* * *

Margot rode the subway, something she had been doing for years with relative unconcern. But now she stared at the array of faces around her, wary as she had never been before. What if this crazy madman wasn't inside the theater? What if he was waiting outside, deciding now to pick people off individually?

Her gut clenched, and she shut her eyes, trying again to picture the faces of the people Maria had named who had been sitting in the cafeteria. But who said it was one of them? People came and went all day long. She hadn't been in the cafeteria at all yesterday. She had stayed near Frank and helped him and the other officers while they interviewed everyone who had received a death threat. She vaguely remembered eating a power bar at some point, and drinking from her water bottle, but that had been it until she and Frank had shared dinner.

Once again she shuddered and looked around nervously. Debi and Liza had both gotten notes, and they were both now in the hospital. Damn. She hadn't given Frank a chance to tell her how sick they were or which hospital they were in.

She pulled her cell phone from her bag, her eyes continuing their anxious circuit of the subway car. She typed out a text to Liza, knowing it might take a while to go through.

Are you ok? Are you really in the hospital?
What happened and what can I do???

. . .

She pressed send and waited, staring at the screen and chewing on her bottom lip.

She and Debi had never been all that close, but Margot had always liked her. She was supposed to go to the girl's wedding in two days, and the poor thing was pregnant, for god's sake.

Hey Debi. Are you ok? Is there anything I can do? Please tell me everything's all right.

She added a fingers crossed emoji and a heart and pressed send again.

Margot arrived at her stop and got out, phone still in her hand as she held her bag tightly to her side. The phone vibrated as she reached the steps to the street, and Margot stepped out of the rush of people and looked down at the words from Debi.

Thanks Margot. Im ok & more importantly the babys ok. They kept me overnight to make sure but Im already out and were on our way to Pauls. I was vomiting a little last night but they put me on IVs and now Im fine

Margot let out a deep breath and a small moan of relief. Thank God.

She sent back a smiling heart emoji with the words *I'm so glad.*

Then she stared at the phone, willing a similar message from Liza, but the screen remained blank, no reassuring bubbles of imminent response appearing.

Frustrated, Margot tucked her phone into her pants pocket and pulled on her mittens. Even down here, several feet from the actual street, the air was still biting cold. Emerging a moment later, she walked the two blocks to her apartment building, eyes darting in all directions in an attempt to both avoid the sludgy piles of filthy snow and to look behind her for a bogeyman in pursuit.

Her hands shook as she took the card from her phone pocket and entered her building, shooting one last glance behind her. She was filled with an irrational but over-whelming sense of relief that there would be a warm ball of affectionate fur awaiting her.

A persistent and totally illogical feeling of unease simmered in Frank as he continued his work at the theater. Margot was a big girl—*a grown woman, for god's sake*—he reprimanded himself, who had lived and worked in this city for years.

This was a bizarre case, though, and there seemed to be no rhyme or reason to the list of victims or to the assaults that had felled them.

Samples had been taken of all the unwrapped food on the premises, and everything remaining had been removed for temporary storage in case further testing was necessary. Even the already opened packages of coffee beans had been taken, much to the sweet cafeteria manager's distress. The entire cafeteria and kitchen area had been dusted for prints, and Ms. Bofil had been sent home with reassurances that the ink stains on her own fingers would fade in time. More than one officer would be looking into every aspect of the woman's background, but Frank was confident she was exactly who she claimed to be, a hard-working woman devoted to feeding the colleagues she had come to regard as family.

The air samples that had been analyzed from Tuesday night had come back negative, but they were still waiting on the new ones taken this afternoon.

He and the other police and FBI officials had once again questioned the few remaining company employees on sight and were attempting to reconnect with everyone who had been at the theater yesterday. Paul had apparently rushed Debi to the hospital early that morning. When he soon after received news from other employees falling ill, he had immediately sent out an all-staff message for everyone to stay home.

Frank flipped through his pages of notes, trying to see a detail he might have overlooked. A star of the company was dead. A stagehand was gravely injured. The company doctor had been sickened but was due to be released from the hospital today. Dozens of dancers had received death threats, and now at least ten people who had been at the theater yesterday had become sick enough to merit a trip to the hospital. Some of those sickened had been recipients of the threatening notes; some had not.

What was he not seeing? Was there a definitive link among these various victims, or were they just random collateral damage?

One thing was crystal clear. The Empire Ballet Company itself was taking a massive hit. He made a note to check if anyone had looked into the company's financials. Could this be some kind of warped and perverse insurance scam?

Who stood to profit if the company collapsed? Who

would suffer the most? Frank didn't know a damn thing about dance companies. Were they privately owned? Were there shareholders? He had been dumbstruck by the number of people involved in putting on the ridiculously extravagant fairy tales, so there were obviously big bucks involved at all levels.

He stared at his notes but caught himself checking the time on his phone for what had to be the tenth time in only a few minutes.

Would she have gotten back to her apartment by now? *Fuck.* He was losing all sense of professional detachment. He frowned at his notes again, trying to focus. But she was absolutely not responsible, of that he was as certain as he was of his own name. Yes, she had been the last one to touch that blasted bouquet—Jesus. What if *she* had decided to smell it? He pushed the thought aside. She had been physically close to him when Rocco had fallen and when the people who were sick today had been in the cafeteria yesterday. Perhaps that very proximity had kept her safe, but now she was alone and quite possibly still in terrible danger.

He told himself to stop thinking about her, to do his job and maintain professional detachment, but his eyes went to his phone again, anyway. Cursing himself, he typed out a text.

Did you get home ok?

He was a fucking idiot. It didn't matter how certain he was of *her* innocence. Someone was behind all this shit, and he had to get his act together and start figuring out who that someone was.

```
        Yes.  Thanks.
```

Huh. Was she pissed at him? Everything had seemed fine in the cafeteria, and then all of a sudden she had left.

He chewed on his lip, trying to remember exactly what had happened. They had been going over the list of people who had been in the room. At some point she had asked him about her friends' condition, and he didn't think he had answered her.

He took a second to text his boss for updates and then stared at his notes yet again and narrowed his eyes. Some of the stagehands had been in the cafeteria, and it was one of their own that had been injured. He had to check out where they congregated and kept their stuff. And the cranky wardrobe mistress. Did she have an office? What about the people "upstairs?" Had their offices been checked?

Frank groaned and rolled his head, trying to loosen his stiff neck. He was so damn tired. Wouldn't it be great if he could just open up a locker or desk drawer, find a bottle nicely labeled "poison," and the case would be closed?

Yeah, right. And the winning lottery ticket might miraculously appear in his back pocket. Fuck, why not make it spring at the same time, as long as he was fabricating a new reality. He straightened up and tried to force himself to energize. Margot was gone, and he had to find someone who could point him in the direction of the stagehands' . . . room? lockers?

Nothing yet back from his boss. He sent another text to verify the parameters of the search warrants and set off to check with whoever was left in the damn building that he still hadn't fully learned to navigate.

The unexpected time off from the theater was disconcerting. Hard to know what the precious perfect ones were going through when everyone was being told to stay home. The fucking wedding was probably still on—but how to find out for sure? That was when Paul would find out what it was like to have his future ripped to shreds before his eyes the way Maddie's family had.

Arizona was never going to happen. Just getting back at Paul would be enough. Years of hating him from a distance, unable to make him pay. . . those days were finally coming to an end. He'd gotten away with a career and even a totally undeserved good reputation, but he sure as hell wasn't going to be allowed a happily ever after. Maddie hadn't lived to become the ballerina she was meant to be, yet the guy who had taken it all away had gotten everything. Enough of Paul, his stupid ballet company, and now his own ballerina princess. Enough.

7

Friday Evening

P aul's fiancée had been released from the hospital, as had two other dancers. The rest were still in various degrees of serious or critical condition, all suffering from what appeared to be an ingested poison.

Frank had spoken with Debi, Nyoka, Liza, and Dylan, the four dancers now recovering at home. Debi recalled eating only a spoonful or so of soup yesterday, and the two other women said the same, although they both had also had coffee from the Keurig machine. None of the three had had any of Maria's specialty coffees, and they all remembered eating some of the individually packaged Saltines. Having each received a written death threat, they reasonably said that they had been too upset to eat more than a few mouthfuls of anything. But it had to be the soup. It seemed to be the only commonality among them. And no one who had received one of the notes, but had not eaten in the cafeteria, had fallen ill. The other hospitalized company employees were still too sick to be interviewed. Some of them had received the notes and others had not.

Paul sent Nguyen a message asking again if there were any test results. But it was 8:30 on a Friday night, so he doubted he'd now hear any more before Monday morning.

Maria's supplies and storage areas had been searched, and nothing had turned up. Hardly surprising, since Frank had been certain, less than five minutes after meeting her, that the kindly older woman felt nothing but motherly love towards "her" dancers and colleagues.

Neither had anything unusual been found in the administrators' offices, the business offices, the communal dressing rooms, the janitorial closets, or the tool and equipment rooms. Either the perpetrator was a stealth ninja, or it was someone operating in plain sight whom no one was noticing.

Employees at the theater used their chipped IDs to enter the building, but there were no records of when they left. He and Margot had been among the last to leave the theater on Tuesday night, but neither he, nor apparently anyone else, had thought to make a final check of who was in the building before he left to drive Margot home.

Tonight he knew precisely: there was one uniformed officer on site, waiting for the four-member cleaning crew to finish, and he would stay the night in addition to the normal overnight security guard. The late-night crew that usually worked after a performance had been told to stay home.

Frank walked to his car in the garage, thinking about the first time he had left the theater three nights ago. Margot had been a stranger then, an intriguing enigma. But on Tuesday night, with Yuri's body removed and the apparent one-and-done murder under investigation, he had been swept up in a totally uncharacteristic level of concern for a stranger and thought only about the beautiful grieving ballerina. His preoccupation had perhaps left the perpetrator time and space to continue his work, and who knew what else might be still lurking even now in the shadows of the cavernous theater.

He sat in the car, hesitating. He needed to go home, eat something, and get a good night's sleep. That was what he needed to do. That was absolutely what he was going to do.

He stared at his phone. Six down from the top of his most recent message: Her name and "Yes.Thanks."

She was safe in her apartment, and he needed to go home.

Seconds passed as he continued to stare absently at his screen. "Yes.Thanks."

What if someone else had her phone? What if this fucking murderer had been lying in wait for a new victim when she had left the theater?

So, asshole, are you going to call everyone in the company, just to verify that each and every one of them is safe?

He checked his email and then the police logs for any incident reports from the last twelve hours that might have links to the ballet company. Nothing. His boss had specifically said to stop kissing murder suspects. But she wasn't a suspect. He knew that, and he had made sure his boss understood that important detail. And calling to make sure she was all right wasn't kissing, anyway.

He pursed his lips and looked at Margot's message one last time before switching to the phone icon and tapping her name. *He was such an idiot.*

Her voice was hesitant. "Hello?"

"Margot. It's me, Frank. I'm about to leave the theater and I wanted to make sure you were okay."

"Yes. I'm fine." A few seconds of silence. "Thanks for checking. You've been there all day, then?"

"Yeah, but we're done here for the night. I'm about to

head home. Unless something else comes up, I shouldn't have to come back."

Another quiet pause.

"You're still feeling good, right? No nausea?"

"I'm fine. Or as fine as anyone could be."

"Have you eaten?'

"No. I'm not really hungry. Laska and I have been curled up on the sofa watching *Friends*."

"*Friends*? The tv show?"

"It's kind of like comfort food."

"Huh. Would you like me to stop by with some real food?"

Another moment of quiet.

"It's not stopping by, Frank. We live in opposite directions, don't we?'

"Well, not *exactly* opposite."

"But I'm not *exactly*, or even a little bit, on your way home."

"No. But you haven't eaten, and I'm starving."

He felt the seconds tick by and tried to imagine her face. Was she exasperated that he had called? Indifferent? Happy, maybe? He hit his head softly against the car headrest. He was pathetic.

Her voice was quiet. "I can make soup and sandwiches again, if you'd like. Or there's the leftover Chinese from last night."

"Sounds perfect. I'll be there in half an hour, if that's all right with you."

There was another pause.

"Okay. That would be nice. I'll feed Laska and take her outside and then have the food out when you get here."

A jolt of fear shot through him. "No. Wait for me to get there, and we'll take Laska out together."

"Dammit, Frank. I don't want to live like this—afraid of my own shadow." Her voice was raw with anxiety.

"It's okay, Margot. We're going to catch him, and it will be over soon. These things sometimes take time, but we're going to get him. You get the food ready, we'll take Laska out when I get there, and then we'll have a nice, quiet dinner."

* * *

Frank arrived in just under thirty minutes, and Margot buzzed him in, then waited at her door. "Not bad for a Friday night in New York. That car of yours works magic."

Frank stood before her, feeling as cold, wet, and tired as he probably looked.

"No magic. The rain on top of the snow out there is disgusting, so I think most people are being smart for a change and staying in. I'm already wet, so give me Laska's leash, and I'll take her out."

"Are you sure?"

"Of course."

"Okay, then, thanks. Wine or beer when you come in? I'm sorry I don't have anything stronger."

Frank hesitated a moment. He was tired, and he was driving his official car, but one beer wouldn't hurt, especially since he wouldn't be leaving again instantly.

"A beer would be great. We'll be back in a minute."

He took Laska out and she did her business quickly, looking up at him reproachfully as she squatted. She didn't seem to care for the obnoxious weather any more than the rest of them did.

The dog shook her furry little body fiercely in the elevator, and Frank sighed. His feet were wet and cold, the bottoms of his pants were splattered with muck, and his back was unusually stiff. He closed his eyes for just a moment while the elevator ascended and tried to imagine a hot, tranquil sun blazing down on a sandy beach. The elevator dinged. No sun, but a fascinating and beautiful woman had a beer and food waiting. He could forego the beach.

* * *

"Still no tomato soup, but I found some noodle soup in the back of the cupboard that I thought would go with the Chinese."

Margot spoke while trying to dry off the wriggling Laska. Frank took off his coat and shoes, and Margot looked up at him.

"Oh Frank, you're soaked. Let me get you a towel so you can at least dry your hair off."

"I'm fine. Don't worry."

But she was already gone and then was back again almost instantly with a soft blue towel. He took it from her, and the odd intimacy of the exchange seemed to hit them both at the same time. Margot watched him intently as he toweled off his face and head, and then she reached up and pushed a wayward strand of hair from his temple.

"I wish I had some sweatpants big enough for you. You'd probably be better off without those damp clothes." She colored then and looked away, seemingly conscious of the possibilities surrounding her suggestion.

"It's okay, really. I'm fine." He held up the towel. "This was perfect. Where should I put it?"

She gave him a small smile. "Here. You put this one on the back of the door handle," she held up the towel she had used on Laska, "and I'll take that one and put it in the bathroom."

Frank did as he was told and then followed Margot to the bathroom. "Give me a second to wash my hands, and then I'll help you with the food."

Five minutes later they were seated once again at the small table. They both ate a few mouthfuls, and the silence grew strained. Margot put her soup spoon down and looked at Frank, the right side of her lower lip caught nervously between her teeth.

"Are you here to keep an eye on me because I'm still a suspect?"

A snort escaped Frank.

"Jesus, Margot. Of course not."

She looked towards the wall, not meeting his eyes.

"Okay. Then why are you here?"

He looked down at his own barely touched food and took in a slow breath.

"I don't know. Believe me, this is not how I normally behave during an investigation. But I needed to know for myself that you were okay, and I didn't like it that you had gone home alone."

Now the eyes that finally met his were bright. Was that defiance or something else?

"I've gone home alone every night since I was about seventeen."

"Maybe. But not when someone's been threatening to kill you. And not when you've gone through a horrible week in so many other ways."

Margot continued to watch him, her eyes wide and intent.

"And I guess I just wanted to see you again. You left kind of abruptly this afternoon."

Margot released a breath and squeezed her eyes shut for a few beats, then looked at him again.

"I know. I'm sorry. That wasn't fair after all you've done for me—coming to the studio this morning and then letting me tag along to the gym. I. . ." She stopped speaking for a moment as if trying to find the right words. "It just got to be too much, sitting there in the cafeteria, listening to the idea that someone might have put poison in the food for any one of us to eat. I cannot understand that kind of evil, and I can't understand how it can be happening at the theater."

Margot looked down at the napkin clutched tightly now in her left hand.

"You hear about horrible stuff on the news all the time, and I know it's your job to deal with violence and murder, but this is a ballet company."

Frank stood up and moved towards her, wincing ever so slightly at the stiffness in both his leg and his back.

But she noticed, and a look of concern flashed over her face. "Oh, Frank. You didn't even get to finish your workout today, did you? I got to take my dance class, and all you wanted was an hour in the gym, and you couldn't even have that, could you?"

She stood up as well, and he reached out and took her hand in his while touching the fingers of his other hand lightly against her cheek.

"It's been a really shitty week for both of us. You want to maybe put this food away and cuddle up on the couch a while and watch another episode of *Friends*?"

She tilted her head and narrowed her eyes. "Seriously? You want to watch *Friends*?"

"Not in the least. But I'm all for the cuddling up on the couch part, and I most definitely don't want to watch the 11:00 o'clock news."

Margot laughed softly.

"Okay. You've got yourself a deal. Help me carry this food back to the refrigerator. Maybe it will look more appealing tomorrow." She gave a rueful laugh. "Dancers spend half their lives trying to figure out how to lose weight. Now I'm not a dancer anymore, and I seem to have lost all interest in food. But I'm not sure even I could market a 'watch your friend die on stage and then live in terror yourself' diet."

Frank reached out again, the need to touch her, to feel

even the brush of her hand against his, overwhelming his common sense.

"You're still a dancer, Margot."

She looked about to argue, then seemed to think better of it. She moved into the kitchen, scooped the food back into the little white cartons, and put the dishes into the dishwasher.

"More beer?"

"No thanks. I've still got half a bottle. Come sit."

He tugged her towards the loveseat and she reached for the afghan folded over the back. He put his arm around her and pulled her close, her head slipping into the crook of his shoulder like a jigsaw piece falling into place. They worked together to spread the afghan, and she aimed the remote at the tv.

"Let's see if there's a good movie on before I subject you to anything painful." She flipped through a few channels and stopped when the vibrant sights and sounds of *West Side Story* appeared on the screen.

Margot gasped in delight. "Oh, do you mind? I love this."

Frank smiled. "Fine with me. I probably saw it a hundred years ago, but I haven't seen it since."

He pulled her closer and felt a sense of release pass over him. It *had* been a shitty week, but at this precise moment, he felt better than he could ever remember feeling. She fit against him so perfectly and smelled like a childhood memory wrapped up in sunshine. He inhaled slowly, his eyes closed. He'd relax here just a short while, and then he'd head home.

* * *

Frank didn't snore, but he did make weird little purring sounds. Margot had sensed him falling asleep almost

177

instantly, and she had been happy that he felt comfortable enough to do so. She couldn't remember the last time she had watched a movie with a friend, couldn't remember ever having felt so at home and at ease with another person.

She herself had not slept but had gotten caught up in the famous story of love and heartbreak, and it was the tears streaming down her face at the end that finally propelled her to slip carefully out from under Frank's arm and go after a tissue. She remained standing then, watching him, unsure what to do.

Wake him and send him back into the cold?

Leave him here and hope he wouldn't end up with even stiffer muscles?

Wake him and bring him into her bedroom? Into her bed?

The thought sent a shiver through her. He had come here, totally exhausted, to make sure she was all right and to spend time with her. That had to mean something important, didn't it? Did it mean he wanted to sleep with her? Did she even know how to read signs in a man?

The kiss they had shared last night had been so unexpected and such a moment of goodness in this otherwise nightmarish week. But was it right to take advantage of something that might not be real outside these bizarre circumstances?

She realized she was standing still in her living room, staring at a sleeping man and a pretend-sleeping dog. Laska had seized the opportunity and jumped up and snuggled in tightly against Frank on the loveseat. She looked at Margot, her eyes visible through the narrowest of slits, as if trying to convince her that she was now far too tired to move.

Margot glared back and then tried to force herself to do something. She was exhausted but not at all sleepy. The movie had wrung even more despair from her, a cruel reminder that happily-ever-afters were unlikely. Kissing

Frank had been delicious, but were they any more likely to end up together than Tony and Maria?

The only way to know was to see if there was anything between them when he wasn't trying to track down a murderer in her world—a world that realistically wasn't even hers anymore, but one which he had made crystal clear was not his. So, sleeping with him now would definitely not be a good idea.

She nodded her head, trying to force the thought to take root. His features, not movie-star perfect, but intriguing, pulled at something inside her, even in sleep. His face was covered by a light stubble, and she realized again how very tired he must be. But she wished, suddenly, that she had stayed in the gym to watch his aborted workout, wished she knew what he looked like under the conservative clothes he always wore. He was probably at least eight inches taller than she was, didn't seem to carry an ounce of fat round his middle, (even asleep his belly looked tight), and he had broad shoulders and a confident posture. She studied his hands, now lying at rest in his lap, and thought that if the rest of him resembled his long, strong, and well-manicured fingers, he was probably pretty darn hot all over.

Stop, she told herself. You just decided that now wasn't the time. If she wanted to see if there could be anything between them, this nightmare had to be behind them.

Without conscious thought she had moved to the top shelf of one of her bookcases and taken down the notepaper she kept there. There had to be something they weren't seeing.

It was far chillier in the room without Frank's body heat and the afghan, so she went to her bedroom and found a sweatshirt, then went back and tucked herself into the armchair next to the loveseat. She shot a last resentful and envious look at Laska, then forced herself to concentrate.

Liza had finally called late that afternoon. She had been released after a few hours on IV fluids, and all she wanted to do now was sleep. When Margot tried to ask about what had happened, Liza told her they'd talk about it tomorrow. She chewed on her lip, thinking about everything that had happened since Tuesday night.

"Empire Ballet Company." She wrote down the words and stared at them, thinking absently of the little girl she had met that afternoon. Everyone—or at least many young girls— wanted to be ballerinas when they grew up. Most of the male dancers she knew had spoken about their own instinctive love for dancing, leaping, and twirling that had started early in life and perplexed those around them. That passion to dance, from all that she knew and had heard from others, was always strong and pushed all other interests out of the way.

So, what if there was someone working at the company who was a thwarted would-be dancer? Would that be enough to compel him to kill? Or maybe her? She couldn't imagine such a thing, but there was obviously some kind of super strong passion of some kind motivating such evil. She tried to picture the myriad workers she passed every day but paid no attention to. The stagehands she didn't know, the cleaning staff, the wardrobe assistants, the women who took care of pointe shoes and tights . . . could any of them be failed dancers holding a grudge? Should she and the other dancers have made more of an effort to get to know them?

Margot's shoulders ached from the tension the thought evoked. She had loved her job, loved dancing, performing, and learning new roles. But there was nothing relaxing or stress-free about a dancer's life. Even in the best of companies, competition for parts was always intense, worries about funding led to cuts here or there, both in terms of personnel and supplies, and each pulled muscle or bad landing brought immediate and often illogical fear of an aborted career. Then there were the real injuries that dancers often tried to ignore or hide, desperate not to lose any momentum or standing. Physical discomfort somewhere in the body was a constant, and often there was real pain, with dancers popping ibuprofen pills for breakfast, lunch, and dinner. Schedules were often frantic: late night performances made getting to morning class on time a never-ending battle, classes ran late, rehearsals ran late, call times were adjusted to go over last-minute changes . . . almost everyone she knew who danced felt exhausted on a daily basis. But were there support staff out there jealous of them, who perhaps resented their fame? And if so, how could she or anyone else know who it was?

She thought about *West Side Story*. Turf wars, ethnic rivalries, revenge. . . there were so many excuses for hate. She couldn't think of any ethnic rivalries in the company. Dancers came from all over the world, as did so many of the people working in the theater. If there were lurking ethnic issues, she couldn't see how attacking random people would help. Turf wars? She supposed there could be a corps member, or members, who desperately wanted to advance, but even as she tried to imagine all the dancers who had passed through the corps in the last few years, she couldn't think of anyone who would fit such a picture.

What were they not seeing? Revenge? Revenge for what? And against whom?

Who was being hurt the most by everything that had happened since Tuesday night? Yuri definitely. But Yuri was gone now, and nothing that had happened subsequently could hurt him further. The thought of Yuri made her remember the service planned for tomorrow. Did Frank know about it? He probably did—he seemed to know everything that was going on. Would he be going?

Yuri hadn't been religious, but people from the consulate

and other Russians in the city had arranged a service at the Russian Orthodox Church. After that his body would be flown home to Russia, and Damien had texted that he was planning to fly to Moscow for the burial.

Margot stared at her notepad. She had written the name, Y U R I, followed by a question mark, and she stared at the letters, absently thinking about poor Damien having to adjust to a world without his beloved.

But if someone had wanted revenge against Yuri, the violence should have stopped. So who else was being hurt?

They all were, obviously. Not her, Margot, really—she probably less than anyone. Tuesday was supposed to have been her last official appearance for the company, even though she had promised to help out in other ways for a time. So maybe it made sense that the police still considered her a suspect.

Yet she had received a death threat, and she could have eaten food in the cafeteria. Hell, she could even have been stupid and tried smelling a bouquet of fake flowers herself right there on the stage in front of thousands of people. Did it mean something that both she and Debi had received the same death threats as the other dancers, when neither one of them was technically still dancing? She had to mention that to Frank.

The very thought drove her to her feet, and she paced around the small room, Laska lifting her head ever so slightly to watch.

The entire company was in danger, and the financial livelihoods of every single person who worked there, from the people who cleaned the studio floors at night to the highest paid stars. So what was the fucking point? Who would win by destroying the company?

"Hey. What's going on?" Frank's voice was sleepy, and she watched as he stretched and yawned.

"I'm sorry. I didn't mean to wake you."

"I didn't mean to fall asleep." He squinted in the near darkness. "Did the movie end?"

"Yeah. Same sad, stupid ending. Everybody died for nothing. And I've been trying to figure out what's going on at the Empire. I don't want the same thing to happen there." Her words came out harshly, and she felt immediate contrition.

"I'm sorry. You maybe were getting the world's shortest break from your job, and I'm dumping it all back on you again."

Frank yawned again. "No worries." He stood up, and Laska gave a resentful whine. Reaching down, he soothed the dog gently on her shoulders. "You're a sneaky one. I seem to remember someone else being tucked up against me when I closed my eyes."

He rolled his shoulders, moved his head from side to side, and gave one more giant yawn, as if forcing himself to revitalize.

"I shouldn't have checked out like that. I don't suppose you figured it all out, though?" His words were light, but Margot gave a resentful groan.

"No. I didn't. I can't make any sense out of it whatsoever, and it's making me crazy."

Frank walked over to her and put his hands lightly on her shoulders.

"Margot. Stop. We'll get him. Sometimes there's a bizarre crime that we don't solve and nothing else ever comes of it. But something like this—with ongoing acts of violence—it will come to a head. Either the perpetrator will slip up and we'll catch on, or he'll escalate and do something in the open. Either way, we'll get him."

"But that sounds like it means more bad stuff has to happen."

"Well, yeah, except the goal is to figure it out before more bad stuff happens. Which is why I should get going. I need to spend some serious time and effort tomorrow going over the backgrounds of this giant pool of suspects." He touched her face, stroking her cheekbone with his thumb.

"None of this is spur-of-the-moment violence, which means someone's put a lot of thought into planning it all. And nobody does that without some kind of internal justification, logical or not. So somewhere there's an impetus to all this—we just have to identify it."

Margot rubbed her face against his palm, wishing he could stay, wishing this were all behind them. But she forced herself to straighten up.

"So, research tomorrow? Will you be going to Yuri's funeral?"

"I think so. It will be the absolute safest place to be in the city, that I can guarantee. Between diplomatic security, the FBI, Russian security thugs, and the NYPD, not to mention the press, nothing bad's going to happen. But I want to watch who's there and see what all transpires. You're going, right?"

"Yes. I told Liza I'd check how she's feeling in the morning, and maybe we'd go together."

Frank touched her face again gently. "Text me, would you, please? Let me know what she says and what you decide to do. And whatever it is, please use a ride service. Don't use public transportation or stand out on the street to hail a taxi, okay?"

Margot nodded and tried to keep her features expressionless.

But Frank continued to gaze down into her eyes, and she couldn't look away.

"I can't remember the last time I relaxed and watched a movie with a friend."

Her laughter was choked. "You didn't see any of it."

"Okay, true. But I really enjoyed not seeing it with you."

Absurdly, her eyes filled yet again with tears, and she bit her lip. "A friend?"

"A very good friend. The best I've had in a long time."

Margot nodded and then looked down, unable to meet his eyes any longer. But he tipped her chin back up and held her gaze as he lowered his mouth ever so lightly against hers.

The kiss was soft, gentle, and over far too quickly.

"Text me in the morning, okay?"

She nodded, unable to speak.

"Goodnight." He gathered up his things, dressed in silence, and then was gone.

8

Saturday Morning

Investigators have brought charges of vehicular manslaughter and DWI against Jason Brandt of Framington, after the car he was driving hit and killed seventeen-year-old Madeline Dimond. The young woman was struck by Brandt's car on the morning of May 21, only a few hours after Dimond and several friends left the banquet hall where they had attended their senior prom. She was declared dead at the scene by paramedics. Her date for the evening, eighteen-year-old Paul Cashman, told the police that he and Ms. Dimond had left the after-prom gathering at Westbrook Park separately (an unofficial and unauthorized use of the park, city officials confirm). He was unsure why she had still been out as she had told him she was going to a sleepover. Maya Hansen, a friend of both Dimond and Cashman, was with Dimond at the time of the accident and received serious but non-life-threatening injuries.

Frank stared at the screen. He had been at the computer for what felt like days, but was only about three hours, trying to

find anything that might shed light on the violence infil-
trating the dance company.

This decades-old newspaper article concerned the
Empire's Artistic Director, Paul Cashman. His prom date
twenty-five years ago had been killed by a drunk driver, and
now his pregnant fiancée had received a death threat and
been treated for possible poisoning. Frank hadn't come upon
any mention of an earlier marriage for Cashman.

He flipped back to the bio notes he had on Paul, studying
the earliest dates. It looked like Cashman had spent the acad-
emic year that culminated in the prom tragedy dancing as an
intern for a German dance company and then had moved to
a corps position in an American west coast company the
month after the death. He must have known the young
woman earlier and returned to the New Jersey suburb just
for the prom?

Frank chewed on his lip. Sad, yes, but there probably
wasn't any link between the two freakish occurrences. He
checked Debi Judson's file again. She was twenty-three, and
Paul forty-three, so the likelihood of her having any connection to the earlier incident, before she had even been born,
was next to impossible. Debi Judson had grown up in Texas,
begun her dance training at a school affiliated with Ballet
Austin, and had only moved to New York to join the Empire
Ballet four years ago at the age of nineteen. Nothing there.

He moved on to the notes he had taken on the seemingly
endless list of Empire's employees. Having to sift through the
intricacies of people's lives was an unfortunate necessity that
was sometimes fascinating, often boring, but always invasive.
Almost all the dancers' bios were similar in their accounts of
peripatetic obsession to dance. Probably as a result, more than
a few of them were facing financial hardship, and he had seen
horrifyingly high credit card balances, rampant late fees, and
numerous instances of families taking out second and third

mortgages, but nothing that screamed motivation for murder. Among the musicians, the teaching and administrative staff, and the board of directors, there were enough human weakness stories to populate a soap opera. DUIs, custody battles, tax evasion, even pending malpractice suits against one board member. Ordinary sad, sordid, frustrating events, but nothing —NOTHING—jumped out as a red flag signaling murder.

Frank glared at his notes for what had to be the hundredth time. There was some bad shit there, but none of it looked like something that could be resolved by attacking the company as a whole. Anyone in financial straits would be loath to see a decent source of reliable income go up in flames.

His eyes returned to the decades old article that mentioned Cashman. Out of curiosity and frustration, Frank decided he'd do a quick search on Madeline Dimond and Maya Hansen and then get ready to go to Yuri's funeral.

Fifteen minutes later his eyes were still riveted to the screen. Madeline Dimond's father, Jack Dimond, now deceased, had owned a pest control company, and Maya Hansen, if it was the same Maya Hansen, was a California legislator famous for her flamboyant lesbian life-style and her active support of LGBTQ issues.

Frank checked the details again. It had to be the same Hansen: her age was right and her bio said she had grown up in northern New Jersey.

He leaned back in his chair. Pest control meant pesticides. Pesticides meant poisons. The chemicals found on the bouquet and in the soup seemed to be an unorthodox combination of numerous lethal substances, most of them indisputably poisonous.

He checked his phone. If he was going to make it to the funeral, he'd have to get going. He gave one last glance at the screen and made a note for himself to look into the Dimond family again later. And if the opportunity presented itself, he'd ask Paul about the incident directly.

* * *

The smell of the incense was overpowering, and the dense press of bodies all clothed in heavy winter garments seemed to make breathing almost impossible. Frank scanned the congregants, seeing an array of New Yorkers from all levels of society.

The church had no pews, so mourners huddled together in varying levels of confusion. The company dancers were almost uniformly dressed in black, many of the women in leggings and fashionable boots and the men in snug fitting pants and short, stylish jackets. Even from a distance Frank could see that several of them looked unsure as to what was going on. Standing nearby were company administrators Frank had spoken with in the last several days, and he concentrated on trying to attach names to the various faces so he could remember later who had attended.

The darkly attired mourners were in stark contrast to the church itself. The Orthodox cathedral presented a spectacular panoply of bright colors: icons of every size lined the walls and the area behind the standing priests, and gold sparkled from every surface, shimmering in the light of hundreds of candles.

There were several rows of stern-looking Russians, men and women, all in long heavy coats, with many of the women wearing hats of one kind or another trimmed with fur. They, alone, seemed to understand the service, even though one of the bearded priests in ornate robes sporadically translated words into English. Some older worshippers stood among them, weeping and rocking back and forth and seeming fiercely sorrowful over Yuri's passing.

A few photographers rimmed the back and sides of the large, high-ceilinged sanctuary, and a group of quietly crying teenage girls stood awkwardly together, some of them holding small bouquets clutched in their hands as if uncertain what to do with them and looking completely out of their element.

Frank could make out Margot in the crowd, standing next to Liza and a man he didn't recognize. Margot had texted him an hour ago, and he'd replied that he might be late and not to worry about saving him a spot. Margot, Liza, and the unknown man stood close to Paul Cashman, who had his arm around a woman Frank assumed was Debi. They had spoken on the phone, but he hadn't been the one to interview her on Thursday.

His eyes travelled over the rest of the dancers. Most of them he recognized, although there were a few people who had the posture and bearing of dancers but seemed older. Probably retirees or teachers.

Maria from the cafeteria, Andy, the stage manager, a few men he thought were also stagehands, and several other figures he recognized but couldn't specifically identify stood further back, as if uncertain of their place in this foreign environment.

Double checking that the sound was off, Frank took a few quick photos. He'd enlarge them later and try to match names with faces. It would be interesting to see if anyone whose presence would normally be expected had not attended.

The two priests seemed to drone on and on, one swinging his smoking incense burner back and forth near the casket as a group of elderly women in quavering voices sang in what Frank assumed was Russian whenever the priests stopped speaking. Frank could understand nothing, but the phrase *Gospodi Pomilo* seemed to be repeated over and over. It was simultaneously soothing and suffocating, and Frank struggled to take a breath, wondering how long the surreal experience would last.

He obviously wasn't the only one feeling the intensity. Paul Cashman was now actively supporting the woman Frank assumed was Debi, and the two were trying unobtrusively to make their way to the exit. As Frank had remained close to the heavy doors, he opened one as quietly as possible and held it while Paul and the woman exited, then stepped out after them.

"Everything all right?" he asked.

"Yeah." Paul's voice came out in a whoosh of exasperation and relief. The woman leaning into him looked completely undone, and tears were running down her pale face.

"Are you sure? We can call an ambulance if you need one."

"No, no, I'm fine. I just couldn't breathe in there." The woman's voice shook, but she took a deep breath and seemed to pull herself together by sheer force of will. Frank saw some of the same steel he had come to recognize in Margot and remembered that this woman, too, had been a dancer.

Frank caught himself inhaling deeply as well and marveled at how exhilarating the bitingly cold air felt after the cloying incense.

"I found it pretty hard to breathe in there myself, so if you're just out of the hospital, it had to have been particularly oppressive."

She looked at him, a small frown on her face as she struggled to place him, and Paul hastened to explain.

"Debi, this is Detective Sutton. He's been investigating Yuri's death, the death threats, the poisoning . . . all the fun we've been having this week." Paul was obviously trying to keep his tone light, but Frank could see the dark shadows that threatened to overwhelm the man's eyes. The Artistic Director seemed to have aged years in just the three or four days Frank had known him.

"Oh yes, of course. You called yesterday, and I remember seeing you at the theater on. . ." her voice trailed off. "God, this has been a messed-up week. Today's Saturday, right?"

She looked up at Paul, who returned a look of such naked tenderness that Frank dropped his eyes and absently touched his screen to check the time.

"Yes, it's Saturday. Are you still ready to take me on for good in less than forty-eight hours?"

The two seemed to have momentarily forgotten him, so Frank flicked to his messages and frowned.

"Fucking hell."

Paul and Debi's heads both turned to him, and he grimaced, the line between safeguarding official information and sharing personal news with the intimately concerned blurring yet again.

"Fred Miller, the electrician, died in the hospital this morning. He apparently had long-standing heart issues and only recently finished chemo for throat cancer. So, whatever he and you," he looked at Debi, "whatever the hell you were fed on Thursday did him in."

"Oh, Jesus." Paul's face was one of utter despair.

Debi closed her eyes briefly but then seemed almost to grow taller before Frank's eyes. Now she was the comforter, reaching to gently turn Paul's face so that his eyes met hers.

"It'll be okay, darling. We'll get through this. And yes, you better believe I'm going to marry you on Monday."

Frank found himself looking down at his phone yet again, an unfamiliar feeling of jealousy and longing sweeping over him. Despite the shit swirling around these two, the love between them was palpable.

He cleared his throat. "I'm going to go back in and stay 'til the end, but I'll need to talk to you again later today, Paul."

Paul nodded. "Of course. You have my number. I'm going to take Debi home and make sure she's okay, and then I'll probably go back into the office. I guess I've got to contact Fred's family and then work with Felicia to get out some kind of statement."

Paul's countenance was still heavy, but Frank could see that Debi's support had bolstered him. These two deserved more than the mess they were currently enduring. *Who the fuck was doing all this and why?*

He pulled one of the heavy doors open and once again scanned the backs of everyone in the church and checked out the perimeters. Two closely-cropped men in short black jackets standing in the posterior corners of the room glared back at him, their eyes narrowing suspiciously. Russian security of some sort, obviously, but were they official agents from the consulate or privately hired thugs? Cynically he wondered if there was any real difference.

Karli Mason, the detective now working from home while on bedrest for pre-term labor, kept insisting they weren't taking the Russian angle seriously enough. But all the Russian figures Frank knew of, who had died of "mysterious causes" throughout the world in recent history, had business, journalistic, or political backgrounds. Nothing in Yuri's file had indicated censure from Russian authorities. Yes, he had been open about his sexuality, and yes, Russian society, at least publicly, had failed to evolve like the rest of the world, but Frank still couldn't see that as a motive for killing him. And as far as he knew, all the other Russian victims world-wide had been taken out individually, without collateral casualties. The victims at the ballet company one way or another now numbered in the hundreds. The financial impact would persist for months, if not years. The CFO had told him yesterday that ticket reimbursements alone would wipe out much of their liquidity. Even now he was unable to pay hourly staff who were now not working. If they couldn't get back into production soon, the very existence of the company long-term was in jeopardy.

The thugs continued to eye him warily, but no one else seemed to be looking around the church.

Frank turned to his phone again, bringing up the list of the company's executive officers. After Paul's name came an Executive Director, an Assistant Artistic Director, an Artistic Administrator, a General Manager, a Director of Marketing. . . the list went on and on with at least ten more positions. And this was just the bigwigs. He looked at the group standing together and counted twelve figures. He'd have to try to match them up later, and then try to figure out who might have brought a spouse or partner.

There were at least thirty dancers and probably about fifteen people standing near Maria and Andy. Frank recognized the music director and a few men and women he vaguely remembered were musicians. He narrowed his eyes and tried hard to match titles and positions from the odd angles of heads and profiles visible to him. He saw an energetic looking older woman bouncing ever so slightly as she stood. That was the physical therapist.

All of these people were here to mourn the death of a foreign-born guest artist, taken out at the peak of his career, at the end of a well-publicized performance honoring Margot.

A stagehand remained hospitalized and paralyzed, a medical doctor was still recovering from inhaling toxins, an electrician was dead from ingesting toxins, and numerous dancers had had the wits scared out of them with written death threats. What was the connection? What was the motivation? What in hell was the end game for whoever was behind all this?

Frank chewed on his lip and continued to stare at the assortment of figures. At the front of the church one of the priests switched again to English. He had a long white beard, a generous girth, and he spoke about the blessings Yuri had given the world and said that his talents had been a gift from God. He admonished the worshippers gathered there today to hold the love of Christ the Redeemer in their hearts and to continue to pray for the soul of Yuri Ossipov.

Frank sighed inwardly and pursed his lips. He had no real use for religion of any kind and had arrested far too many supposed believers over the years. His eyes again roamed the mourners. He doubted that few, if any, of the ballet company personnel shared the priest's religious convictions, and indeed, many of them looked merely exhausted. If Yuri's soul actually still existed on another plane, he doubted the rituals being performed here and now made any difference.

The service at last came to an end. The Russians in the know lined up to pay their final respects at the casket, crossing themselves and some leaning down to kiss the closed wooden coffin, while many of the company attendees appeared content to quietly depart. Frank stood aside and watched the mourners leave. Some met his eyes and nodded an acknowledgement. Others seemed intent on getting out as quickly as possible.

It took a while for the sanctuary to empty. The young girls whispered together for a few moments and then moved en masse to put their flowers on the floor near the stand holding the coffin. Then they moved out, many of them still crying. Their devotion reminded him of girls he had known long ago in high school pining over rock stars. Frank had never imagined ballet stars capturing that level of passion, but there seemed to be a lot about dance he was learning on the fly.

His eyes instinctively moved to find Margot again, and as

their glances met, that unfamiliar surge of rightness flared up inside him once more. He shouldn't care, shouldn't seek her out, shouldn't feel this sense of shared intimacy with someone he only knew because of a murder investigation. But with a sinking recognition of both panic and exhilaration, he realized it was too late.

A week ago he had not known Margot Johnson existed, but now their eyes met and communicated wordlessly as if they had known each other forever. He understood she would wait for the others to leave and then join him. She had become not a suspect, not a witness, but a partner. And as simply as that, the thought made him free to concentrate again on the words, gestures, and behaviors of the dozens of people now leaving the church.

* * *

The service had been draining. Margot had spent the interminable ninety minutes remembering Yuri over the years. He had been excited at partnering with her in Paris when she arrived there for an international gala two years ago, and she had been both surprised and touched that he remembered her from the Empire's visit to St. Petersburg a few years earlier.

"Of course, I remember you! You dance like a butterfly camel!"

She had stared at him, utterly confused. "A butterfly camel?" Despite his accent, she was pretty sure she had heard the words right, but they baffled her.

"Yes, yes. A camel is strong and never falters, and a butterfly makes flying look beautiful and effortless. That is you when you dance."

Margot had continued to regard him, her eyes wide in

shock. Both his assessment of her and his odd command of English amazed her.

"Where did you learn to speak English?" She had blushed as soon as the words were out of her mouth, afraid she might have offended the handsome young dancer.

"Oh, my boyfriend and I love to watch American movies! Come meet him. I told him I would be partnering a wonderful American dancer named Margot, and he got so excited by your name. He wants to know if you are related to Margot Fonteyn?"

And so had begun an improbable but always joyful friendship. Yet Yuri had been the true butterfly—always moving from one encounter to the next with boundless enthusiasm.

Knowing he was paired with her for her final performance had given her confidence and comfort. He danced with precise technique combined with bottomless energy and exuberance, and his partnering was among the best she had ever experienced. He lifted her effortlessly and securely, his hold during turning sequences was unfailingly perfect, and his eyes always held a spark of mischief. And now he was gone. His body lay in that polished wooden box at the front of this ornate and totally foreign church, surrounded by the cloyingly sweet smell of incense. Nothing in this claustrophobic environment fit the Yuri she had known, a never-fussy embodiment of youth, vigor, and joy.

When the service finally ended, the reassuring sight of Frank near the doors seemed like a lifeboat in a turbulent sea. Struck by an odd thought, Margot shot a last puzzled look toward the coffin. She and Yuri had formed an instant, unlikely bond, irrespective of their age and cultural differences. It seemed a similarly improbable bond had formed between her and Frank, and she wondered if in some crazy, inexplicable way, Yuri was looking out for her.

She stared more intently at the casket, sending all her love towards her lost friend. She knew Yuri, the essence of him, was not in that box. She could only hope that he was at that very moment making some bystander in the hereafter laugh and marvel at his effervescence. But maybe, just maybe, a tiny bit of him was still around to give her strength and lift her up the way he had always done so magnificently on the dance floor.

Frank was standing a few steps away from the doors, phone to his ear, when Margot left the church with Liza and Kevin. She stopped, and Liza gave her a questioning look. Margot angled her head slightly in Frank's direction, and Liza shook her head but smiled.

"If you see my old friend, Margot, say hello from me, would you?"

Margot raised her brows, but Liza was on a roll.

"Fifteen years I've known you? Probably longer, but since our age is now a data point entry in need of constant revision, let's stick with fifteen. Never, ever, ever, have I known you to be swept off your feet like this."

"Who said I'm swept off my feet?"

"Your whole face says it, girl! See? Look at me. I'm with Kevin." She held up their interlaced hands, and Kevin looked slightly confused. "You know I'm with Kevin and Kevin's with me. There might as well be a neon light hanging over our heads. It's obvious. Well, that same 'it's obvious,'" she dropped Kevin's hand to make air quotes, "is hanging over your head, shining just as brightly."

Margot looked at her friend and felt a blush come to her cheeks.

"We're just friends," she said, and Liza laughed.

"Oh, you keep telling yourself that, sweetie. But in fifteen years, I haven't known you to spend time with all that many friends, either. Just be careful, okay?" She leaned forward and pressed a kiss on Margot's cheek and then was off, Kevin in tow. He turned and smiled at Margot and gave a small shrug.

"She's right, you know. She always is!"

Then they were gone, turning the corner toward the subway entrance.

Margot frowned, multiple thoughts competing for her attention. Was Liza labeling something she herself had been afraid to name? Or was her friend maybe totally off base for once? Or was Margot perhaps giving off vibes she had no right to give off? Or might Yuri somehow actually be looking out for her and helping her find a real-life partner?

She stood, metaphorically and physically frozen by the cold and by the number of 'ors' swirling through her head. Frank finished his call, slipped his phone into his pocket, and came over and took her gloved hand.

"That was certainly intense. I've been to several department funerals in the last few years, and they're always gut-wrenching, but the ones I've been to have all at least been in English or Spanish and free of that incense." He gave a small shudder, but then his eyes softened as he looked at her. "I'm sorry; that was rude. Are you doing okay?"

She looked at him, and the 'ors' receded. Whatever the heck 'this' was, it had an integrity of its own. Frank's hand had seemed to reach for hers without thought and his concern was real.

"Yeah, I'm okay. A little wrung out, that's all."

"Why don't we go get a coffee? I've got to get back to the precinct, but I've got a few minutes."

She gave him a small smile, and the skin around her eyes was stiff from the tears she had shed. The sensation caused her to squeeze her eyes tightly shut for a second, and then she took a large sniffled breath and nodded.

"Yup, that sounds good." They both looked around, perplexed, and when their eyes met, they laughed quietly.

"Looks like neither one of us knows the neighborhood. My car's just down the block. Let's go get warm for a sec, and we'll figure out what's nearby."

Letting go of her hand, Frank pulled her against him and held her around the waist as he steered her towards his car. Margot let her head rest lightly against his side, the zipper on the breast pocket of his jacket cold against her cheek.

Fifteen minutes later they struck gold and found a table open at a Starbucks.

"You said you don't keep good coffee at your apartment, but you like coffee shop drinks. What frothy, foamy, creamy concoction can I get you?"

Margot was touched. Her own mind was racing a mile a minute, but he had remembered something unimportant she had said in passing.

"An oat milk latté would be great."

"Nothing more complicated?"

"Nope. That'll do."

He went to the counter and Margot took off her coat and sat down. It was a cold and bleak late Saturday afternoon in mid-town Manhattan, so the shop was far emptier than it might have otherwise been.

When Frank returned with their drinks, Margot was sitting with her elbows on the table, fingers interlaced and pressed hard against the space between her chin and bottom lip. He was bound by his professional duty to try and identify the murderer. But she was pissed off. Frank had told her about the electrician's death during their walk to the coffee shop, and her anger had built with every step they took.

She held the paper cup between her palms and tried to absorb its warmth and quiet her inner turmoil. Then she looked directly into Frank's eyes.

"Did you learn anything from the service? I saw two of Yuri's Russian friends that I remember being at his place once, but they never looked in our direction. Do you think that means anything?"

Frank looked back at her, his amber eyes intense. She noticed tiny age lines at the sides she hadn't noticed before and realized they were seated closer together than they had been at her apartment. Absently she decided that his eyes were actually an astonishing mix of brown, gold, and just a hint of caramel—a bit like the outside of a sticky bun. At the moment they were drawn together in frustration, and though she shared his preoccupation and was seething inside, she wondered for an instant what he'd be like if he could relax completely.

"Were they people you'd call friends? If you were running into them under other circumstances, would you or they strike up a conversation?"

She thought for a moment.

"No, probably not. I don't even remember their names."

He nodded briefly.

"But the Russian angle: did Yuri ever mention harassment of any kind? Was he on good terms with the consulate? Did he hang out with Russian friends often?"

Margot looked out the window at the gray piles of hardened snow that bordered the street and the narrowly cleared sidewalk and searched her memories. His apartment had been filled to the brim with friends from all walks of life at the Russian Christmas party he had held in January, and she was pretty sure the two she had recognized at the funeral had been there then. But she had been to gatherings at his place on a few other occasions, at parties he had thrown on the rare times when Damien was in town, so she couldn't be completely sure.

"There were always a couple Russians, men and women, but they all spoke some English. Damien is French, of course, so he didn't really know any of Yuri's Russian friends. But everybody seemed to get along fine. The Russians always brought vodka, of course, and they used to yell something like '*dodnya*,' that Yuri and Damien turned into a kissing game."

She looked down, overcome for a moment by sadness.

"This is all so wrong. Yuri was about joy. He should have lived to be a hundred."

She turned her gaze back to the ugly street. Her tone was harsh when she continued. "Whoever wanted to hurt him is the antithesis of joy. We need to look for darkness."

Frank waited for her eyes to return to his.

"And he never mentioned difficulties with anyone from the consulate or from the Russian government?"

Margot shook her head.

"So, then, who is darkness at the ballet company? Can you think of anyone?"

Margot chewed on her lip.

"I really can't. I've been wracking my brain, nonstop, but I can't. Dr. Han is usually super serious, but he's nice. Some of the lighting crew act grouchy when Paul or one of the choreographers asks for changes after they think everything's finalized, but they only grumble and make a few off-color remarks that they pretend they don't want anyone to hear, but they really do, and then they're fine. A few of the teachers spend three quarters of every class yelling at us, never smiling, never saying 'good job,' but that's just their way. Bettina's always cranky, but we're all used to her."

"Why do the teachers yell?"

"I guess because they assume it will make us work harder and better. And strangely, it usually does."

"Why is Bettina always cranky?"

"Who knows? Usually it's over some accident, like a rip in a costume, or make-up getting on a costume, or one of us leaving a costume on the wrong rack, which we always do."

"Those seem like relatively minor infractions."

"Of course, they are. And they all happen at every performance. So, as I said, we're used to her. We do something wrong," she made air quotes, "Bettina glares at us and spits out comments about responsibility, and we all nod and promise to do better."

"Okay. Anyone else?"

Margot shook her head as she tried to think.

"We had cockroach problems when people were leaving food in the dressing rooms last year, and everyone was sniping at everyone else. And there are always minor hissy fits in the fall when the new health insurance deductions are posted and stuff like that. A lot of the interns and apprentices and even some of the corps dancers have to work second jobs to survive, so people are exhausted and on edge and occasionally resentful of the la-de-dah crap that's on display at galas and so forth. But it's all part of choosing ballet. Nobody expects to get rich from it."

He tilted his head and studied her.

"Have you?"

"Have I what?"

"Have you gotten rich from it?"

Margot colored slightly and looked down.

"Yes and no. As a prima, I was paid well, and I've been lucky the last couple years that a few companies have wanted me to appear in their lines of workout clothing and shoes. But that's all just since I became a prima. Before that I struggled like everyone else."

"So, might there be dancers—maybe a male dancer—who will advance now that Yuri's gone?"

She bit her lip again

"Not really. His contract was only for this season, and even if that were part of it, then what would be the point of the death threats and the food poisoning?"

"None that I can think of. But once again we seem to have hit a brick wall."

Margot made a low growling sound.

"This is all so impossible. None of it makes sense."

She narrowed her eyes and glared at Frank.

"*Could* it all be a Russian plot? Are they trying to destroy the Empire Ballet Company so they can replace it with a Russian company? Or maybe somebody on the board owes money to the mob?"

"We're looking into that, along with everything else."

She threw up her hands.

"So maybe it's aliens. Maybe this is the first step in some diabolical plot to destroy culture on earth. Or maybe someone's in love with Paul and is mad he's marrying Debi."

Frank set down his coffee cup and stared hard at Margot, eyebrows raised.

"I'm almost positive we can rule out the alien theory, but can you think of anyone, anyone at all, who might fit that second category?"

"You mean being in love with Paul?"

Frank raised his eyebrows higher and held out his hand as if opening himself to her suggestions.

But Margot only closed her own eyes and shook her head.

"We went over all this the other day, didn't we?"

"You said Debi joined the company. . ." He flipped through his phone, checking his notes.

"About three or four years ago," Margot supplied.

"Whom did Paul date before that?"

"I have no idea. No one in the company, as far as I know."

"What about Debi?"

But Margot just shook her head again and shrugged.

"She was in Austin, before, right?" Frank frowned as he checked his notes. "Do you know if she dated anyone there?

Is there anyone else now at Empire who used to be in Austin?"

Margot frowned.

"I don't think so."

"Was Paul in Austin?"

"Was he ever in the city of Austin? I have no idea. But as far as I know he's never had any professional association with the company."

"Do you know of him ever dating dancers before, anywhere?"

"He might have, but I have no personal knowledge of it. I knew of his reputation as a dancer when I was growing up. It's always easier for men to become known when they're good because there are so few of them. He won a few major competitions and then was both fortunate and talented enough to have pieces he'd choreographed staged at the two companies he danced with before he came to Empire."

"And there was no gossip about his love life during all that time?"

Margot shrugged.

"When you say it that way, yes, it sounds a bit odd, even to me. But I might not be the best one to ask 'cause I don't spend all that much time on social media."

"But you don't know of him ever dating dancers before?"

"You just asked me that! No, I don't."

"Do you know gossip about other dancers? Other male dancers?"

"Yes! No! I don't know *a lot* of gossip. I hear things, like everybody does. There's usually a fair amount of talk about the male dancers, just because there are fewer of them and many of them are rather. . . flamboyant. We all knew about Damien before Yuri got here. And we had a guest choreographer last year who must have slept with half the women in the city." She stopped to think for a minute. "I could probably tell you the orientation of all our male principal dancers and if they're with anyone at the moment. . . . and I'd probably be right about most of them. But there's never been any talk about Paul that I was aware of. We caught on pretty quickly that he and Debi were interested in each other, but I couldn't even begin to tell you how or why we knew."

"What about Debi? Did that choreographer last year get it on with her?"

Margot shuddered and shook her head vehemently.

"No. In fact I remember she was one who thought he was way out of line and tried to warn some of the younger girls about him."

"What was his name?"

Frank's phone vibrated and he let his breath out in a huff.

"Damn. I've got to go."

His eyes darted back and forth quickly between Margot and his phone as if calculating time and distance.

"Go," she said. "I'm fine. I've got to get home and take Laska out, anyway."

"I don't like you going home alone."

Margot stood up and put her coat on. Her fury from a few minutes ago had dissipated, replaced by exhaustion. She looked at Frank and saw a similar fatigue mirrored in his own face and felt a wave of hopelessness sweep over her.

"I'll be fine, really. I'm a big girl and this is my city. I feel bad that we used up this hour and got nowhere, yet again."

"Don't say that, sweetheart."

Frank had risen and looked as surprised by his words as she was. But he moved the few inches around the table and took both her hands in his.

"Text me as soon as you get to your apartment and then again as soon as you're back inside with Laska."

She smiled into his tired eyes.

"Yes, sir, Mr. Detective, sir. Anything else?"

"Yes. Be careful, please."

God, but his eyes were beautiful. How nice it would be if she could keep standing there, holding his hands and looking into his sticky bun eyes. But it was getting dark, she had a dog waiting for her, and he still had a killer to find.

"You, too."

He bent his head and pressed his forehead against hers for a blissful moment, and she tried to absorb the very essence of him.

Frank's phone buzzed again on the table, and he jerked away with an oath.

"It's fine," she said, yet again. "Just go, and don't worry."

He gave a brief nod, then grabbed his jacket and turned towards the door.

"Two texts. Promise?"

"I promise. Go." She blew him a kiss and made a shooing gesture. "Go."

He went.

* * *

Thirty minutes later Margot opened her apartment door and couldn't help smiling at the eager enthusiasm Laska lavished on her. The little dog alternated between running in mad little circles and jumping to place her front paws against Margot's shins as if trying to reach up for a kiss.

"Has it been that long, you crazy little dog?"

Margot had been in her apartment for more than five years and had never been bothered by loneliness. But having another creature greet her arrival with joy was kind of nice.

"You're most definitely a pain in the ass," she said, bending down and fondling Laska's furry neck and shoulders. "But I'm beginning to see why Yuri loved you so much."

She had not been frightened after leaving Frank. Her

mind had circled around and around on everything they had discussed and then come to a reluctant conclusion. She sent Frank a quick text.

```
Home. Taking Laska out. Can we talk in
10 minutes?
```

```
Of course
```

His reply was almost instant.

She quickly leashed Laska and went back down into the dark and dreary night. She hadn't been afraid when she had left the coffee shop, but stepping outside now, she looked left and right before moving down the street.

She imagined shadows everywhere, and it felt like the blasted cold was never going to abate. Yes, it was winter, but it was almost February, and the weather for the last couple of years had always included odd breaks in the cold. Picking her way between the cleared patches and the piles of frozen sludge, checking over her shoulder for any possible assailants, she thought for maybe the first time in her adult life about living outside the city.

If she lived in a house with a yard, like her parents. . .

Damn. She was supposed to go to her parents' tomorrow but had almost forgotten in the week's chaos. They had planned a family get-together to celebrate her final performance, and it had been a long time since she had seen her grandparents or cousins. She normally took the train, but she'd want to take Laska with her, so she'd have to either get a ride or have her mom or dad come in for her.

She mock scowled at the dog, waiting for her to finish. "My mother's going to fall completely in love with you, you little monster, and she's gonna get on my case to move back in with them."

There was absolutely no way she'd do that, but for the briefest minute, the idea of a little house with a fenced-in yard, with no bogeymen threatening to kill her, held enormous appeal. She could start a ballet school, determine her own hours, come home to a loving little dog who could run and play on a nice, green lawn...

A gust of wind blew, and she shivered. "*Come on*, little girl. Let's get back inside."

She dried off Laska's feet, set an alarm on her phone to call her mom in an hour, and then got out a pen and notepad before sitting down at her table and calling Frank.

"You're back inside and the door's locked?"

"Hello to you, too. And yes, sir, of course the door's locked."

"Good. Everything okay?"

"Yes. But I wanted to tell you what I've been thinking. It's not the mob, and it's not aliens. It absolutely has to be someone from the ballet company."

"Yeah..." His voice prolonged the syllable into an open invitation to continue.

"Only someone from the company—someone who knows everything that goes on—could possibly have done all the things they did. I keep thinking about the flowers. In other productions of *Giselle*, other ones I've danced in, others that Yuri undoubtedly danced in, Count Albrect doesn't smell the flowers. Only someone who knew our production inside out would know that was going to happen. You wouldn't have known that, right?"

Frank snorted.

"And that same someone had to be familiar with the exact layout of the backstage and the cafeteria. And only someone who really knows everything that goes on would have known to mail that damn note to me and Debi at our homes instead of to the company with the rest of them."

Margot stopped to breathe and heard Frank sigh on his end.

"That's all exactly to the point, but it leaves us with the same question we've been dealing with all week. Who inside the ballet company hates the ballet company?"

Margot pursed her lips and stared at the empty sheet of paper in front of her.

"Well. . . that's what I'm trying to figure out."

Frank laughed softly. "Me, too. Although as I keep saying, you know them all a hell of a lot better than I do."

Margot groaned. "All right! I'll keep working on it. Sorry to have bothered you."

"Hey, I didn't say you bothered me. I'm glad you called. I like hearing your voice."

A shiver of pleasure ran up her spine and she tilted her head as she held the phone tightly pressed to her ear.

"Me, too."

Frank sighed again. "But I have to get back to work. I set myself a minimum of forty names to get through tonight, and I'm only on. . ." he paused to check his notes. "Number six."

"Oh, God. You're going to be up all night. If I think of anything, I'll call you back, okay? And by the way, I'm going to my parents' house in Morristown tomorrow."

There was a moment's silence.

"So, I guess I won't see you, then. That'll be kind of weird, which is in itself kind of a weird thing to say."

"Yeah." This time it was her turn to put a lot into that lone syllable.

"How are you getting there?"

"I'm not sure. I usually take the train, but I'm going to call my parents as soon as we get off the phone. I'd like to bring Laska with me. If I know my dad, he'll volunteer immediately to come get me."

"That's probably a good idea. Text me in the morning before you go, okay?"

"If I don't discover who the murderer is first."

"That would be even better. Call anytime if you figure that one out. I don't care how late. But text me in the morning in any case."

"I will. G'night."

There was a moment's pause.

"Good night, Margot. Sleep well."

Images from Pretty Boy Yuri's funeral had been shown on the news. All those fancy-dancy people—HA! A pun!—acting so sad. Lousy actors, the whole bunch of them. They'd forget about him in days. That's the kind of shallow, selfish people they all were. But the intrigue! The mystery! The banner across the television screen had read "Phantom of the Ballet?"

What a pack of assholes.

The headaches never ceased now. But it would soon be over. The sexy young reporter—they were all sexy, young, and brainless —had looked at Paul with those big limpid eyes and asked him if the future of the ballet company was in danger.

"Of course not," Fuckwad had answered. "Our mission is to bring ballet to the people of New York and the world, and we will be back doing so as soon as we know our dancers are safe."

His dancers, safe. He hadn't even been able to keep one dancer safe. No. It was his fault Maddie was dead, his fault Yuri was dead, his fault Fred was dead, and it would be his fault when that stupid little dancer young enough to be his own daughter ended up dead. And then maybe the pain would go away.

9

Sunday

Frank's back ached, his neck was stiff, and his eyes burned. He had been staring at his computer screen for more than six hours, looking at birth records, death notices, marriage licenses, traffic citations, divorce decrees, loan applications—searching for some red flag, some hidden connection somewhere that would reveal an avalanche of rage.

But he wasn't finding it, and he was tired. Frank stood up and moved to his mini kitchen, the lengthy immobility causing daggers of pain to shoot up from his stiff ankle and lower leg.

He looked down at his left foot. Knowing he'd be home, he had left his brace off, and now his weight rested almost entirely on his good, right foot. His mind had been completely immersed in the details of people he didn't know or care about, but he was jerked back to the here and now by the aching awareness of his own reality.

Was he actually trying to pursue a relationship with an exquisitely beautiful and enchanting woman, whose every movement screamed physical perfection? When he was an aging cripple? Heads would always turn when she walked into a room. Hell, he had seen the look of rapt worship on the face of that girl by his gym elevator. The brief nanosecond of attention she had captured had lodged in his brain and revisited him as he lay trying to sleep some thirty-six hours later.

That little girl had recognized Margot for who she was—a star. A world-famous ballerina whose talent had demanded and received admiration from even his own totally ignorant and uninterested consciousness when he had first seen her on Tuesday night.

But she's not going to be dancing anymore, he reminded himself.

But she'll always be a dancer. She's kidding herself when she says she won't.

He remembered that absurd thing she had said about seeing music and hearing dance. But it really wasn't that absurd. He could see the dance in her when she sat at a table in her apartment or Starbucks, or when she walked down the street all bundled up in a shapeless winter coat with her dog.

Frank groaned as he rolled his head and tried to loosen his neck and shoulders. He saw the frightened young woman coming back through the curtain from onstage, her arms filled with flowers and her eyes huge and uncertain in her thick stage makeup. He saw the tiny little thing, clad simply in jeans and a sweatshirt, reaching up for a can of soup in her kitchen. He saw the sophisticated but grieving professional whose eyes found his, like one magnet finding another, when she was preparing to leave the funeral service. No matter the circumstance, she exuded grace and beauty.

Not even five full days, and his head was flipping through countless images of this woman who had filled a void in his life he hadn't known was there. He wasn't a beast. He knew his features were decent, his body still fit and trim. Before Brenda had bewitched him, there had always been girls hanging around, calling to do homework together and trying to get his attention. And his buddies in the army, male and female, had harassed him about his Ken Doll looks and teased him about his Barbie back home.

Even at the precinct where he had put up with the good-natured speculation about whether he was gay, straight, or neutered, the implication had been that someone who looked like he did shouldn't be alone.

But he simply hadn't cared. Hadn't cared enough to want to get involved in something that would inevitably, and expensively, turn south. Because almost all relationships went south. It was just a matter of time. And he hadn't wanted to get to the point where he'd have to take off his fucking pants and let someone see his ugly carcass of a leg.

He was fine at his own specialized gym, where almost everyone had some physical challenge of one kind or another. But Margot was used to beautiful bodies and physical perfection. He knew enough about her already to know she'd never let on if she were repulsed, but it would inevitably be there. His first steps in the morning or after long periods of inactivity were always painful and spasmodic. He had been advised time and time again to massage the withered muscles and tendons, but by the time he fell into bed at night, all he wanted was sleep.

And that was the other elephant in the room. He was a fucking cop—one who'd proven over the years that his time and attention belonged exclusively to the city. Someone who worked ridiculous hours and kept his grumbling to himself when his "day off" was ignored. Because what did someone who had no life need with a day off?

And yet. . . somehow, the idealistic, optimistic idiot he had been at nineteen—the one who had signed up to do his patriotic duty and married his forever sweetheart—was clawing at the lid his curmudgeonly self had slammed shut and demanding to be let out.

He shifted his weight and made circles with his left ankle. It hurt. It almost always hurt. But it held him. Odd though, today his whole leg seemed to hurt.

He saw again Margot's face as it had looked as she knelt next to that young girl in the wheelchair by the elevator. It had expressed only interest and kindness. Not pity. He had told her a little about his leg, and she hadn't shown horror or revulsion. Instead she had matter-of-factly recounted being dropped by an asshole. *God.* The very thought made him shudder.

He was pretty confident he could still perform in the bedroom. His nocturnal imaginings of late, both awake and asleep, assured him that his equipment was more than eager for him to pursue Margot. It was the organ above his shoulders that had decided years ago that he was done with women.

Frank's stomach growled and propelled him into movement. He opened the refrigerator and saw a few cans of beer, some wrapped American cheese slices, a bottle of ketchup, and an unopened box of Girl Scout cookies his sister had sent him last spring. Or it might have been two years ago; he couldn't remember.

The freezer wasn't much better. Three frozen pizzas, two frozen Chinese entrées, and several frozen burritos. The realization hit him that he had last stood here on Tuesday night and had eaten an evening meal with Margot each of the three nights after that and had coffee with her late yesterday afternoon. How in the world had that happened? Was he out of his fucking mind or the luckiest man on earth?

He continued to stare unseeing into the freezer until the cold air finally jerked him back to attention. Actually, he felt really cold. He took out a pizza, put the oven on to heat, and then looked at his phone.

5:27. Margot probably wouldn't be home for hours yet. She had texted that morning that her dad was coming in for her.

I sat up in bed last night trying to think about everything I knew about everyone in the company. My grandma always says that gossip is for uninteresting people, but I'm going to tell her today that all those lectures might have kept me from seeing or hearing something important. But of course I won't say that cause I don't want her to worry. I will tell her I've gotten to know a very wise detective who is close to solving the case.

Frank stared at her words from hours ago, and he could see the smile on her face as she had typed the last sentence. God, but she was beautiful.

He blew his breath out in a frustrated hiss. His chest felt kind of funny. He went back to the fridge for a beer. He took a swallow and then stared at the can. It didn't taste all that good. He was hungry, but the smell of the pizza starting to cook made him slightly queasy.

He pressed his hands against the kitchen counter and

stood back a few steps, trying to loosen his back with the cat-like stretches his therapist encouraged. He was so fucking stiff and so tired, and the thought came to him that there was no way he could force down pizza.

Frank turned off the oven, took the pizza out, and stared at it for a moment or two. His brain seemed to be turning to mush, and he shook his head to clear it. The movement hurt, and he realized that his head was very heavy.

He took in a long, slow breath. He felt like absolute shit, but it began to hit him that it might not be the normal shit he felt like after a hard week.

He moved to sit down at the stool he kept as the only chair in the kitchen. His buttocks hurt as they made contact with the stool. *Fuck.* He must have a fever. He had been ploughing through documents all afternoon, his brain working slower and slower, and now he understood why.

Half an hour later he lifted his head and pain shot through him everywhere. He had fallen asleep with his head on his arms against the kitchen counter.

Fucking hell. The goddamn flu.

He forced himself to his feet and made his way to the bathroom.

Fuck. Fuck. Fuck. Everything hurt. He looked in his medicine cabinet and found a small bottle of ibuprofen. The bottle looked old, but he didn't care. He shook out three tablets and swallowed them, then tilted his head under the tap for a bit of water to force them all the way down. He made his way to his bedroom and stared for a moment at his bed.

Thank God his charger was where it belonged. Frank plugged in his phone, sent his boss a quick text telling him that the flu had found him, and then texted Margot.

. . .

Seem to have come down with this damn flu.
Hope I didnt give it to you. Call me when
you get home

He pressed send and then fell back against the pillow. A minute later he struggled to stand up again and limped back into the main room for his laptop. He had to keep looking through the damn files. Something had to be there.

He got back into bed and propped the laptop up near his head. He'd close his eyes for only a minute or two and then get back to work.

* * *

The phone rang several times before Frank finally picked up.

"Hey." His voice was hoarse. "You're home?"

"Oh my God, Frank, you sound horrible. Do you need anything?"

"No. I'm fine. But I keep falling asleep when I need to be working."

"Forget the work. You need to sleep."

"It's kinda hard to forget the work when there's someone out there who may be trying to kill you."

"No one's trying to kill me. I'm almost positive. I keep thinking about it. I don't think whoever is doing this had anybody specific in mind. It's all just randomized violence against the ballet company."

"Yeah. Your ballet company."

"No, not anymore. I retired, remember? I had a party today at my parents' to prove it."

"How was it?"

"It was nice. But you need to go to bed and sleep for real. Are you in bed?"

"Yeah."

"Do you have your computer with you?"

"Uh-huh."

"Well, put it away. Frank? Do you hear me?"

"Okay. Maybe for a little while. What time is it?"

"10:30."

"I really need to go through some more files."

"No, you really need to sleep. How about I call you in the morning, early?"

"No. I don't want you to wake up early just to wake me." His voice sounded muffled, as if he needed to blow his nose.

"I have a dog now, remember? She likes to get up early. Besides, the wedding is tomorrow and I wanted to take a morning class first."

Frank didn't answer for a moment.

"Frank? Are you still there? Are you okay?"

"Yeah, I'm fine." That lie again. "But I hate you going to class by yourself. Are you going to the same place as yesterday?"

It had been two days ago, but she didn't correct him.

"Yes. But I'll be fine. It's supposed to be a little warmer tomorrow and they said we might even get some sun."

Frank grunted.

"Do you have a doctor? Maybe you could get some of that Tamiflu stuff. Or do you have any cold medicine?"

"I took ibuprofen. I'll be fine."

Not likely, given how bad he sounded.

"How about I come by in the morning before I go to class?"

Frank snorted.

"God, no. It's bad enough I might have given this to you already. I don't want to make it any more likely."

"You've been to my place a hundred times now, and I don't even know where you live."

"I'm in the West Village. But it doesn't matter, cause I don't want you anywhere near here right now."

She waited a moment.

"Then you need to go to bed for real now, and I'll call you in the morning. If you feel well enough, you can start working again, and if not, then you'll sleep some more."

Another grunt.

"Okay, Frank?"

She could hear him coughing and wished desperately she could do something to make him feel better.

"Yeah."

"So as soon as we hang up, you're going to put your laptop away and sleep, right?"

"Uh-huh."

"Okay then. Make sure you do it. But please call me if you need anything, all right? Promise?"

Another grunt.

"Good night, Frank. I hope you feel better."

"Night, Margot. Love you."

Margot stared at her phone, the call disconnected. Had he just said what she thought he had said? She shook her head. Not possible. Absolutely not possible.

She found herself pacing around the room.

He had said her name, so he wasn't confusing her with anyone else. Right? But maybe he was really, really sick and not right in the head. But he had said her name, had talked rationally about her class tomorrow, and had said he had taken ibuprofen.

"Love you."

Not "I love you," granted, but still. No one had ever, ever, said those words to her, with or without the "I." Her parents had, of course, and her grandparents, and probably her cousins, and friends from dance said it to each other all the time.

But no male, talking directly to her, had ever said those two or three words. Every relationship up to now had been superficial. Some fun, some less so, but none of them had actually meant anything. All of her focus, from about age three on, if her mother was to be believed, had been on dance.

And now, in the course of a week, she had danced her final performance, and an incredibly sincere, caring, and pretty hot guy had said he loved her.

It had to be the fever. Didn't it? Maybe he was sicker than he thought. Should she call someone? But who? She knew he had a boss, but then everyone had a boss. It wasn't like she could simply call 911 and ask to speak to Detective Sutton's supervisor. She knew he had a mother and a sister, and probably (maybe?) his mother had the same last name, but a lot of good that would do her since she had absolutely no idea where the woman might live.

She paced some more. She lifted her phone and stared at it, deliberating.

Should she call him back? That would be dumb, since she'd just told him to go to sleep. Text him? No—if he had done what she suggested, that would be stupid, too.

She stared a little longer at her phone. This was insane. He was sick and had spoken without thinking, and she had to let it go and focus on what was important. Laska was already waiting for her on the bed. She needed to get her bag ready for class in the morning. And she should probably get out everything for the wedding, too, since there wouldn't be a whole lot of time in between the two.

Spending the day with her family had been like being in a different world. There had been close to twenty people at her parents' home, all loud and loving. Her cousin's young boys had delighted in Laska, and the dog was now completely exhausted. She was pretty tired, too, come to think of it. And so stuffed with food. Her mother had made three pans of lasagna, one completely vegan, and there'd been garlic bread, salad, and a huge cake that read "Way to Go, Margot!"

She had talked about the week's horrors with her dad on the drive to her parents' house, but the topic hadn't come up during the rest of the day. Thanks to the horrible weather, the flu epidemic, and the current scandal at City Hall, the incidents at Empire weren't grabbing all the headlines. Both her parents were extremely interested and anxious, but her father admitted that the rest of the family was probably largely unaware, and they had agreed to avoid the topic as much as possible.

Instead, her family had peppered her with questions about her future. Her father's mother suggested she go on a cruise and think about what she wanted to do, maybe finding a nice young man at the same time. Her mother's mother, still incredibly young and limber at eighty-seven, wanted her to enroll in a yoga teaching program at her yoga studio. Her paternal grandfather had taken an instant liking to Laska, but then had said to her: "A lively dog like this needs children to play with. How about it, sweetie? Harry has given me great-grandchildren; now it's your turn."

Margot had merely laughed at her grandfather, whom she adored. "You've been saying the same thing to me for years, and now you're using my dog? One thing at a time, Grandpa!"

Both her parents had been in the car for the drive back into the city, and the ride had been quiet. She knew they were worried—about the murders, about her future—but they had always been both supportive and trusting in her ability to make her own decisions. Her mom had brought up the idea of college again but hadn't pushed. Her father's "I think I've got about five years left before I retire, so if you want a tuition break, you'll need to start soon," was the same line he'd been using for years. She wasn't sure he'd ever retire.

Her mother had gotten out of the car when they arrived at her building and watched while Margot walked a few steps with Laska. Then she had hugged her fiercely.

"We love you, Sweetheart. Please be careful this week. Whatever you decide to do, we'll support you. You're still in touch with the detective you told us about, right?"

Margot nodded.

"Then listen to what he says. There's obviously more than one crazy person in this city, but this is the first time anyone's targeted dancers."

"Then it's a good thing I'm not a dancer, anymore, isn't it?"

Her mother had only shaken her head and hugged her once more. "Just be careful."

So what was she doing this very moment? Checking her ballet bag for class in the morning. Even she had to recognize the irony. Why was a "not a dancer" going to dance class?

Now was not the time. She would figure this all out next week--or whenever. She wondered if any of the rehearsals she had promised to help with in Paul's absence would now take place. That would depend, no doubt, on whether there were any more murders. Margot closed her eyes and tried to take a deep breath. She was in her own apartment, and she was safe. But the simple truth was that it would all depend on whether or not they caught the son-of-a-bitch behind all this.

Margot stood still. She had insisted to Frank that it had to be someone within the company. But there was no "son-of-a-bitch" in the ballet company. Or if there was, he must have some kind of split personality.

"Fucking-A." She said the words aloud, but there was no

one there to hear her bad language, and Laska had wisely gone to bed already.

She had been at Empire for almost ten years. If she couldn't figure out who was behind all this, how could the police?

She put her dance bag by the door and moved to her bedroom closet. The wedding was at 3:00 at St. Bartholomew's, and the reception would follow in a downstairs section of the church. She hadn't been inside a church in years, and now she was ending up in one twice in one week. A wedding was better than a funeral, though. She had originally thought to wear one of the super-sleek, form fitting dresses she kept for galas, but given all they had recently been through, she lifted out a green, woolen, long-sleeved dress her mother had found at a consignment shop. The dress was simple, elegant, and warm. She found a pair of sheer black pantyhose and her black heels. She next went to her jewelry box. Her dad had bought her diamond stud earrings for her first Sugar Plum Fairy role more than twenty years ago, and to this day they were her favorite earrings. She chose a gold chain with a rose pendant and a simple gold bracelet. There. That was done.

She had everything out and looked around, her bottom lip caught in her teeth. There was nothing else to do. Everything was ready for tomorrow. She hadn't figured out who the murderer was, despite her determination, and she should just go to bed.

But she was wide awake. She had spent the day with her family, celebrating the end of a fabulous career, that she, herself, had chosen to end. What kind of fucking idiot was she? She had no real plans, someone had killed people she knew and cared about, the weather sucked, and a possibly delirious police detective had said "love you" to her.

Margot sat down on the edge of her bed and pressed her

face into her clenched fists, her elbows propped on her lap. Laska lifted her head, stretched out her furry little body to almost two whole feet, and then came over and stuck her head against Margot's chin.

"Has the whole world gone mad, little one? I keep asking you that, and you don't answer."

Laska remained mute, her stubby tail thumping against the bed as Margot patted her.

"You're right. It has, and there's nothing we can do about it. Bed it is."

She went and brushed her teeth, washed her face, and climbed into bed. Laska curled right into her side.

"Did Yuri let you get away with this?"

No answer.

But she didn't mind. She put her hand on the dog and felt its steady breathing. For this precise moment in time, she had nothing to complain about. She was warm, dry, comfortable, and had a little bundle of affection pressed up against her. Tomorrow would have to take care of itself.

* * *

He was gazing down into Margot's luminous eyes, his hands on her cheeks and his erection pressing against her belly. She was so beautiful and so warm. So very warm, almost burning. But other hands—long fingers, in shiny black gloves—reached out and grabbed her around the throat and pulled her across the stage. Frank tried to get to her, but his legs were being held, and he couldn't move. She was pulled farther and farther away, and it was no longer a stage but a desert, and then she was being thrown from a cliff and he couldn't run . . .

Frank awoke with a hoarse cry, his legs tangled in his sheets. He was hot, beads of sweat on his face, neck, and down his back, and he hadn't been able to save her. He looked around blindly for a moment, overcome with horror and guilt, and saw his laptop on the floor next to his bed.

A dream. Just a horrible, addled dream. He shook his head, then groaned. His head ached. His throat ached. Everything ached. But now he was cold. He reached for the tangled mess of sheets, but they were drenched with his sweat. He sat up and rocked back and forth. He had to pee, but he stared in confusion for a moment at his erection. He had been about to make love to Margot, and then she had been taken.

"Oh God." He put his head in his hands and continued to rock for a minute more. He finally pushed himself to his feet and limped to the bathroom, shivering. He'd have to put on some sweats and sit in a chair for a while until his sheets dried off. He was too tired to change them and too cold to think about anything else.

Ten minutes later he sat in the chair, staring at his closed laptop. He had to work, had to figure out who was trying to kill Margot.

No. Stop. No one was trying to kill Margot, specifically, or anyone else—he was almost sure. They were likely trying to destroy the ballet company, and if he could only figure out why, he'd probably have his killer.

He was so cold and so tired. Maybe if he just closed his eyes for a few minutes and thought about it, he'd figure it out.

1 0

Monday

The sun actually made an appearance on Monday morning. Margot glanced at it in disbelief as Laska picked her way through the piles of partially melted muck. Gross. Sunlight was wonderful, but the mess on the white dog's feet and legs was disgusting. For the millionth time she pondered the impossibility that she was now a dog owner. But without Laska, she would probably never have slept last night, so she'd just have to deal with dirty paws.

Back inside she looked at the time, trying to decide whether to call Frank or wait. But she'd promised.

"Hey."

He sounded worse.

"Hey, yourself. You're really sick, aren't you?"

"Yeah. No. It's this same crap everybody's been getting. I'll be fine in a day or two."

"Are you sure I can't bring you anything?"

"Yes. I'm completely sure. I don't want you to get sick. What time is your class?"

"Ten."

"And what time is the wedding?"

"Three."

He was silent for a moment, but Margot could hear how muffled his breathing sounded.

"Frank, listen. If you're in the West Village, I can grab soup from a deli near the studio and come down in a cab. I can even have it wait for me while I drop if off and then go the rest of the way home before the wedding."

"No. Absolutely not."

"Then I'll come by after the wedding. It will be on my way home, anyway."

"Only if it was July and you were going on a ridiculously long run. Otherwise, it's two cabs or rides you have to depend on, for no reason. Because I'm fine. You need to go straight home after the . . . is there a reception?"

"Of course. But it's at the church, right after the service."

"Good. Then you need to go straight home after the reception."

Margot waited a moment before answering.

"Are you always this bossy? I think it was easier when I was a suspect."

Frank started to answer but got hit by a wave of coughing.

"Never mind. It doesn't sound like talking on the phone is doing you any good. So just listen. I'm still trying to figure things out, but I haven't come up with anything yet. I'm taking the subway to class, coming home, showering, and then I'll take a cab to the wedding. And yes, bossy-man, I'll come straight home afterwards. But if you change your mind and need anything, text me, okay?"

"Okay. Yes. Thank you. And Margot, I'm sorry. I don't

mean to be bossy. I'm worried, and I don't know how to do this . . . this kind of thing. And I should be out there. Where's the wedding, again?"

"St. Bartholomew's. And don't worry. I think we'll be pretty safe in a large church in the middle of Manhattan."

"How is that different from a large theater in the middle of Manhattan?"

Well, he had her there. But this was a private wedding, and she was pretty sure there were no killers on the guest list. *Please, God, don't let the killer be on the guest list.* Margot tried to relax the muscles that had instinctively tightened at Frank's words.

"You need to rest, drink tea, and forget about all this for a few days. Everything's going to be fine. There'll probably be plenty of police in the area anyway, right?"

"Yes, but as soon as we hang up, I'm going to call Mackie and make sure he has it covered."

She remembered her scattered ideas from last night. Mackie was presumably Frank's supervisor.

"What's your mother's last name?" The minute the words were out, she felt foolish.

"My mother?" His tone was confused. "It's Sutton, of course. Why?"

"Never mind. I know it sounds stupid, but I was worried about how sick you sounded and thought about trying to call your mother."

Frank started to laugh, but it immediately turned into a hacking cough.

"God forbid. You'd play right into her 'You need someone to look after you' routine." He had tried to alter his voice, but due to his already strained throat, he made his mother sound like a strangled chicken.

"I said it was stupid. Never mind!"

Neither spoke for a moment.

"Please call me if you need anything."

"Text me when you're home from class and before you go to the wedding."

They had spoken simultaneously, and Margot laughed.

"You go back to bed and stop worrying. I have a busy day and a fierce watchdog here to protect me when I get home."

"Just be careful. Be aware of who's around you at all times, and don't go off anywhere alone. I'll talk to you later."

They disconnected, and Margot was appalled at the disappointment that coursed through her. No "love you." It had probably been the fever talking last night—an automatic response to someone like his mother or sister or maybe even a girlfriend who cared about him. He had never acted like someone who had a girlfriend, but anything was possible in this crazy world.

She had to get going. It *was* going to be a busy day, but going to class was really the only way she knew to start a day. It was where she felt safe and like herself. Where she belonged.

* * *

Margot was walking down the aisle in a beautiful white gown, and Paul was waiting for her, love shining in his eyes. Frank thrashed about, trying to get to her, to stop her from marrying the wrong man. But the aisle in front of him got longer and longer, and Margot moved closer to Paul.

Frank sat up, trying desperately to call out, but his voice was hoarse and unintelligible. She couldn't marry Paul. That would be all wrong. *He* loved her. She should be marrying *him*.

Reality slowly flooded back to him. Margot was not marrying Paul. It had been another senseless, fever-induced dream. And what the fuck was he thinking? Did he really love her? Tears slipped from his eyes and his nose ran. He knew he had a fever from the way his skin felt like it was being pricked by thousands of needles. He reached for a tissue, but the box was empty, the floor covered with earlier discards.

He tried to concentrate. He had to think about the murder and the possible suspects. But the image of Margot walking down the aisle kept pushing rational thought aside. He had never contemplated remarrying, and even the word sent a shiver of horror through him. But stronger than his reserve was the sudden realization that he never wanted to say good-bye to Margot Johnson.

He wanted to share meals with her, wanted to hear her talk about ballet shoes being dropped by drones, wanted to walk that silly dog with her, and carry that ridiculously heavy dance bag for her. He wanted to kiss her and taste her and feel her small, lithe body on top of him and underneath him.

Jesus. Frank forced himself to breathe. *Get up, asshole.* Wash your face, blow your nose, take more ibuprofen, solve this damn case, and then there might be time to figure out if there was any hope for something permanent between him and Margot.

Twenty minutes later he was standing in his kitchen, waiting for the cup of water in the microwave to boil. He had found tea bags in the cupboard. There were several pantry items on his shelves that his mother and sister had bought when he first moved in that he had never touched. But the thought of coffee at the moment made him nauseous.

Images from his fever dream kept running through his mind. *Get your head out of your ass.* She's not marrying Paul. Paul was marrying Debi.

Frank narrowed his eyes, squinting at the microwave. He wished his head didn't throb so much. He and Margot had talked this damn case to death, but at the coffee shop the other day they had honed in on the idea that someone was trying to hurt Paul.

He needed to learn more about Paul's past. The water boiled, and he took the mug out and put in the tea bag. The water sizzled over the top and splashed onto the counter. He stared at it dumbly. He wasn't even sure he had ever made tea before, but he thought the teabag was supposed to soak for a while. He went and got another sweatshirt to put on top of the one he was already wearing. He was so fucking cold.

* * *

The ballet class had been gloriously distracting. Certainly not difficult, but several of the wealthy, middle-aged women who regularly took the morning class had danced in their youth, so the centuries' old pattern of barre, center, and across the floor work moved at a good pace.

Margot thanked the teacher after the reverence and smiled and nodded at several of the dancers, but she didn't stay to chat.

Heeding Frank's last words, she kept alert as she walked the few blocks from the studio to the subway. The sun had stayed out, miraculously, and given how many moments of her life had seemed gray this week, she was sorry she didn't have more time to soak in the comforting rays. It might have been nice to walk several more blocks before descending into the subway, but she had to get home and change for the wedding. She'd take Laska out again quickly, in case the reception ran long.

She looked around once more when she exited the subway, but the sunlight somehow made the insane events of the past week seem unreal. There were no bogeymen waiting to jump her, just busy New Yorkers trying to go about their normal lives. Maybe it was all over. Maybe whoever it was had had some kind of melt-down that had made him temporarily vicious, and it was now done. She stopped a minute to think. Yuri had died on Tuesday night. Rocco had fallen on Wednesday. They had received death threats on Thursday, and the food that had sickened Liza, Debi, and poor Fred had been put out on Thursday as well. All of that could have been planned on Tuesday or maybe even Monday, or maybe even ages before that. Nothing else had happened since. So maybe it *was* all done.

She became aware of people brushing against her as she blocked the sidewalk. She'd have to mention this idea to Frank later tonight. Maybe if nothing else happened, they could simply assume it was a "one and done" kind of thing, and everything could go back to normal.

A bus took the corner sharply just as she was stepping up on the curb near her apartment building, and her leggings and boots were splattered with brown muck. The sun chose that moment to disappear behind an ominous looking group of clouds, and Margot shivered and looked around nervously. She was being totally naïve. It hadn't been "one," and it most likely wasn't "done." Numerous lives had been permanently altered or ended. No surprisingly bright, and evidently short-lived, late January sunshine could change that.

She blew out her breath in an exasperated sigh as she looked down at her filthy boots. Should she clean them off before leaving for the wedding and carry her shoes, or should she be reckless and go in her heels, hoping she could avoid the mess that was everywhere outside? She suddenly felt overwhelmed and exhausted. If she wore her boots, where would she put them when she changed into her heels? And what if the murderer *was* on the guest list?

* * *

Everything's fine. Hope you're feeling a little better. I'll call you when I'm back home tonight if it's not too late.

Frank grunted when the text came in and then forced himself back to the documents he had pulled up. After the incident in New Jersey when his prom date had been killed, Paul had moved to the Pacific Northwest. There he had risen through the ranks, gaining renown both as a dancer and a choreographer. There were pictures of him at charity events, often with another dancer on his arm and sometimes with an obviously older female patron close by his side. But Frank couldn't find more than two pictures of him with any specific female and no references in the gossip records to a girlfriend. Or a boyfriend. It was the ballet world, after all.

Paul's Instagram profile was professional, as was his Twitter account. He had a public and private Facebook page, but it looked like they were rarely updated. Since his arrival at Empire several years ago, there had been surprisingly few mentions of him in the New York gossip pages—print or electronic. Again, there were numerous pictures from galas and fund raisers, but he was often photographed in group shots with other dancers.

Frank checked Debi's accounts. Lots of glamorous ballerina shots from Austin and New York. Typical pictures of a vibrant 20-something-year-old female smiling brightly with friends in restaurants, tourist sights, and cuddling a cat. Tweets about performances, foam rollers, resistance bands, lambswool, other dancers, and *Game of Thrones* and *DWTS*. Frank shook his head. Why would anyone want to Tweet about foam rollers, and what was with the lambswool? There was one shot on Instagram of Debi and Paul together, but otherwise, there was almost nothing personal anywhere.

He rubbed his forehead, trying to find anything important in this sea of incomprehensible nonsense. He desperately wanted to close his eyes again, but fear was gnawing at him. He hated Margot being out alone with the killer still on the loose, and his spidey sense was telling him that shit was going to hit the fan. Or maybe it was his fever making him crazy.

He had to get away from social media. He went back over records he had searched before: no arrests or complaints filed against them or by them. No financial red flags. Their credit reports were both good: no student loans or high credit card balances.

He looked at his phone. He'd take his laptop back to bed with him, rest for a short while, and then get going again. He wanted to have something by tonight. The ballet company needed to get back in business; Margot wanted to do what she had promised to do while Paul was away. And he needed a day off and to get back to a more normal caseload.

The trip to the bedroom took an unbelievably long time. He tried to hold a blanket wrapped around him with one hand while carrying his laptop and water bottle with the other. He hurt everywhere and wanted to sleep for a hundred years.

The bed was a rumpled mess, but he was too tired to care. He got in and attempted to prop himself against the wall with a pillow, with the laptop open on the bed, but he couldn't stop shivering. He slid down deeper and tried to pull the blankets more tightly around him while still being able to reach the trackpad.

It had to be about Paul. Margot had said so, and she knew the ballet company, right? The nightmare image of her moving down the aisle flashed again in his mind, but he pushed it away. He wished he could see her and know she was safely at the wedding.

Goddamn it! He had left his phone by the armchair. He was too cold to get up and go get it. But what if she called? What if something happened? He closed his eyes for a moment, trying to decide what to do. He'd work for a few minutes and then get up and get his phone.

Eyes blurry, he forced himself to study the screen again. He pulled up the story about the incident after the prom and then looked up the pest control company owned by Paul's date's father, Jack Dimond. Fighting off the need to close his eyes, he searched for Jack Dimond and the girl's mother, Marina Dimond. There were death notices for both parents. They must have both died relatively young. Frank blew his nose and squeezed his eyes tightly, willing himself to stay alert.

He read both notices. Jack had died two years ago of a heart attack. He had been out on an exterminating call and had apparently pulled his truck over to the side of the road and died. Well, that was pretty decent of him. Dimond had left one daughter living in New Jersey and a brother who lived in Virginia. The death notice mentioned an older daughter's tragic death and described how the drunk driving incident had brought the small New Jersey town together and led to reduced speed limits and increased sobriety checks, especially during spring and summer months.

Marina had died in the aftermath of an apparently prolonged battle with cancer ten years after her older daughter had been killed. She had been survived by her husband, a remaining daughter, Bettina Dimond, and a brother and sister, Harold Galick and Allison Galick.

Frank pushed his laptop aside and rested his head against the pillow. He would just close his eyes for a minute or two. The story was a sad one, and he wondered if Paul had kept in touch with the family. He had to have been close to the girl to have come back between living in Germany and moving to the west coast only to attend a prom. Death was horrible when it took young people like that. He imagined the family trying to pick up the pieces—heartbroken parents and a little sister.

A little sister. *Wait.* He struggled to remember. The sister's name had been Bettina. Was that right? That was a pretty unusual name. He pushed himself up and pulled his laptop close once again, tapping the trackpad to wake it. The articles he had just read were still on the screen. He stared again at the mother's death notice. He hadn't paid attention to the line that read née whatever, but now he did. Her maiden name had been Galick, and she had been survived by a brother and sister with the last name Galick.

That cranky woman from the ballet company. Wasn't her name Bettina Galick? He sat up straighter, the blankets slipping off, and accessed his synced notes that he had made earlier that week.

Bettina Galick. Wardrobe mistress. At the coffee shop when Margot had been talking about nasty people at the ballet company, she had mentioned Bettina but said everyone was used to her.

Frank's breathing grew rapid. Her father had been an exterminator. Her sister had died after a date with a much younger Paul. She had to be the killer.

Frank stood up and swayed, reaching to hold on to the bedframe. He was dizzy and still so fucking cold, but he had to warn Margot and had to call Mackie. He pulled the blanket from the bed and wrapped it around himself before going back into the main room. His phone was on the floor by the chair, and Frank was hit by another wave of dizziness as he bent down quickly to get it.

He had to call his boss immediately, but he hit Margot's

number first. It went straight to voicemail. *Fuck*. She was in a church, at a wedding, so it made sense her phone was off or on mute. He flipped to his boss's number and waited impatiently for him to pick up.

Jesus Christ. Another fucking voicemail. He hit the redial once, then two more times. A noise that sounded horribly like a whimper escaped him. He had to do something. He limped quickly back into the bedroom, sat on the bed, and searched his laptop for the contact information for all of the dance company employees. He found Bettina's number, entered it, and pressed call. Voicemail. He stared at his phone in horrified disbelief. Was this another nightmare?

He tried his boss again, and Oh, God, *thank God*, he picked up. Frank rasped out what he had learned, and Mackie's "Goddamn" sent another shiver of fear through him.

"So let me get this straight. This woman, Bettina Galick, you said? She's a wardrobe mistress at the ballet company, and her father was an exterminator, which would give her access to poisons, and her sister once dated the company director and died after going to the prom with him? Fuck, that's a mess. What the hell is a wardrobe mistress? Never mind. Where is she now, do we know?"

"I tried her number and got no answer. But I'm afraid she might be at the wedding."

"Oh, Jesus. Hang on. Let me call the guys who are over there now. It was St. Bart's, right?"

"Yeah."

"You have a description of her?"

Frank struggled to remember. "Kind of mousy looking. Long, graying hair, I think. Someone you'd barely notice."

"And her name is Galick, but what was the other name?"

"Dimond. That was her last name growing up and the name of the pest control company."

There was silence while his boss presumably called the uniformed cops doing security at St. Bartholomew's.

"Okay, I've let the guys know. The wedding ceremony started about half an hour ago, so they're keeping an eye and will see if she's there after the service ends."

"Walter, you have to stop her. She's obviously crazy. This is some kind of insane revenge for something that happened twenty-five years ago and seems to have been a complete accident."

"We're on it, Frank. You sound like absolute shit. But you figured this out, and we'll take care of it. Take some aspirin and to go bed."

"Goddamn it, Walter. Margot's there, at the wedding."

"Margot? Your Nancy Drew? Jesus, you've got it bad. Go to bed. We'll take care of it. Your ballerina girlfriend will be fine."

Mackie disconnected and Frank stared at his phone. He tried Margot's number and again it went to voicemail. *Fuck, fuck, fuck*!

He couldn't to this, shouldn't do this. He had no arrest warrant, no right to tell a member of the public anything the police had learned in an investigation. He could very well be fired. But he had no choice.

```
Its Bettina. She had access to the poisons
and motive. Shes super dangerous. Get out
of there ASAP
```

He sent the text and stared at his phone. He'd be disciplined for sure if anyone found out, but he didn't care. He just hoped Margot saw the text and got out of there.

Another wave of shivering hit him and he sat down

heavily in the chair. He should go there, go to St. Bart's and help them take down this crazy woman. He remembered how Bettina had glared at him when he had asked her for directions in the theater. If Margot got anywhere near her, the bitch wouldn't hesitate to knock her down. Or worse. He shouldn't have told her. She would be safer not knowing. He should go there, *now*.

He stared at the time on his phone, trying to think, trying to work out what was the smartest thing to do. If he left now, it would take him at least a half hour to get there, probably more. He wasn't dressed, was a disgusting, unshaven mess, and he didn't know if he could drive. He rocked back and forth and wanted to cry; he didn't remember the last time he had cried. He needed to do something, and there was not a goddamn fucking thing he could do.

`Please call as soon as you see this`

He hit send, and then wrapped the blanket tighter once more. He'd sit and wait and hope to God she would call him soon.

11

Monday Afternoon

St. Bartholomew's was both an historic landmark and a
beacon for music lovers due to its world-famous pipe
organ and its magnificent choir. Visitors came from near and
far to marvel at the elaborate stained glass windows, admire
the architecture, and hope to hear music. But it was also a
neighborhood church, and as Margot entered, she was
relieved to see security guards separating wedding attendees
from tourists, who were directed to side areas and the gift
shop.

Though Debi had grown up in Texas, it turned out her
New York grandparents were life-long members of St. Bart's,
as the locals called it, and a Monday afternoon wedding
wasn't all that hard to squeeze in. The church was huge, but
Debi and Paul had desired only a modest wedding, so the
usher who accompanied Margot led her past what seemed

like countless empty rows before they reached the small group congregated at the front of the sanctuary.

Liza had seen her and was beckoning to her, and Margot slipped into the row and pushed her bag under her seat. She stared for a moment, confused. She had expected traditional church pews, but the seats were wooden chairs. The thought flashed through her mind again: two odd church experiences in one week. *Please God, let next week be a boring one.*

"Are your boots in your bag, too?" came Liza's whisper, as she reached over and hugged Margot.

Margot nodded, her eyes wide in shared exasperation. The muck outside was just too much, and at the last minute she had dumped out the contents of her dance bag, lined it with a plastic garbage bag, and now her dirty boots lay stuffed inside and a tiny black purse, big enough for only her phone, a small comb, and her lipstick, hung over her shoulder.

Kevin smiled a greeting. "This place is amazing, isn't it?" he whispered.

Margot nodded, looking around and smiling. It was beautiful. When she had checked the location, she read that the church attracted almost as many visitors as St. Patrick's, but Margot had never been inside before.

The front of the church was quickly filling up. Margot studied the family members of the bride and groom, seated in the first few rows on both sides of the aisle. She realized she knew very little about either Paul or Debi outside their lives at the company. It looked like Paul had at least two brothers, and Debi's extended family was enormous.

Several girls from the corps were there, as well as two beloved ballet mistresses, the music director, the assistant artistic director, the executive director, the general manager, and four of the principal male dancers. Margot was surprised and pleased to see Maria from the cafeteria sitting across the aisle. She always shared love and affection with everyone, in addition to food, and it was nice to see that Paul and Debi recognized her friendship.

Bettina was there, seated in the same row as Maria, with an empty seat between them. That was a little odd. Margot had never known Bettina to be particularly friendly to anyone, and she was certainly not aware of any close relationship between the wardrobe mistress and either Debi or Paul. But maybe inviting her had been a professional courtesy. Bettina worked hard; she had obviously costumed Debi often, and Paul depended on her organization and skills.

The music coming from the phenomenal organ died away as a minister came from a side area to stand front and center. A moment later he was joined by Paul, dressed in an elegant black tuxedo. Instead of the traditional wedding march, the first notes of Bach's "Jesu, Joy of Man's Desiring" began to resonate throughout the magnificent church. Family members in the first rows stood and turned around, and the rest of the congregation followed suit.

A young girl dressed in a gossamer pink dress walked slowly up the long aisle, carrying a basket of flowers. She was followed by one young woman, who looked a lot like Debi, dressed in a knee-length lavender-colored dress, and a groomsman in a dark gray tux. Behind them stood Debi, arrayed in a simple but exquisite A-line white gown, her arm on a silver-haired gentleman, who looked like he was holding back tears. They moved slowly up the aisle in step to the hauntingly beautiful music, and Margot could see the love and joy shining in Debi's eyes as she walked toward Paul.

The service itself lasted only about forty minutes. There were a few inspirational readings, a young man sang "Make Me a Channel of Your Peace," the bride and groom spoke vows that no one sitting anywhere near Margot seemed able to hear, and then it was over.

The congregation was directed to stand and turn to a hymn for the recession. More breaks from tradition—no Mendelssohn. Kind of a shame because it probably would have sounded extraordinary coming from the famed organ. Margot dutifully opened to the page and then put the book back down. She didn't know the piece and couldn't sing, so there was no point. She wanted to get a picture of Debi and Paul, anyway.

She got her phone out of her purse as the last bars of the hymn's introduction were played and turned it on.

Two texts were visible on her screen.

```
Its Bettina. She had access to the poisons
and motive. Shes super dangerous. Get out
of there ASAP
```

```
Please call as soon as you see this
```

Margot stopped breathing and felt an actual chill run up her body. She stared at her phone, momentarily frozen, and then glanced across the aisle to where she had seen Bettina. Everyone in the church was standing, eyes turned to the bride and groom, but Maria, who was in the chair closest to the aisle, was still seated, a look of absolute terror on her face. Next to her, standing, Bettina held what looked like a large pistol in her right hand, with the open hymnal in her left hand, partially hiding the gun from sight. But Margot was directly across from them and had an unobscured view.

Oh God Oh God Oh God. The words ran through her mind as she stood, petrified. Bettina had a gun, and Paul and Debi were going to walk right by her. What could she do? She had to do something. Could she throw her phone at Bettina? What if she missed? It was an odd angle, and Bettina might shoot *her*. Or maybe she meant to shoot everybody, anyway. Margot had no clue in the world as to how many shots a gun like that might hold. *Fuck, fuck, fuck, fuck, fuck*—the singing had begun, and Paul and Debi were starting to walk, hands clasped, huge smiles on both their faces.

Margot took a hiccuping breath. She had to do something, *NOW*. Debi and Paul would be near them in just seconds. Trying not to draw attention to herself, she pushed her phone against Liza, who took it, a questioning look on her face. Margot bent down quickly, grabbed the dance bag that usually weighed at least twenty pounds but now held only muddy winter boots, and threw herself across the aisle, less than ten feet in front of the approaching newlyweds. She pushed the bag against the hymnal, knocking the book and the gun into Bettina's startled face, pushing her back and half falling against Maria.

"You bitch!" yelled Bettina. She was struggling to get up from where she had landed against the unsuspecting guests in the row behind her. The organ music continued, but Paul and Debi had stopped moving, and all around people were gasping and turning to look.

"Help me!" Margot yelled, and Kevin was beside her and then on top of her, reaching out to hold Bettina down, pressing her against the back of her toppled chair as the people in the crushed row tried to move away. Bettina's right hand still held the gun, but it was pressed tightly against her chest as Kevin pinned her arm.

"Let go of me," she hissed, trying to thrash her way free.

Margot felt Maria's hands steadying her as she attempted to slide out from under Kevin's weight without dislodging his hold on Bettina.

And then the gun went off.

Screams came from all around, and finally the music stopped playing.

"Everyone down, now!"

Cops were there, guns drawn, and someone was hauling Margot backwards. She saw the blue of uniforms, heard more screaming, but everything sounded distant, the retort of the gun going off so close to her head making all noises sound like they were coming through a tunnel far away.

"Are you hurt, Miss? Miss?" She blinked and realized the man standing in front of her had asked the same question multiple times.

She stared at him, confused. Was she hurt?

"I don't think so. Are Paul and Debi all right?"

"Are they the bride and groom?"

She nodded.

"Yes. They're fine. They're right over there." He pointed towards the front of the church, where three more police officers stood, with the wedding party and most of the guests crowded together on the ground behind their defenders in the same area where Paul and Debi had made their vows only minutes earlier.

"Did she hurt anyone? The gun went off—I couldn't stop her." As she said the words, a terrible trembling swept over her. Her knees gave way, her hands shook, and she felt herself starting to hyper-ventilate.

The policeman held her by the shoulders and moved her to a chair at the end of one of the rows, guided her down, and gently pushed her head towards her knees."

"Just breathe—nice slow breaths. No one's hurt. It looks like you and that fellow prevented a real disaster." He kept one hand on her shoulder and called out to paramedics who were entering the back of the church. "We need a blanket up here."

A moment later she was being wrapped in a silver foil

blanket, and more people in different uniforms were asking if she was all right. She nodded, teeth chattering, the continued ringing in her ears making everything seem unreal and distorted.

She forced herself to take a few slow breaths and carefully raised her head, willing the shivering to stop. She stared in some surprise at her lap. She was still wearing the green wool dress, the one she had picked because it was warm. She had to get herself under control. She was okay. She hadn't been hurt. No one, it seemed, had been hurt, and Bettina was being led down the aisle of the church, her hands in handcuffs behind her back.

Margot caught a glimpse of her face before she was turned towards the exit. Where a few minutes before there had been rage, there was now a look of utter defeat and despair. The cranky wardrobe mistress was gone, the fanatical killer was gone, and in their place was a pathetic shell of a woman who seemed to have aged years in only a few minutes.

A man in an overcoat appeared in front of her. "Are you Miss Margot Johnson?"

She nodded.

He held out his phone. "I'm Walter Mackie, and one of my men would like to speak with you." He handed her his cell phone."

"Hello?"

"Margot! Are you all right?"

Frank's raspy voice sounded frantic.

"I'm fine. It's all okay." She began to cry, tears running down her face as if a dam had been unleashed. "You figured it out, Frank. You did it, and Paul and Debi are alive."

"Oh, Sweetheart. Shhhh. Don't cry." His own voice sounded thick with tears, and Margot sniffled and tried to get herself together.

"Is it really all over?"

"Yes. We're pretty sure it's all over."

"Oh God, Frank. She had a gun. She was going to kill them with a gun. At their wedding." Her tears started again, and Margot pulled the foil blanket tighter around herself.

"But you stopped her, Margot. I heard you went from Giselle to Super Woman and saved the day."

"No, I didn't do anything. I just couldn't let her shoot Paul or Debi, Frank. They looked so happy, and she wanted to destroy that." Her breath hitched as she tried to stop herself from losing it completely.

"Shhhh. I know. But it's over. You saved them. You saved everybody. When I think how you could have been killed . . ." his voice broke and there was quiet, his own choked breathing the only sound.

Margot closed her eyes and held the phone pressed tighter to her head. "Is it really okay, Frank? I'm sorry I didn't see your text earlier. And I guess I didn't do what you asked me to. I don't even know where my phone is right now."

"Liza has it. I was talking to her on it and listening to the screaming and heard the shot. I thought you were dead." Again, his voice broke off, and Margot heard him blow his nose.

The man in the overcoat turned back to her, and Margot realized he had been standing a foot away the whole time, probably hearing everything she had said.

He gestured to her, his eyebrows raised, as if expecting her to finish up.

Margot forced in another few syncopated breaths and tried to loosen the death-like grip her fingers had on the borrowed phone.

"It's still pretty crazy here, and I think your boss wants his phone back."

"I know. I can't even imagine how long you'll be stuck

there while they get everything written up. Don't hang up before you give the phone back because I have to talk with him a minute. But Margot, call me the minute you get home, okay? Promise?"

"Uh-huh. I will. Promise."

"And Margot. I love you. I know you might not be ready to hear that yet, but when I thought I might be losing you. . ." his voice cracked again, and she could hear how he struggled to go on. "I love you. And if you don't love me, that's fine. Or if you need time, that's okay, too. I just wanted you to know."

The tears had started again, and Margot bit down hard on her lip to stop its trembling.

"I love you, too, Frank. But you're you, and I don't know who I am anymore."

"Oh, Margot. I know exactly who you are. You're an incredible athlete, an artist, and an amazingly kind and intelligent person. You helped me and fed me all this week, and today you proved you're the bravest woman in the world."

His voice was still hoarse and cracked, but she had no fear now that his words were fever-induced.

She tried to stop crying, tried to find some way to deny his absurd utterances, but all she could do was hold the phone tighter and try to force air in and out.

"I know this has been a lot for you. Don't worry about us right now. You need to take care of you. You're going to give the phone back to Mackie now, and then you're going to concentrate on breathing for a few minutes, all right?"

She nodded, no thought to the fact that he couldn't see her.

"I'll make sure someone brings you something to drink, and you just take your time when they need to take your statement, okay?"

She sniffled and nodded again.

"And then you call me as soon as you're home. One of the officers will give you a ride. You got all that?"

"Uh-huh. Thank you, Frank."

"There's nothing to thank me for. I'll talk to you soon."

"Okay. I love you." She whispered the words.

"I love you, too."

She handed the phone to Mackie, who tilted his head and gave her an intense, assessing look before he turned his back to her and walked a few steps away towards the rear of the church.

Margot sat still for a moment. Her hearing felt more normal now, although her head ached abominably from all the tears, and she knew her face was blotchy and swollen.

A policeman was photographing the rows on the side where Maria and Bettina had been what now felt like hours ago. Margot saw her dance bag lying on the floor amongst the upturned chairs and wondered if she could retrieve it.

She stood up slowly, a sense of utter exhaustion sweeping over her. But as Frank had promised, a different policeman was coming towards her with a can of Coke.

"Here, Miss. Inspector Mackie said you should drink this."

She took it, a little surprised. She never drank soda. But she popped the tab, took a sip, and felt the delicious sugary effervescence pervade her senses. She'd do whatever they needed her to do, and then she'd go home. Laska was waiting for her.

12

Six Weeks Later

The spot of moisture against her left cheek felt cold and clammy.

"Yuck!" Margot's head came up abruptly. She gave a pitiful little whimper. "I did it again."

Frank chuckled and pushed her head back down onto his chest. "I keep telling you, I don't care if you drool on me."

"Well, I care." Margot growled in mock humiliation and reached across to pull up a corner of the sheet. She wiped the drool from her cheek and Frank's chest, their arms tangling as he simultaneously tried to push her head back down.

"Stop moving. You feel perfect just where you are."

Satisfied that enough evidence of her sleepy abandon had been absorbed, Margot settled back down against his warm body, her arm across his torso.

"I appreciate your super-human energy, but there's a time

and place for everything. And right now, your place is right here."

"Right here?" she teased, her fingers moving gently across his belly. "Or maybe here?" She allowed her hand to slip a little lower.

Frank arched his back ever so slightly and groaned his approval. "You're an insatiable little witch, aren't you? And you've put your spell on me and turned me into a sex-craved monster." He gave a theatrical roar and rolled them over quickly, pinning her beneath him.

"Is this what you wanted? Should I remember that as soon as the drool starts, I'd better get ready for another round?"

She pretended to push against his chest.

"That's a horrible thing to say. I don't drool that much."

His head bent and he began nuzzling her neck, evoking a contented purr of delight.

"I don't know. It sounds like a pretty effective means of communication to me."

Margot gave herself up to his caresses. They could continue this conversation later on. Right now, words were totally superfluous.

The last six weeks had brought a blur of changes to her life. The investigation into Bettina's actions had been both exhaustive and amazingly uncomplicated. Bettina had journals dating back decades in her New Jersey home, with huge sections again and again excoriating Paul for his supposed role in her sister's death.

Paul's account was completely different. He and Maddie Dimond had started ballet class together in first grade and had been friends throughout their childhood and teenage years. But as they grew, Maddie's fondness for her school friend, Maya, had gradually morphed into something more passionate. Paul hadn't cared. Many of the girls from their dance classes and from school had crushes on him, which he reciprocated with fervor. He and Maddie cared for each other and were the best of friends, and they teased each other regularly about their love lives. But theirs was a conservative town, and Maddie's parents were never shy about expressing their vocal distaste for "those kinds of perverts."

So, Maddie and Maya had hidden their love, and Paul had gone along with the charade that he and Maddie were sweethearts whenever she asked. He had been overjoyed to finish his last year of high school via correspondence when the ballet company in Germany had offered him an internship. As the end of the school year approached, Maddie had written to him, begging him to stop at home before he moved out west and to pretend to be her prom date. Paul had wanted to see his family and friends anyway, and so he had agreed.

He had picked her up at the Dimond house, posed for the obligatory pictures, and then they had gone to prom. There he had partied and danced with all his old friends whom he hadn't seen in a year. Maddie told him her parents understood that a group of girls were having a sleepover after the dance, so they weren't expecting her home. After the prom officially ended, a large group of them had gone to continue partying in a local park, where he admitted that alcohol and pot had been shared by all. He had left the gathering at about two, saying good-bye to Maddie and Maya, who only had eyes for each other.

The next morning his parents had woken him to tell him the police needed to speak to him. He had been shocked and horrified to learn of his friend's death. He and Maddie had been friends for more than ten years, and he was genuinely heartbroken to have lost someone so dear to him.

The police questioned him about all that had gone on

after the prom. He tried to walk a fine line between telling the truth and not getting anyone in trouble. Yes, he had had a beer, but no, he didn't know if Maddie had had anything. Why had he left her there? He was flying to Washington the next day, and Maddie and her girlfriends had left the park when he did—he heading home in his father's Toyota, and Maddie and a group of girls walking to the sleepover at a house near the park.

Since an arrest was made quickly, and the issue of drunk driving became the focus of the tragic story, interest in Paul's part of it all quickly faded.

He had delayed his departure for Washington to attend Maddie's funeral. He had loved her, not as a girlfriend, but as a dear friend he would never forget. He had been startled, though, when Maddie's younger sister, Tina, came up to him after the burial.

"It's your fault," she had yelled at him, tears running down her face. "If you had stayed with her and taken care of her, she wouldn't have been killed. I thought you loved her." The accusation and hatred in Tina's tone had shocked him.

"She was with her friends; they were going to a party," he had tried to explain, but she wasn't interested.

"Boyfriends don't leave their girlfriends after a dance. They take care of them. I hate you!"

She had turned then and left, and Paul had not seen her again until his second year at Empire. He had had no part in her hiring, but someone from HR had brought the new wardrobe mistress to meet him while showing her around. He had stared at her, thinking he knew her from somewhere, but not sure where. She had been introduced as Bettina Galick, not Tina Dimond, and it had taken him a few weeks of passing her here and there to figure out who she was. He stopped her on the day it finally came to him.

"Tina, I didn't realize it was you when we were introduced. Why didn't you say anything?"

"There was nothing to say. You have your job, and I have mine."

She had been polite but distant. He had attempted on several occasions to ask about her family, but her responses were curt, at best. She had taken only a day or two off when first her mother, and years later, her father, had died. Both times, Paul had sent flowers that went unacknowledged.

Then in December she had stopped him in the corridor. She had smiled at him—a rare occurrence, indeed—and said that she had heard congratulations were in order. He had been a little surprised, since he and Debi hadn't announced anything publicly, but he had been in the dance world his whole life and knew there were no such things as secrets. He had thanked her, and when he and Debi had discussed the wedding, he had reluctantly suggested they invite her.

"Really?" Debi had questioned. "She's never been particularly friendly."

"I know. But she's not friendly to anyone." He gave Debi the barest account of the twenty-five-year-old tragedy and then held her tightly in his arms.

"It actually took me years to get over all of it. I never loved Maddie that way, but she was my friend, and a part of me did feel guilty that I hadn't stayed with her that night. After that, I never dared—or cared—to risk my heart with anyone. But then you danced into my life."

And so, they had agreed to invite Bettina to the wedding, mostly out of pity for the unhappy woman with no family or love of her own.

But Bettina's diaries proved that she had never stopped blaming Paul, and her desire for revenge had only increased as time went on. She had kept track of his career, often writing of how Maddie should be starring in ballet performances and not him, and she had mapped out her career intentionally to eventually meet up with him.

She had ranted in the police car about how guilty he was, and then she had gone silent. Her trial was scheduled to begin next summer, and rumor had it that her lawyer was going to plead insanity.

The police had contacted Representative Maya Hansen in California, and she had corroborated Paul's story, adding that Maddie had been the love of her life.

It appeared that everything that had happened at the Empire—Yuri's death, Rocco's injury, the food poisoning, the death threats—had indeed all been done with the sole intent of damaging Paul's reputation and future. News of Debi's pregnancy and upcoming marriage had apparently caused something to snap in Bettina's addled mind, and she had lost all sense of reason.

Paul and Debi delayed their honeymoon departure for a week, allowing Paul to direct the ballet company's first performance three days after the wedding.

Margot had stepped in as planned when the newlyweds left, and she found she enjoyed the administrative and coaching aspects of the job.

But Margot had unexpectedly found herself enjoying something else even more. On the day after the chaotic wedding, Margot's parents came into the city, and her mother cooked food in the tiny kitchen and suggested repeatedly that they would love to have her spend some time at home with them.

Margot had resisted. She admitted that she and the detective she had told them about were "seeing" each other, and with Frank's concurrence, promised her parents they could all meet as soon as he was over the flu.

The following morning, she had gotten up, talked to Frank on the phone, gone to class, and then thought about it being Wednesday. The schedules and patterns that had ruled her life were gone, and each day's decisions were now her own. Rehearsals would begin at the theater the next day, and she planned on being there in order to go over details with Paul. But Margot remembered the little girl, Nida, telling her she went to the gym for therapy every Wednesday and Friday. Another call to Frank, and within minutes, the head physical therapist from his gym had called to tell her she was welcome to come by and meet with Nida, as long as the girl's mother agreed.

And so had begun a totally unusual and unexpected friendship. With Allison's approval, Margot watched Nida's therapy, and then, using her phone's music, she showed Nida some simple dance moves she could do with her arms. Nida had been ecstatic. Margot returned on Friday, and another young girl in the gym asked if she could "dance," too. Not sure how it had all come about, Margot was now teaching a "dance" class for children at the gym three times a week and absolutely loving it.

Both the flu and the winter cold had subsided, and Mackie had rolled his eyes in mock disgust and agreed that perhaps Frank's schedule should include regular days off, seeing as he was now more a "family man" and not a robot.

Margot was still working with the pointe shoe company —"We don't drop shoes from drones!"—she told Frank again and again, laughing as he never failed to insist that he knew what he had heard. She enjoyed the work far more than she had expected and spent time speaking with and encouraging dancers of all levels, including, most wonderfully, those trying on pointe shoes for the very first time. She didn't know what else her future might hold, but for now, she was content.

Except for when Frank brought her to heights of pleasure she had never imagined possible and whispered of how he loved and adored his ballerina Superwoman. Then she was far more than content.

She had stood on a darkened stage, aching with fear and sorrow at a dear friend's death, and a miracle had made an unscheduled entrance. Margot dancing as Giselle was no more. But Margot loving dance to the very core of her being and spreading that joy to others was a work in progress and a passion continuing to grow and evolve. And Frank stood by to partner her every step of the way.

ACKNOWLEDGMENTS

As always, I could not have brought this book to life without the constant support and encouragement of my husband and my sister. They make me believe my words are worth waiting for, and for that I am supremely grateful. They also pick lovingly and tirelessly over my manuscripts, and for that, I am eternally in their debt. Any remaining mistakes and awkward phrases are mine alone, but many of the good parts are thanks to their prodding.

I also am indebted to my wonderful writer friends, especially those I work with online, day-in and day-out, led valiantly by the gifted and always encouraging Keely Thrall.

And huge thanks to my brother, Gene Swift, who answers my cries for technical help and makes my website and my online presence possible.

To my three uniquely talented and amazing children: I go to sleep each night and wake up each morning grateful to share a world with you.

And to you, my readers: knowing you find pleasure in my work brings me incomparable happiness. If you've enjoyed any of my books, please email me and let me know. But the greatest gift you can give me, or any writer, is a review telling the world what you liked. Your reviews on Goodreads, BookBub, or wherever you buy books help make my work more visible and encourage the publishing world to take the books we love seriously. Thank you for your help in ensuring that my books remain available for new readers to find.

ABOUT THE AUTHOR

MEG NAPIER writes love stories: short stories, long stories, suspenseful stories, and stories of intertwined souls loving through time. When she's not writing, she's listening to books she wishes she had more time to read, taking long walks with her dog, avoiding housework at all costs, fussing after her husband (near) and her children (far), and wondering what kind of delicious dessert she can get away with today.

Look for her at MegNapier.com or through the social media links below—which one of these days she'll learn to embrace.

facebook.com/MegNapierAuthorPage

twitter.com/NapierMeg

instagram.com/megnapierauthor

About the Artist

Sally Schaedler has been sharing her beautiful artwork and illustrating books for years. She has also been a dear friend to my family, and I am blessed beyond words that she was willing to jump into the fray with a relatively unknown author. Find her work at http://sommerstudios.com/

ALSO BY MEG NAPIER

Second Drop, a short story found in LOVE GONE VIRAL, a Covid-19 Anthology

Second Draft, a short story

And coming in 2021: SECOND SIGHT, a heart-wrenching story of love that defies time.

CPSIA information can be obtained
at www.ICGtesting.com
Printed in the USA
LVHW081053070121
675978LV00022B/451